Lana Fray

-AND-

the Grand Plan

Typeset by Amanda Ashton in 9pt Heuristica
www.ashtondesigns.co.uk

Edited by Abby Hagyard and Darcie Byrd

Cover Design by Mary 'Graphicagirl' Gale

Printed in the United States of America

For Brandon, my love;

Sheila & Walter for the inspiration to
always follow my dreams;

To my Dad & Ann for giving me the
love for books and adventure

and the many friends & family who
offered their unwavering support.

To: Group Message
From: Lana Fray
Subject: The GRAND Plan

Hey guys and gals!

Okay, so you all know that I'm actively seeking Mr. Right, right? (Well, you do now!)

My 30th birthday is just around the corner and the only thing worse than having no one special in my life is that none of these "find your guy" deals that seem to work for everyone else have worked for me.

Anyway, this morning I had a brilliant epiphany! What's the point of having great friends if you don't reach out when you need them? And what's the point of having money if you can't/don't/won't do something with it to make you happy?

So I'm done with these "find your guy" scam artists. As of right now, I'm reaching out to my friends with a great offer: If you set me up on a date with my future husband (AKA the man of my dreams) within the next four weeks, I will give you five thousand dollars on our wedding day. Seriously!

I know some of you will think I'm crazy, but I'm counting on the rest of you to know me well enough to realize that this is no game. I'm on a mission!

Let me know ASAP if you have any serious candidates. I will be scheduling dates via email immediately.

Thanks!
Lana

Sigh

I sent this out to 100 people.

What was I thinking...

Introduction

*T*en minutes? It was ten minutes ten minutes ago!

Pulling at the too-short bangs I'd thought would be a great style shift last night, I glance away from the sizzle reel footage I'm screening to check the wall clock for the thousandth time.

You'd think a veteran TV producer would have her PhD in Calmness and a ton of Patience, but no. In my Reality TV world, Calm is what you get right before all Hell breaks loose. And as for Patience... well, let's just say that it's not one of my strong points.

While we're on the subject, why is Patience a virtue? Why can't hurry-the-!#$%-up be a virtue?

Sigh. I glance at the clock again. Oh yay. We're down to nine minutes. Back to the footage. What I'm wondering is whether to kill myself now or wait and let the Bossman do it. I mean, come on: A reality show about guys who work in cement? Seriously? What was I thinking?

Okay, I know exactly what I was thinking. Stuck in traffic, the sun beating down making everyone sizzle, staring at those hunky construction guys with their shirtless, toned bodies slick with sweat, it was a total Chippendale's moment with *Sexy And I Know It* blaring from a passing stereo.

What I *should* have done was keep my fantasy moment to myself, but Nooo. As soon as the Bossman gave me grief for showing up late, demanding fresh ideas as penance, I rose to the bait. The last thing I'd expected? *Get me a sizzle reel, Red, an' we'll see about lettin' you run with it.*

So I did, God help me, because telling the Bossman to shove it would have been a suicidal career move, and now I'm nine – no, make it eight – minutes from getting the go-ahead on a project I don't want, exposing people who are too nice, to being featured in the kind of sleaze TV Bossman will produce.

And while we're setting the record straight, my name isn't Red. It's Lana Fray. I was born and raised under the blue skies of Boise, Idaho where I inherited my red hair and rebel ways from Grandma Helen, who still answers to the nickname *Hell on Wheels* and she's 73.

I came to Los Angeles fresh out of Boise State's fledgling film school (Go Broncos!) to Make It Big as one of those producers who Makes A Difference, but somewhere along the way my quest to expose the raw injustice of Man's Inhumanity to Woman got derailed. Ten years later, I'm on the verge of turning thirty and all I've got to show for my Tinsel Town adventure is an okay rep as a freelance producer, a growing hatred for reality TV and not ONE man I would take home to meet my mom. Hell, I don't even have someone I'd introduce to my fish.

Gawd, I can't believe this is me talking like this. For one thing, I have GREAT friends. For another, I work with FABULOUS people. And my life suited me perfectly FINE right up until my 29th birthday. One day I was on top of the world and the next day I'd become one of those limp creatures you see reading gothic romances, obsessing on Mr. Right, and eating too much chocolate cake.

Okay, no. That's crazy. Even with the flu, I'm not the limp type and I wouldn't call it obsessing when an intelligent single woman sensibly conducts a thorough investigation of the dating scene. Offering rewards after Love eluded me like the plague? Okay, yeah. THAT's obsessing.

My GRAND Plan came to me in one of those aha moments people talk about. Okay, it was the morning after *another* date-from-hell adventure and I was desperate, so no jury would convict me. I mean, the guy actually leaned over and licked my face, in the restaurant. Because why? Because I was "sweet enough to eat." No, I'm not making it up. Who says stuff like that?

Anyway, I'd checked my email before leaving the apartment and Ta Daa: there was a note from my bank confirming a $5000 credit, thanks to a commercial I'd hated producing so much that I'd put it out of my mind as soon as we'd wrapped.

Found money, I'd thought! And since I'm not strapped for cash, I should do something totally crazy with it. Like... Hey! Buy a horse! Why not? I grew up around horses in Boise. And what little girl hasn't always wanted a pony? The horse may have issues, though. My schedule is pretty crazy. And how will *My Friend Flicka* feel about life in a two-bedroom apartment in Studio City, even if it is on the ground floor and does have a small, private patio out back?

Okay, so no horse. What else could I do with the money? Well, figuratively speaking, I could buy a better man than the men I've been dating, I thought with a laugh. And then I stopped laughing and sat up in my chair. AHA!

Not that I'd actually *buy* a man, of course. I mean, there's a name for people who do things like that. Just shout out, *'Who wants to be the Next Reality TV Star?'* and you'll find them wedged between the *'I'll eat/wear/say/do anythings'* and the *'I already dids'* of this world.

But seriously, I could put up the five grand as a finder's fee! That wouldn't be the same as buying, right? And it would be so much more satisfying to invest in a thank you to a friend instead of all those monthly memberships, funeral flowers and wedding gifts.

I could offer it to the first person to introduce me to Mr. Right before my birthday and make it payable on my wedding day! It would be a cross between match-making, bounty-hunting and viral hits. A game where I was the only woman and everyone who entered had an equal chance to win. And considering my track record so far, seriously how much worse could things possibly get?

I was so excited, it didn't occur to me that my hapless happiness plan was remarkably like the shows I produced: monstrous creatures that defy best laid plans, whose relentless Ground Hog Day sameness and OMG outcomes are shaped by the outrageous behaviors of the amateurs featured on the show.

What I also failed to see was that I was pinning my hopes of everlasting love on the questionable motives of the 100 email recipients who received my limited time offer and the one-track attitudes of the men they chose to ask me out.

I know. Looking back, I should have gone with the horse.

Week One

Thursday, Day 1

*B*lue skies and the loss of wide-eyed innocence aside, one of the things I *don't* miss about Boise, Idaho is the winter. The beautiful boys of the Endless Summer they call Los Angeles stole my heart over eight years ago.

But what about the gridlocked traffic, you ask? What about the Road Rage? Nope. All I need is a shirtless road crew breaking a sweat pouring cement and I'm cured.

And right here, right now, I'm stuck in a bumper-to-bumper snarl just a few feet away from five gorgeous, tanned bodies and I'm hopelessly late, so why not sit back like any normal, red-blooded American girl, take off my TV producer hat, and enjoy the view?

"Take OFF my TV producer hat???" Producer Girl Who Never Sleeps gives me a mental slap. There'll be none of that crazy talk when I'm thinking 'cement' as in cement shoes... As in cool Mafia wise guys reveal hot bodies covered in sweat... As in *Fuggedabouddit Jersey Shore* meets *Magic Mike!*

With Mae West in my head (*Nice workin' with ya, boys*), I'm out of the car, broken field running across three lanes of traffic, giving my card to the guy who looks like he might be in charge.

"Hey guys," he grins, pulling out his own card and handing it over. "You wanna get famous? This girl's a big time Hollywood producer."

Their whistles and laughter are suddenly drowned out by honking horns. I turn back and see that everyone ahead of my blue Cabrio has moved 50 feet and everyone behind me is having fits.

"I'll call you!" I yell to the boys as I dash for my car. In reply, they bump fists and wave.

Back in the car, I glance at their card. Muckers Cement. Forming and finishing since 1929. Giovanni Vitale, Proprietor. I'm thinking Brando, DeNiro, and Pacino, their family gone straight when another convertible cruises by blasting *Sexy And I Know It* from its stereo. Oh yeah.

I'm having so much fun with the idea that it takes a billboard ad for online dating to remind me of the AHA inspiration that I've dubbed The GRAND Plan. When I reach the rundown slum where I'm currently working – because no one in reality TV wastes money on nice digs – I slide into my office, draft my email and blast it off to 100 lucky recipients before I chicken out.

In seconds, I've got mail, but no time to look. I race to the boardroom, late for my production status update meeting with Nolan (my partner), Carlton Bozmund (*aka* Bossman) our Executive Producer, and our line producer, Irv (*aka* the money man for the production company).

Running his fingers through his who-does-he-think-he's-kidding dye job, Bossman growls, *"You better have a good reason for being late that will prove I shouldn't ship your sorry ass back to Boise?"*

"Imagine *The Godfather* meets *Greensburg*," I hit the ground running, "or *Jersey Shore* meets *Magic Mike*, if you like. We follow a Sicilian Mafia family that went straight when a young Giovanni Vitale came to America in 1929, saw how Henry Ford and his cars were changing America, opened a cement finishing biz and started building streets, sidewalks and bridges. The gamble paid off and today, they're in every Mall, parking garage and Public Square in LA."

Before anyone can jump in, I deliver the hook: "You get road rage. You get graft. You get greed and corruption. And… you get the hottest bodies in town. It's called *Meet the Muckers*."

Everything stops. In unison, every head swivels from me to Irv to the Bossman, who stares at the stained tile ceiling. "Get me a teaser reel, Red. We'll see about lettin' you run with it."

Nolan grins as we head back to our desks. "Where did that come from?"

"Traffic jam on the Ten. I took Olympic and voila: road construction."

"Fifty bucks says we've got next season's hit."

"No deal," I laugh.

My partner, Nolan, is a heart-breaker whose moves are wasted on me because he's my mom's sister's kid. She moved them both from Boise to LA when he was six so she could get out from under her deadbeat ex and maybe make her fair-haired, green-eyed boy a star. She's living in Florida now, thanks to husband number four, and Nolan is very glad. She was one of *those* stage moms and that kind of stuff can wear on a kid.

We've reached our office when the intercom squeals and Bossman's voice fills the room. "When I figure out who is gluing cans of tuna to my desk, there will be Hell To Pay!" There's a crash as the loud speaker phone slams back into the cradle.

"What's that about?" I ask.

Nolan shrugs. "There was one can when he got in. Sounds like they're multiplying."

I narrow my eyes. Nolan has a reputation for pranks.

Catching my glance, his hands go up. "It ain't me, babe!"

As we check our emails – I'm up to twelve replies – Nolan laughs. "Five grand? What gives?"

I'd had a pat answer ready, but I find myself telling the truth. I mean, he's my cousin. He'd know a lie the minute it left my mouth.

"The clock's ticking," I tell him. I can feel myself getting anxious just thinking about it. I can also feel my arms flailing all over the place – a typical me move when I'm losing it.

"I thought I'd be married to the love of my life by now; have beautiful kids; be travelling the world doing Real Work, changing lives. The reality is that I'm working in a dump and getting yelled at by a bubble-bellied jerk that colors his hair with shoe polish, stinks up the place with his revolting snacks and doesn't give a shit about anything but his own bottom line."

Surprisingly, he doesn't laugh it off. "I get it. Just... look, be careful, okay? You need to really look at these guys before you go out. I don't want to be called to the hospital in the middle of an awesome date with a super model, you hear?"

I can't help smiling. "Yes, dad. Nice to see where your priorities lie, by the way."

He shrugs with a grin. "So talk to me about cement."

The easiest way to describe our partnership is that I'm the one who comes up with the ideas and Nolan helps make them come together. Though he's older than I am by a few years, he's much happier watching my back than taking the lead. So I do the pitching, develop the themes, direct the shoots and take the meetings while Nolan serves as sounding board and partner on things like auditions and organizational details...and he's also great at keeping us on track when I veer off in a million directions.

On location, he wanders all over the place, looking like he's lost in space. After a while, it's easy to forget he's even there and people forget to be self-conscious around him. But when we debrief after a session, it's always Nolan who noticed the crazy wonderful things people were saying or doing that everyone else missed. Later, he wades through tons of footage and finds those quirky moments, blending them into the episode to turn so-so scenes into ratings gold.

By the time we've sketched out a few obvious scenarios – jealous husbands, bad checks, corrupt city officials, natural disasters – and I've got a meeting lined up first thing tomorrow at Muckers Cement, it's mid-afternoon. We decide to take off early. Nolan is busy with plans for his big birthday bash tomorrow night and after I check my emails, I'm off to Girls Night.

As he clears his desk, I ask, "See you later?"

If he doesn't have plans, Nolan sometimes tags along when I get together with my three best friends: uber-tall Swedish ice-goddess Katarin (Kat), who runs a millionaire match-maker service; curvy, curly-haired Jewish princess, Mitzi, who sells commodities under the unforgiving eye of her ruthless I-always-wanted-a-son stock trader dad; and beefcake gay BFF, Jonah, a California native son whose serious passion for hiking led him to launch a wildly successful outdoor gear franchise. Add a pint-sized spitfire from Boise who produces reality TV and Girls Night is never dull.

"You'll be at the pub?"

Looking up from a text from Mitzi, I shake my head. "No. It looks like we're at Mitzi's."

"If I can make it, I'll bring wine."

"I've always liked that about you," I reply and he favors me with his killer surfer dude smile.

An hour later, I toss my bottle of Chardonnay into the car and rumble on down the road to Mitzi's. I know I'm in for a special private session. When she saw the GRAND Plan email, her first move was to cancel our regular table at the pub and text us to meet at her place at seven. Then she'd texted me privately. "I need you here as soon as you can. It's urgent."

As I park my car I wonder if my Plan is the urgent issue or if it's her good-for-nothing boyfriend, Tad the Cad, up to his usual tricks. Whether we lead with Tad or not, I know I'm going to get an earful, but given the replies I've been getting, I'm pretty sure their concerns will soon be followed by "Have I got the guy for you!"

Tad the Cad wins. The big surprise is that Mitzi is all smiles for a change because their latest fight – when she'd found Tad's laptop open to an online dating site – has been resolved. "It was a total misunderstanding, Lana. He was just being polite."

When I choke on my wine, she hands me a napkin. "Stop it! It was an old account he'd totally forgotten about. When he suddenly started getting messages, he was just writing to tell them his status had changed. Honestly, he was so cute! He even sent me gorgeous flowers!"

Will it do me any good to remind her that he bought the damn' flowers with her money? Nope.

Mitzi chose a commodities career path because it feeds an insatiable need to punish herself. Does she surpass any normal person's wildest expectations? Absolutely. Does her success make up for the fact that she was born a girl instead of the boy her father always wanted? Never. Does it come as a surprise that the men she falls for are arrogant, insensitive and unforgiving? Not at all.

Mitzi switches gears before I can ruin her moment. "AND I forwarded him your email. He thinks it's a great idea and says he's got the perfect guy."

"WHAT?" Now I'm wearing my wine. This is just getting better and better.

"Oh, Lana, I'm sorry."

"I should hope so!!!" I said patting my chest dry.

"Well, you don't need to go all *verklempt* on me. I mean, your top is cute, but it's hardly Versace."

"I'm not talking about my top," I tell her through clenched teeth. "I chose the people I sent my email to for a reason! I didn't ask them to forward it to every Tom, Dick and Tad on the planet."

Mitzi's back goes up. "Really? And what part of 'I'll pay you thousands of dollars to find me a guy' did you think *wouldn't* bring out the worst in people? If you're lucky, it won't go viral!"

I'm on my feet and ready to walk out the door when it suddenly occurs to me that she might be right. Mitzi has blinders on when it comes to Tad, but in every other respect her people sense is infallible. That's why she's so successful.

"Friends don't do things like that!" I say hotly.

Now it's Mitzi's turn to choke.

"Okay, *my* friends don't do things like that. Is that better?"

"Lana, your friends love you to death, but we're only human. We'd never hurt you deliberately, but that doesn't mean it doesn't happen. I'm sorry I passed your email on to Tad without checking with you. I know he's not your favorite person. I also know what he was like before he met me. I messed up and I'm sorry."

I'm hugging her when the doorbell goes and Jonah makes his grand entrance. "I want all your cast-offs, girlfriend! Did you really send a hundred emails?"

By this time I'm so embarrassed, I just nod.

Jonah grabs Mitzi and executes a flawless twirl and dip. "Mitzi, dahling, look deep into my eyes. Can't you just taste all those glorious men?"

One of the qualities I love in Jonah is the way he says the things everyone else is thinking. How he turns the most awkward moments upside down is all in his delivery. I only wish his search for love had the same happy outcome. Here's a guy who loves the outdoor lifestyle, craves the big sky and wide-open spaces, and launches a brilliant business in a competitive, testosterone world. What are the chances he'll find the special someone who will see and love the funny, funky girlie side of him too? Slim to none.

As Mitzi pours wine for him and I go in search of soda water to spritz things up, Jonah calls after me, "I want details, young lady. How many replies have you had? How many dates have you planned? When do I get my turn?"

Before I can answer, Mitzi's dog, Ginny, starts barking.

Kat side-steps the pooch and offers her cheek to Jonah for a kiss. Kat is as unlucky in love as she is with dogs. She runs a match-making service for the rich and famous, but she can't make a match herself. The man she'd finally picked a year ago actually left her standing at the altar in front of her family, the media and all her big-name celebrity friends.

"Slip a mickey into the dog's kibble," Nolan offers on his way in. His attitude has all the high-maintenance hotties running after him in droves. He loves the attention, especially since it keeps him safely out of reach of anyone smart enough (and real enough) to be a truly great partner.

With Nolan joining the group, we look like we're about to shoot one of those glamour hair commercials. Mitzi's got masses of long chestnut waves. Kat's high cheek bones and wolf grey eyes are framed by a platinum blonde mane. Jonah's Irish roots blessed him with thick curly black hair and piercing blue eyes. Nolan is the green-eyed, honey blond surfer and I'm the slim-hipped tomboy with a million freckles and strawberry red hair.

In the ten years I've been in LA, this has become my family. There's nothing they won't do for me and the feeling is mutual. Who could ask for anything more? Okay, I could. I want The Man of My Dreams. So sue me.

As I reach for one of Mitzi's snacks, Kat clears her throat and shoots me a look. Oh joy. It looks like Family Court is in session. Let the third degree begin.

"You couldn't ask for help first? You couldn't find anything better to do with that kind of money than spend it on some jerk that's going to leave you at the altar and break your heart?"

Jonah weighs in. "Kat, honey, you're projecting. Lana's not going end up with your guy."

Kat shakes her head. "She's telling everyone she'll pay for a husband. It's like prostitution."

Jonah grins. "Careful, girlfriend. Remember how you make your living."

"I make discrete introductions!"

To my surprise, Mitzi jumps in on my side. "Cut her some slack. It's her money."

"I'm just saying--" Kat tries to protest.

Mitzi cuts her off. "Do you have any idea how happy it makes me when I can do something nice for the guy I love? What's the point of making money if you don't use it? What's the point in putting up with an impossible father every freaking day, or working for a jerk like Lana's boss?"

Nolan taps Mitzi on the knee. "Why don't we let Lana tell us what she was thinking?"

"I'm feeling like an idiot now, but the only thing I had on my mind was how to improve my chances of meeting someone fabulous instead of all the someones I've wanted to slap silly. Until Mitzi opened my eyes a few minutes ago, it never occurred to me that people would jump all over the money thing."

I get up and start pacing. "The reason I emailed those people is that I like them. I get who they are and I respect them. We've known each other a long time and that means they get who I am, good and...well not my finest features. To me, meeting people through them means better odds for success than filling out a bunch of computer generated questionnaires because this group knows the kind of guy I'm looking for. And if one of them does find my Mr. Right, after all the crap I've been through, doesn't it make sense that I'd want to thank them? I mean, if it turns out to be one of you, can't I thank you?"

"Lana, we couldn't take your money," Jonah says.

"So you I'll pay in cast-offs and I'll work out barter deals with the others."

"Now you're talking!" he grins.

"It's not funny," Kat says. "People do crazy things for money. Look at your shows."

"What are you talking about?" Nolan nearly chokes on his wine. "Lana's not looking for monsters. She's looking for someone nice. We don't do shows about them. Who'd watch?"

"I just think we'd have come up with a better plan if she'd discussed it with us," Kat replies.

I think back to her heartbreaking moment, standing alone at the back of that church with her neat ball of pink roses as she realized that her groom wasn't there. And I remember the long months that followed as she searched for a way to move on. I understand where her concern is coming from and it makes me realize how lucky I am to have such great friends.

"What if I promise to let you check out any guy I'm seriously interested in?"

"I am SO there for you, honey!"

"Jonah!" Kat throws up her hands.

"What? It's the kind of friend I am," Jonah grins.

With no way to top that, I raise my glass: "To the GRAND Plan," I say.

Jonah raises his immediately and Mitzi follows. Nolan gives Kat a nudge and, after a deep sigh, she makes it unanimous. After we drink, Mitzi's the first one to set her glass down.

"Now talk, sister. Who's first and who's next and how many are you seeing after that?"

Friday, Day 2

*F*riday morning is the reverse of Thursday. We don't hear a peep from the Bossman until we check in at Slum Central, well past noon. By that time, Nolan and I have met the two Muckers who basically run the show. Gina, in her late twenties, has been in the driver's seat since her mother passed away. To do this she had given up her career in the military to step into her mother's shoes. Her mentor is her grandfather, Giovanni, who originally launched the business and now serves as elder statesman and watchdog.

Through Gina, we learn that her Uncle Mike – the guy I spoke to on the street – supervises the work crews and her father, Angelo, takes care of their equipment. Gina's older brother, Giovanni Junior (aka Junior), handles sales so he's usually on the road. A younger sister, Maria, does their book-keeping from a home office and a kid brother, Antonio, is out of the country at the moment. We don't get to see any of the crews but that doesn't matter. Even without the beefcake component, the Muckers are great and Nolan is pumped. On the drive back to the office, we're talking non-stop.

"I like the idea of shooting Gina's office as a situation room. We can jazz it up with a few of her military trophies to highlight the active duty life she left behind."

I'm nodding. "I agree. You don't hear much about women on the front lines and I can't remember any stories about female sharpshooters."

"No kidding. Here's a title for you: Deadlier than the male."

"Is that from personal experience, cousin?"

"Don't ask," he laughs. "Let's get back to staging. Those city maps with the colored flag pins she uses to mark their jobs will look great."

"You know, a young woman calling the shots, especially in that kind of business is a nice twist," I add. "People won't see that coming."

"Yeah, with the kindly old Godfather as mentor."

I shoot him a murderous look and he grins. "Come on. You know it's what everyone's thinking."

"Not gonna happen," I tell him firmly.

"Okay, then you're gonna hate my next idea."

"If you say mandolin theme music, I'm tossing you out of the car."

"Please. Do I look suicidal? I'm thinking we feature what's his name in the teasers."

"Giovanni. But, she said they call him Poppi, remember?"

"Yeah, whatever. Talk about a fashion hound, by the way. I wanted to ask him where he shops and would he take me with him next time, but I had a feeling he was going to say 'Milano' and I wasn't sure you'd let me take the time off. D'you think he can read?"

"In the first place, if anyone's going to Milan it's me. And what's with the "can he read" kinds of questions... of course he can read. What are you talking about?"

"Narrating the sizzle."

I grin. I start thinking over the idea of a sizzle, being the quick, energetic video that we will use to sell a TV show to the network. Then imagining Poppi narrating it is interesting. "Armand Assante just off the boat—"I say out loud.

Nolan fakes a husky Italian voice. "—itsa, whad do you call him, fine-a ting, bella."

"So you're saying we have Poppi narrate the beginning and any transitions that need it... then we come up with a Poppi-ism as the button, so basically he bookends the show and fills in any gaps. I love it!"

"That way, we don't have to include him in anything nuts. We just cut in the advice he gives."

Continuing his thought I say, "So we don't compromise him with the sleazy Mafia stuff Bossman's going to try to slip in. Nice!"

"I'm kind of curious about this Antonio guy, though."

"Why?" I ask.

Nolan shrugs. "I'm just wondering where he fits in. And why he wasn't there."

It's my turn to shrug. "Who cares? Maybe he's shy. Or he's a dud."

Nolan's voice goes husky again. "Or maybe he's-a wise-a guy."

"Nolan!"

Nolan grins. "So you'd say no deal to any references to family with a capital F, even if we could use them to bring the Bossman down a peg or two?"

Wow. It's a tempting thought that I push firmly away. "How's about we get on a conference call with Trent, my brother, the prison warden, and ask what he thinks?"

"Oh geez. Okay. Not funny. You win."

I shake my head. "They don't call you Mr. Sensitive for nothing."

He grins.

"Speaking of sensitive," I shift topics, "what's happening with your birthday party tonight?"

Nolan laughs. "The only thing I'm going to say about it is wear something fabulous."

"Why?"

"Wild horses will not make me talk. Just plan on looking hot. And speaking of hot... what's the update on the GRAND Plan?"

"Twenty-two," I tell him.

"Dates?" His blue eyes widen as his jaw drops.

"Mmmm, let's call them discrete inquiries. So far I've got five actual dates on the calendar."

His face lights up. "Give!"

"The first is a musician named Skylar. He's meeting me for coffee on Saturday. After that, I've got dinner dates with a German art critic named Lotar, a cameraman named Jeremy who just moved here from New Orleans, and a DJ named Doug. And..." I take a deep breath and plunge ahead... "I'm having a drink on Monday with a plumber named Jason who's a friend of Tad's."

Nolan's head snaps around. "Not Tad the Cad!"

"Yeah."

"Are you insane?"

"It's just for drinks. What's he gonna do, steal my purse?"

"All I'm saying is, I don't trust anyone who calls Tad a friend. Everything about that guy stinks, you know what I mean?"

I'm in total agreement. Mitzi's boy toy totally gives me the creeps.

As we slow down to make the turn for Slum Central, a foul odor hits us. We're still half a block away and my eyes are watering so badly, I can't see the road.

"Jeez, pull a U-Turn, Lan! Get us outa here!"

"I'm on it!"

As I get some distance between us and IT, recognition sets in. "Nolan, that was pure skunk."

"Are you sure?"

"The number of times my dog came home reeking, it's not something you forget."

Nolan tries calling the office. "No good. I'm getting voice mail."

"Try the Bossman."

"Right," he punches the number and then nods at me. "Yeah, it's Nolan. What's happening? Really? When? Wow. No, no. We're good. Anything you need from us? Okay. See you Monday."

Nolan disconnects and sits there, shaking his head.

"Hello?"

"Sorry. Someone put a skunk in Bossman's trunk. The car's a write-off. And they have to fumigate the whole place so he sent everyone home. He wondered if anything had happened to us. He's called the cops, but no one can get near the place."

He's quiet for a minute or two. "You know, I don't like this."

"I don't imagine the Bossman is all that crazy about it either."

"That's not what I mean. I thought the cans of tuna glued to his desk were funny – I mean, he's such a jerk with his ripe cheese and garlic sausage snacks in the editing bay, leaving us to work in that stink – but there's something seriously nasty about a prank ruins a $70,000 car and shuts down a studio."

"No kidding."

He turns in his seat and locks eyes with me. "Promise me you won't go in there alone after hours until they clear this up. This town is full of crazy people and we know the Bossman isn't famous for making friends."

He's right on all counts. "Okay, okay... you got it...Dad. I promise."

I drop Nolan at his condo and head back to my apartment. With the afternoon suddenly free,

I decide to pamper myself with a lazy bubble bath. Showers are the best way to scrape off the dirt, but nothing beats a bath when you need some time to decompress.

First things first, though. After tossing a few gourmet flakes into the fish tank, I check my messages. Everyone else in the world can go wireless all they want, but my mom Shirley insists that I keep a landline, just in case. In case of what, I don't know but I just go along with it. Keeping a land line is easier than wrangling an angry Shirley. And since I love her to death, what's the harm in indulging her craziness? I punch in the code and wait for the beep.

"Lana? Are you there, dear? It's your mother. (pause) Shirley."

I shake my head. As if I would confuse her with anyone else...

"That unfortunate girl who can't keep a job – you know the one I mean, I can never remember her name – she took those yoga classes with you and then tried her hand at scrapbooking, and when that didn't work out she got that job at the reptile zoo – what IS her name? Jane? Jody? Something like that. Anyway, I bumped into her at the library this morning – imagine my surprise to find her at the library – and she said the most astonishing thing. Even for her. Of course, I didn't believe her for a minute. Even if you do have a tendency to take in strays, as I told your dad, you'd hardly need to reach out to her, of all people, to find a man. What IS her name? Monica? Melanie? Honestly. So listen, dear: if you do feel you need to run a classified ad to find someone, your dad and I are fine about it, but I think Trent is a little worried. You know how he fusses. If I've told him once, I've told him a thousand times, you dated Billy years before he turned to a life of crime. But does he listen to me? Not Billy, dear. I don't think Billy has ever listened to anyone. Your brother listens to me all the time. He listens and nods and smiles and then goes back to fussing about every little thing. I'm sure it's a quality that stands him in good stead at the prison, but it

gets on my nerves. All right, dear. I have to go. Your dad wants to take me to look at a horse. Give my love to Fish."

For all her wackiness, I love my mother to bits. Once you dig through the random chatter, there's a logic in the way her mind works that can't be denied. Even my decision to call her Shirley made perfect sense to her.

It happened by pretty much by itself, really. A logical outcome of random events that happened when I was still in kindergarten. We went to the park one afternoon and I can't remember now if I'd hurt myself or discovered something cool. All I remember is that when I yelled 'Mom', every woman over the age of fifteen came running. What a terrifying sight! So the next time I needed her, I yelled 'Shirley' and guess who I got? Exactly. When her friends quibbled about it, she was great. "Well, we both *know* I'm her mother, dear. There's no need to belabor the point."

While I wait for the bath to fill, I boot up my laptop and find four new replies. The first one is from Trent. I'm already grinning when I open it.

Sometimes I wonder if you were adopted! Mom wants me to let you do your thing, but I'm seriously thinking of flying down, putting you under arrest and dragging your crazy redheaded ass back to Boise. Seriously, if you're doing this for real, send me their names BEFORE you go out with them and I'll run them through our database. If they've got a record of ANY kind, you are NOT going out with them. I don't care if God himself sets you up. You got that? Love, Trent.

The fact that Trent works in law enforcement gives his threats a deeper meaning. All things considered, thinking back to some of the boys he scared off in the past, I'm getting off easy.

Email number two is from Tad the Cad.

I always wondered what it would take to get a girl like you but I never had the courage to take the risk. Since last night, when you agreed to meet my buddy, Jason, I've been having a hard time getting you out of my mind. But that's my problem, not yours. Between us, Jason's a better choice. He's worth a lot of money.

I close my eyes tight, trying to get the icky, crawling feeling on my skin to subside. I think for a minute, not sure what to do. In the end, friendship wins: I have to call Mitzi. I pull the phone out of my purse and I'm actually hitting her speed dial code when it rings and it's her.

"Hey, Mitz—"

"That bastard!" she cries.

"What?" I catch myself looking over my shoulder, wondering if she somehow read my email.

"I never want to see that son-of-a-bitch again, Lana, and if you know what's good for you, you'll tell his buddy Jason to go to hell!"

"What's wrong?"

"He said I was fat," she sobs. "It's the Investors Gala next week and I tried on the dress I'm planning to wear and he said – that good-for-nothing loser – he said I looked like a dumpling."

"Honey, what—"

"Who tells a woman something like that?" Mitzi yells into the phone.

"I'm—"

"I'll tell you who. A guy with a death wish, that's who."

"Can you—"

"A guy with every goddam thing he owns – which isn't much, let me tell you – sitting at the end of my driveway in garbage bags, that's who. And if he doesn't get back here before garbage pick-up at 3, he'll be wearing what he's wearing right now till Hell freezes over or he finds another sucker who will put up with this crap." Mitzi says with fury bleeding though the phone.

I decide to wait until her rant has run its course, so I say nothing.

"Hello? Lana? Are you there? Goddammit, I can't even get this *farkakte* phone to work."

I hear all kinds of clatter as she wrestles with her phone. When I hear a series of beeps as she pushes button after button, I open my mouth to speak. The next thing I know, she hangs up.

I hit Jonah's number. He answers on the first ring. When I ask him to drop everything and rescue Mitzi he says she'll be fine by the time he brings her to Nolan's party. Not for the first time, I wish he liked girls… with red hair, that is. I give my head a shake and climb into the bath. Since Nolan warned me to dress for success tonight, I'm guessing boots, jeans and a dressy top won't do. I'm mentally reviewing my pathetic closet for options when I suddenly sit up, slopping suds everywhere. In all my grand planning, I'd never thought about dating clothes. First thing tomorrow, with or without the girls, I have to hit the shops! The thing is... I dread shopping. I can only hope someone will help me figure out what to buy!

I'm in my car two hours later, still thanking my lucky stars that I thought of clothing before the dating games begin, when Lady Luck smiles on me twice. As I turn the corner and head up the block to the club hosting Nolan's birthday bash, a car pulls out of a prime spot right out front and I slide in. My slick manoeuver earns whistles from two great-looking guys and a handful of pedestrians. Smiling as I step out of my car, I catch my heel. I'm about to go down in a jumble of legs, tall boots and red hair when one of the guys leaps forward and grabs my hand, saving me from disaster. The whistles change to applause as my heroes escort me inside.

The first person I see inside is Nolan, who greets me with a smile. "So much for my surprise."

At my puzzled look, he laughs. "Lana, meet my skydiver buddies, Ethan and Van. Guys, this is the crazy, fabulous woman I've been telling you about."

"Well that's relief," says the blond guy named Van.

"Yeah," dark and handsome Ethan laughs. "Now we don't have to tell Nolan's cousin we're already smitten with a damsel we just rescued.

"What's with the 'we' stuff, buddy?" Van asks. "I didn't see *you* pulling her to safety."

Ethan rolls his eyes. "Oh, brother, here we go. Can I buy you a drink?" he asks me.

"Wine please," I laugh. "And thanks!"

"May I have this dance?" Van takes my hand.

"I'll grab a table," Ethan says. "Go have fun."

Out on the dance floor, Van breaks the ice. "Nolan says you're a producer?"

I nod and smile. "What about you?"

"Business stuff," he replies. "No big thing. My real love is skydiving. Have you ever tried it?"

I shake my head.

"We go every Sunday. Want to come?"

"Sounds great!" I say and promptly start wondering what our kids will look like.

There's only one down side to this: I'll be throwing myself out of a plane thousands of feet in the air to be with this marvelous man and I'm scared to death at the mere thought of flying.

As the music ramps up, I put Sunday out of my mind and concentrate on having fun. Song after song, Van matches me, move for move. After several songs, he says, "Drink?"

Just as I nod yes, the music ends. Before I can move, he dips me to the floor. Wow.

Back at the table, Ethan hands me the wine I'd asked for. When Van tells him that I've agreed to go jumping on Sunday, Ethan gives me two thumbs up.

"I'll be shooting the video." Ethan says with a smile.

"Is video your hobby?" I ask.

He shakes his head. "I'm a freelancer. Sometimes, when it gets crazy, I think it would be nicer as a hobby. But then the adrenalin kicks in and I wouldn't change careers for the world."

"Really," I murmur. Nolan and I could use a cameraman. I wonder if he's any good.

Just then I hear Mitzi's fabulous laugh and I remember all the books I'd read on dating. I realize I need to give these guys a little space. When I plead the need to spend some time with the birthday boy, Van asks for my phone number. On cloud nine, I drift back to Nolan's table.

When I see Mitzi's face, I'm very happy. Jonah's cheer-up magic has come through as promised. When he sees me smile, he gives me a wink. At the same time, I catch Nolan's wave from the corner of my eye. He's just coming back to the table with Kat, who has the kind of sparkle in her big grey eyes that makes me wonder if she's just won some kind of prize.

"Kat's met a man," Nolan murmurs into my ear. "His name is Trevor. He's getting their drinks. Jonah says he's gay. I think so too, but we're not going to spoil her fun."

"Got it," I nod and change the subject. "You sure know how to throw a party! Those skydiver guys are hot!"

"Hey, what's a birthday without presents? Looks like you were a hit." He smiles.

"I'm even going skydiving with them!" I say with a big grin.

Knowing my fear of heights, Nolan laughs. "Bartender!" he exclaims. "This calls for a drink!"

Before things get too crazy, I manage a quiet moment with the girls, telling them my shopping plans for Saturday. I seriously need some fashion help and, as it turns out, everyone's up for a tomboy transformation.

It's not long before Van takes me for another dance marathon. Back at their table, I learn that Nolan has spilled the beans about my fear of heights. Is Van concerned? Hell no! He does his best to terrify me even further with stories about jumps gone haywire. Finally, Ethan takes pity on me and changes the topic. That's when I learn Ethan will be filming me and Van is certified to give tandems (whatever that means). Ethan assures me that they'll be tracking me every step of the way.

When a sudden yawn hits me, I realize how tired I am. In all the excitement of launching my GRAND Plan, meeting the Muckers and dealing with office pranks, I haven't slept more than a few hours the last few nights. So I say my good-byes to my rescuers, give Nolan a cousinly birthday kiss, confirm tomorrow's shopping date with the girls and head out the door.

Saturday, Day 3

*M*ost women love shopping. They also love to cram their closets full of every fashion item imaginable. Not me. As far as I'm concerned, if jeans, a cute top and boots don't work, I don't need to go. But I've got a perfect man to find, and if I have to go through Hell to get fitted out in dating clothes, I'm willing to suck it up.

This was my thinking before the gang arrived. When Jonah says his *start where you are* shopping strategy begins in my closet, I'm having second thoughts about the whole thing. Grumbling that it sounds more like Psych 101 than a wardrobe make-over, I trail after them as they head for my closet.

"You know I don't have anything good in there," I complain. "Can't we just hit the shops and get it over with?" My protests fall on deaf ears. "What about brunch?" I say brightly, hoping a direct appeal to Jonah's stomach will shift this agony into second gear. I might as well be invisible.

Humphing back to the living room, I boot up my laptop and check for messages. Alright! Ten more replies. As I weed out the impossibles, I forget everything else. A few minutes later, I'm amazed at the results so far.

In addition to the musician I'm having coffee with later today and the dinner dates with the art critic, cameraman and DJ, there's Tad's electrician friend, a Beverly Hills hotel owner, the son of a French diplomat, a personal trainer, a car salesman, an agent and the skydiving date with Van and his friends. Things are looking up!

Sunday	Monday	Tuesday	Wednesday	Thursday	Friday	Saturday
				WEEK ONE[1] The Plan	Nolan's[2] Birthday	Skylar[3]
Skydive -Van[4]	Jason[5]	Doug[6]	Henri[7]	WEEK TWO[8] Frank	[9]	[10]
[11]	Jeremy[12]	Lotar[13]	Paavo[14]	WEEK THREE[15]	[16]	[17]
[18]	[19]	[20]	[21]	WEEK FOUR[22]	[23]	Oscar[24]
[25]	[26]	[27]	[28]	DEADLINE[29]	RESULTS[30]	My[31] BIRTHDAY

Hours later, feet sore, bank account thinner, I'm done. The only thing that saved the day was that it was time spent with my pals. Now I need some quality 'me' time before my first GRAND Plan date. What with Mitzi's endless rants, Jonah's high energy and Kat's new man raves, I'm ready to kick back and relax before my Mr. Right, Mr. Forever, Mr. One-and-Only adventure begins.

This reminds me that I need to confirm tomorrow's skydive. As I rummage through my purse to find Van's card and pull out my phone, I realize that my throat is suddenly dry. Stage fright? Seriously? I dial quickly, hoping his machine picks up. It does! Yay!

"Hi, this is Lana Fray. I'm calling about a ticket on straight down airways? I wanted to check out the flight plans for tomorrow and was hoping you could hook me up. Thanks."

Shaking my head at my lame excuse for a message – who, in their right mind, would waste their time on such a dim broad – I'm gathering my parcels and bags when the phone rings.

"Hey, Lana. It's Van. Ethan will pick you up at 7AM sharp. We'll be heading into the desert to reach our destination. You'll need warm clothing and your credit card. It's $200 for a tandem jump, and $100 for the video. We'll be gone all day. Need to know anything else?"

"Uhh, no." I mean, what else could I possibly need to know about heading off into the desert with strangers and jumping out of a moving airplane? How to notify next of kin? Who to put in my will?

"Good. Text me your address and I'll see you in the morning."

"Okay, I--"

But he's already hung up. Wow. What have I gotten myself into? I text him my address anyway because... You know what? To be honest, I've no idea. I realize that I'm wasting my time trying to second-guess my sanity and safety, so I call Nolan. He's not home so I leave a message.

"Nolan? Lana. Skydiver Van just called. Here's the thing: First thing tomorrow morning, I'm supposed to go to the desert with these guys and if they don't rape and kill me and bury my body out there, the plan is that I give them $300 to push me out of an airplane and video my demise. Am I crazy? Are they? I mean, how well do you know them? Will you feed my fish if something happens and I'm never heard from again? On second thought, y'know what? I'll just call and cancel. Maybe I'll change my phone number. That's no big deal, right? Shit! I just gave Van my address. Dammit anyway. I've got my first GRAND Plan date tonight so I won't have time to move. Wait! I know! I'll call my brother and get him to run their names through AFIS or their prints through CODIS or whatever the hell-it-is that he does to find fugitives. Yeah. That's the best idea. Thanks Nolan." And I hang up.

My phone rings immediately. It's Nolan. "What I like best is the way you handle pressure."

"I'm over-reacting?"

"Ya think? Have a bubble bath. Enjoy your date. And do me a favor, try to relax and just have fun tomorrow. Okay?"

"Fine then." I hang up in a bit of a huff. I know he's right, but seriously? Who does this kind of thing? And really, telling me to relax just irritates me more, even if I know he's totally right.

Luckily, Nolan knows me well. The bath was just what I needed to cool my jets and, by the time I sort through my new clothes and choose a casual sweater to go with my favorite jeans and boots, I'm back in the right frame of mind to meet Contestant Number One. This guy, Skylar, apparently makes a good living as a studio musician, according to my referral pal. So he's not a musician for the fame or the women. He's in it because he truly loves music. I'm excited: a man with Soul!

A few minutes later, as I stroll up the street to Café Aroma where we're scheduled to meet, I'm wondering if our talented kids will take after him and become rock stars or follow in my tone deaf path and win Oscars instead.

Café Aroma is one of my favorite places. At least three times a week, I spend a quiet hour or two soaking up their cool atmosphere. Even if I had the faintest idea how to make the coffee they sell, drinking it alone at home just isn't the same.

Inside, I toss my book on a corner table by the window overlooking their terrace. One of the café owners– a woman named Penny – waves at me from behind the counter and I head over to pick up my usual brew. I love a place where I don't even need to stand in line to order, because they know exactly what I want. This is very comforting right now, as my stomach is doing more flip flops than a trampolinist trying for the world record.

My choice of table is strategic. I can see the front and side doors without much effort and it's close to the ladies room. You'd think I was a Girl Scout, I'm so prepared.

Moments later, a great-looking guy walks in and looks around, curiously, before lining up for a coffee. He's stocky, dressed in jeans, boots and a great plaid shirt. I like his tussled brown hair, liquid brown eyes and the grin that he flashes my way as soon as he notices me looking. Cute! I'm using all my powers of positive thinking, hoping he's my date, when he heads in my direction with an even bigger smile. Jackpot! I stick out my hand to shake his.

"Hey, Skylar, Rayne was right! You're adorable!"

"Darn," he laughs. "My name is Tony. For a second there, I thought it was my lucky day, finding such a gorgeous woman staring me down."

I blush, totally embarrassed, my mind racing. Here I am waiting for a date and I have a cute guy right in front of me. I can't ask for his info in case my date shows up and sees me. I mean, if some guy was waiting for a date with me and I saw him exchanging info with a hot girl I'd be mad.

And this isn't just some guy I'm waiting for. This is my first GRAND Plan referral. I can't change the rules right out the gate.

Fortunately, I'm saved from having to solve the problem when a tall, gangly hippy looking type in a stained green shirt, droopy jeans and stringy black hair pushes past Tony and plops down in the opposite chair.

"I'm Skylar," he says. "How's the food?"

"Hi" I smile graciously.

"You hungry or did you already eat?"

As he looks for a waitress and Penny heads over to our table, I casually look around for Tony, but he's nowhere to be seen. Damn! Disappointed that he didn't stick around, I push him out of my thoughts and focus on Skylar. We order, me a Roast beef sandwich with a side of fries and he gets the vegetarian hummus sandwich.

As he tells me about the last Phish concert he attended, he keeps staring. Suddenly, he interrupts himself. "Are your eyes always that blue?"

Okay, this isn't terrible. He may be a little scruffy, but he's clearly got taste. Maybe his music and lifestyle will be the quality that makes ours the kind of relationship that lasts. When Penny brings the food and hands me the Tabasco, Skylar's eyes light up.

"You like spicy food?"

At my nod, he suddenly shifts into full-on rant. "Okay, wow! There's this hot sauce called FIRE – have you tried it? It's amazing. Oh, and I can take you to this great wing place – you like wings? – yeah, you eat the wings there and it burns for days!"

I laugh, thinking how cute his enthusiasm is. So what if we're different. This is great.

Penny comes back with a pitcher of water and glasses and as Skylar reaches up to take them from her, a breeze coming through our window wafts a stench of body odor in my direction that makes me gag. A smell this ripe isn't a case of first date jitters. When I take a closer look at his stringy hair and grimy shirt, I realize that he probably hasn't bathed or changed in days. If this is his idea of first date etiquette, what happens when he stops trying? I'm staring at him, wondering what to say.

But Skylar doesn't seem to notice my reaction or the fact that a number of people are looking pale, grabbing their drinks and heading for the terrace.

"Wow, you were hungry," he says.

I look down at my empty plate. I've been eating as fast as I can to get this date over with. As I realize that I must have looked like a starving horse the way I attacked my plate, I blush. Maybe he doesn't know he has body odor. Maybe it's one of those genetic things and no one has ever told him. Maybe I'll just ask him to take a shower next time. I mean, what's a minor hygiene challenge compared to the joy of finding The Perfect One?

Skylar is a total gentleman for the remainder of the meal. Sweet and funny, he insists on paying and settles for a kiss on the cheek when I tell him I don't need an escort home. As he climbs into an okay-looking car I think to myself, *I'll see you again if you call.*

Sunday, Day 4

I'm up before the alarm clock. I'm not a natural early riser, but panic can change a woman.

I try deep breathing. I try role playing. I try coffee. I catch myself glancing more than once at a bottle of scotch my brother left behind on his last visit when my sensible inner voice tells me to grow up.

For my last day on earth, I've chosen a navy blue Alaska shirt and a pair of "oh, what a nice ass" jeans. The shirt will make my blue eyes bluer and the nice ass jeans speak for themselves. I may be a tomboy, but I'm not an idiot. I reach into the back of the closet and haul out a down-filled warm-up jacket I've barely worn since Boise and transfer my I've barely worn since Boise and transfer my basic essentials to a small blue messenger bag. Low-heeled brown cowboy boots, a snuggly powder blue scarf around my neck and a pair of purple knit gloves and I'm all set.

Ethan shows up at 7 on the dot, his friendly grin and bear hug erasing my earlier fears.

"Ready to go?"

"You bet!"

At his big black truck he opens the passeger door with a flourish. "Your chariot awaits m'lady."

As soon as I'm strapped in, we're off. Our first stop is McDonalds, where he orders a bunch of Egg McMuffins with the works. Next stop is a tidy little house with a nice sized lawn where Van is already loading duffel bags into an ancient VW camper.

When I jump out of Ethan's truck and walk over to say hi, I get the kind of welcome any girl would love. Van's eyes twinkle as his lips lightly brush mine. "We'll be off in minute, babe."

Ethan brings his equipment and loads it in through the back window. "Don't worry about the way this old boat looks," he grins. "Everything's nice and clean inside."

When I take a peek I'm impressed. The passenger compartment behind the front seats has been divided in half, with the back serving as a storage area and the front made cozy with a love seat and three matching chairs bolted onto the carpeted floor in place of the typical bench seats. A cooler under the window is filled with bottles of water and power bars. Storage cupboards have been added above the curtained side windows along both sides. I notice that the chairs and love seat have seat belts and side pockets. The only thing missing is a TV, snacks and a crackling fire.

I choose the love seat in the hope that Van will join me. If he doesn't, at least I'll have a great view between the two front seats. When Ethan takes the wheel and Van takes the passenger seat beside him, the view wins. Oh well.

The old camper motor wheezes and whines when we hit the highway and Ethan coaxes it up to speed. In the steady stream of vehicles whizzing past I see nothing but frowns and shaking heads. Conversation is impossible until we exit onto a dusty dirt road that takes us into the desert. As I look around, I see nothing that looks like a place a girl could run to if her life depended on it.

"You worried about something, Lana?" Van asks casually.

"No," I lie through my smile. "I'm just looking at the beautiful desert landscape."

"There's nothing to worry about, you know. You don't have to do anything but fall out of a plane. Everything else will be handled by the wind."

The look on my face must be priceless, because they burst into gales of laughter. If I get out of this alive, I'm going to kill Nolan for setting me up with these heartless beasts. Then I'm going to read Van the riot act. I'm not interested in the kind of husband who thinks my fear is funny and has to be told when the little woman needs a hug. Forget my quality of life for a minute, what kind of message will that send to our kids?

A few minutes later, Ethan pulls over to the side of the road and turns off the engine. He looks at Van. "You bring the shovel?"

"Yeah," Van nods over his shoulder. "It's in the locker above the window."

"Better get it."

Van steps between the seats, snaps open the safety latches and pulls out a grubby cloth drawstring bag. He pulls on the strings and to my growing horror, he takes out a nasty looking shovel head and three handle sections that he quickly screws together.

"Ready?" Ethan asks.

"Yup," Van replies.

"Let's git 'er done," Ethan says.

And the two of them turn and look at me. Suddenly, my mouth is totally dry. I'm trying to remember everything I've heard about abduction, but all I can think of is RUN.

Jumping to my feet, I rush for the door. I'm too late. Van is blocking my way.

"We've got one question for you, Lana." Ethan's voice is soft and somehow menacing.

"Yes?" My voice is a dry whisper.

"You want ketchup on your hash browns?"

I blink as their laughter erupts again. Knowing there's no point in trying to fake my way out of this, I shake my head and smile. "Okay, so can I ask what the shovel is for?"

"When it rains, like it did last night, the parking lot at the Drop Zone turns to mud. The old boat gets stuck every time so we keep the shovel handy, just in case," Ethan explains.

After we've eaten our Egg McMuffins, it takes us another ninety minutes to reach the Drop Zone, which is located near a small desert town called California City. As Ethan pulls up beside a nondescript two story building and starts unloading the gear, Van grabs my hand and takes me to meet the manager (Elsie), the dive instructor (Pete) and the mechanic (Rick) before we go into a hangar filled with furniture rejects so awful the Goodwill folks have probably turned them down. Squares of ratty carpet are scattered around the concrete floor, covered in parachutes in various phases of being packed and checked by skydivers getting ready for their jumps.

After the boys show me how to climb into the dive gear, Pete takes charge of my training. In a blur of fingers and thumbs, he demonstrates the hand signals I'll need and where the pull cord is. Just before he leads me to a platform under a stairway labeled "Mock up", Van steps in.

"I'll take it from here, Pete," he says.

"Better show her the hand signals again," Pete suggests. "I'm not sure she was following."

Van grins and leads me away from the platform, taking me back to the beginning again.

"The first thing to get clear is that you and I are jumping tandem, Lana," he says. "Tandem means we'll be strapped together, so you don't need to worry about getting every step right. The main reason I'm going through the details is to make sure you know *why* each step matters."

What a relief! It's like a ton of worry has been lifted off my shoulders and all of a sudden I can hear what he's saying and follow his lead. When Van is happy with my progress, we go back to the Mock Up platform and he shows me how to kneel in position. After a count of three, we jump together off the two foot high shelf.

"And that's it," he says. "Congratulations, Lana. You're trained."

Over the intercom, I hear Elsie announce '15 minute call' and suddenly everyone is strapping on colorful backpacks covered in arm, leg and chest straps. Van helps me into mine and then takes me over to the others. Outside the door, I can see the plane and my mouth goes dry again.

"Ready, babe?" Van grins.

I'm so scared I can't trust my voice so I just nod.

"Remember, we're going to be joined at the shoulder, waist and hip. I'll be right there with you, every minute."

Van and I are among the first to board and as soon as we're inside, he hooks us together.

"Think of it as a vertical three-legged race," he jokes.

As the plane fills up, he tells me that everyone (except me) has a minimum of 30 jumps and some of them have thousands. I nod and smile, trying to look calm. Inside I'm praying furiously.

I know. Bargaining with God is such a cliché, but what the hey. *If I survive this*, I think desperately, *I will do anything you ask.*

"Van, what if I change my mind and tell you up there that I don't want to go?" I stare hopefully.

"Oh, that's okay," he grins. "No and Go sound the same up there with all that noise so say anything you like." With that he winks and turns to talk to another fun jumper.

I am doomed.

I keep my eyes glued to the floor as the noisy, twenty-minute climb to fifteen thousand feet takes what feels like an eternity. As the plane reaches altitude and levels out, the skydivers start bumping knuckles and pointing at each other. I try to focus on this until a garage-sized door suddenly flies open. I take one look and think to myself, *That's it. I'm going to be sick.*

I watch the first pair of skydivers grab hands and jump head first. The next pair goes. Too soon, every jumper is off and out the door. As I watch someone fling himself out the door in the shape of a cannon ball, leaving an empty space on the bench beside me, it takes a second to register that it's our turn. I feel Van tighten our straps and I snuggle in closer, hoping and praying that somehow this works and I survive.

Am I this desperate to meet a man? I ask myself. *If I'm willing to jump out of a perfectly good airplane, there's no better word to describe me!*

"Okay, Lana, walk like a crab," Van says. "That'll get us to the door."

I suddenly realize that Ethan is hanging outside the door with his camera rolling as Van pushes us to the edge.

Van says, "Count to three, girl."

I take it slow, trying to delay the inevitable. "One... two..."

And BAM, we're flying. I try to scream but the minute I open my mouth, my breath is snatched away. So I close my mouth and breathe in through my nose. When my lungs are full, a screech breaks free for three of the longest seconds in my life. I'm about to faint from fright and then it hits me: I'm already falling. If I'm going to die, there's nothing I can do about it.

The blind panic fades and after a couple of seconds I begin to enjoy the sensation of the wind hitting my face and the freedom I feel as we fly across the powder blue skies. It really is more like flying than falling, I realize, and it's … to be honest, it's AMAZING. Van takes the two of us into a turn that spins us around and, out of the corner of my eye, I catch movement. I turn my head and there's Ethan with the camera strapped to his helmet, catching our every move. And that's when I realize something else: I LOVE IT! Love the freedom, the speed and the adventure of this wild and glorious ride.

Suddenly, I see Van's finger pointing in front of my face. What is it? Oh! Pull! I reach back to grab and pull and… I CAN'T FIND IT!!! As panic rises in my throat, BOOM! Van grabs and pulls the cord and the jolt of the parachute catching the wind is intense – like going from a hundred miles an hour to thirty, with nothing in between.

Now we're floating and it feels like a dream. Van points out different landmarks as the parachute flutters above us.

"You wanna play a bit?" he hells into my ear.

I nod and he yanks the right toggle, sending us into a spin floating sideways and I'm loving every dizzy second. I look down and suddenly the ground is coming at us pretty fast. I don't have time to panic because Van is kicking my legs, yelling 'legs up'! In the next second, he's pushing me into his lap, running madly just before our butts hit the dirt and we're pulled along by our 'shutes in a dusty desert skid.

My heart races and the tears begin to flow. I've just had the most freeing experience of my life and it happened in the arms of an incredible man! Everyone comes running as Van untangles me from the jumble of legs and lines and I leap to my feet. I'm filled with so much energy I can't stand it. These strangers feel like my best friends and I run around hugging everyone. I cheated death! I defied gravity! It was miraculous!

On the ride back, Van joins me on the love seat and puts his arm around me. From high up on Cloud Nine, I sigh, "I'm never going to sleep again. That was incredible."

"That's the adrenaline talking," he says. "I give you ten minutes."

The next thing I know, I'm hearing whispered voices. I open my eyes to find that we've arrived back at Van's bungalow and Ethan is dragging his camera gear to his truck. Van sticks his head in the open doorway. "Hey, Miss Never Gonna Sleep. Hustle your buns. You're ride's waiting."

As I step onto firm ground, he grins. "Wanna come sky diving with us again next week?"

"OHMYGODYES!!!"

"Okay, but try to show a little enthusiasm," Van grins and then gives me a quick kiss. "Ethan says he'll have your video ready by then."

Monday, Day 5

Searching out Nolan first thing Monday, I throw my arms wide and say, "I'm a skydiver!"

While the rest of the office bursts into spontaneous applause, he simply gives me two thumbs up and doesn't ruin my moment with an 'I told you so'. Then I see a fine line crinkling between his perfectly shaped eyebrows. Something's up.

"Ethan just called," he says. "He's looking for a job. What do you think?"

Having a cameraman who isn't on staff at Slum Central is something we've been debating for the past couple of months. The risk is that another player who isn't on the Bossman's direct payroll means more money out of our meager budget. That was one of my smart negotiating points when I took this job, if it's our guy behind the camera, we own the footage and that can mean leverage when it comes time to negotiate contracts. It also makes him loyal to us and our agenda.

I quickly shift gears and run through my memories of yesterday, doing my best to dismiss the stark terror before the jump and the total wow of flying in Van's arms. What I'm left with is the impression of a guy who thinks on his feet, takes no unnecessary chances and blends in with the scenery. Since reality TV is a seat-of-your-pants game played with unpredictable amateurs, a cameraman with Ethan's attributes is worth his or her weight in gold.

"I didn't see any of his work," I tell Nolan, "but I liked his technique. Let's get him in for an informal chat ASAP and see where it takes us. Tell him to bring his resume and reel."

"Will do. Next on the agenda, Bossman wants to see us."

My eyebrows go up. "When?"

Nolan glances at the clock. "Half hour."

"I'll confirm a couple of interviews in case he needs solid proof that we're moving forward."

"And speaking of moving forward," Nolan grins.

"Not counting Van and the guy I met Saturday night, I've lined up ten men for lunches, dinners and drinks. That's a pretty good return since Thursday, don't you think?"

"Unless they're all raving madmen running from the law," Nolan says, "your GRAND Plan may turn out to be the Hot New Thing. I wonder if we shouldn't be following you with a camera."

"Not a chance in hell!" I laugh.

Thirty minutes later, we hear the Bossman yelling the same thing as we approach his office. Nolan and I exchange looks. He taps on Bossman's door before turning the knob. His eyebrows shoot up. It's locked. Something is definitely up.

"Who's there?" Bossman's voice sounds muffled.

"It's Lana," I tell him. "Nolan's with me. You wanted to see us."

We hear a desk drawer closing, murmured words and then the door opens. Bossman stands there, looking pale and tired. Even his shiny boot-black hair seems dull and faded.

"Come in."

As we take our seats I notice that he locks the door before he returns to the safety of his desk.

"I call the cops after the skunk," he says as he drops into his chair, "and they got no time for me. This detective yahoo says, 'There's nothing we can do until something more serious happens', like trashing a $70,000 car and shutting a studio down is some kinda joke to him. But when I say, 'Whaddaya want me to do, die in a fire?' suddenly he's all over me. 'Was I planning an arson? Did I know something I wasn't telling them?' Assholes."

The Bossman falls silent after this and we've got nothing. After a few seconds, I clear my throat.

"So, uhh…" I'm prompting. "You sent for us because?"

The Bossman stares at me, drumming the fingers of one chubby hand on his desk.

"These 'cement shoes' guys of yours," he makes air quotes with a wink. We look at each other and back at him and he raises his eyebrows and nods, like he's giving us some kind of signal.

Then it hits me. He means the Muckers. I close my eyes for a second and take a deep breath to keep my voice calm. "What about them?"

"I'm just sayin'. I'm just floatin' it out there. Wouldn't they maybe know somebody?"

"To do what? Repave the parking lot? Find you a bodyguard?"

"Well… yeah, okay, that too."

"What do you mean, that TOO?"

Nolan clears his throat and I turn to look at him. "I think he wants us to hire a hit man."

My jaw drops. I look at the Bossman. Incredibly, Nolan's right. I can see the look of hope shining in the lunatic's beady little eyes.

"You want me to call people I've just met, people I barely know, and tell them what? That we'll put them on TV and all they have to do in return is put us in touch with one of their wise guy cousins to hunt down a prankster who deserves to die because he put a SKUNK in your car? Have you lost your mind?"

"I said I was just floatin' it," the Bossman says defensively. The room goes silent as the Bossman shifts in his chair. Suddenly, he seems to get hold of himself. "An' remember who you're talkin' to here, by the way. All I'm saying is, you're gonna be gettin' their back story, you never know what comes up. If you heard somethin' we might look into, it's an opportunity we might not wanna ignore."

If I stay in his office one more second I'll do something I'll regret. Through clenched teeth, I tell him I'll keep my ears open. Without even looking at Nolan, I head for the door and grab hold of the door knob. Naturally, I've forgotten that it's locked and I nearly yank my arm out of its socket. Job or no job, it's a very good thing no one says anything. I take a deep, calming breath, twist the damned button, turn the knob and walk out, leaving Nolan to follow suit.

Nolan finds me in the parking lot, burning off my frustration by walking in circles.

"It could have been worse," he remarks.

"You're kidding, right? Tell me you're kidding."

"He could have called them himself. Imagine that scenario, sports fans."

In a blinding flash, I realize he's right. I can even hear that oily voice in my head, 'My producer gave me your card, and since I happen to be looking for a hitman...' I think I'm going to be sick.

Nolan keeps talking. "Wait: There's an upside."

"Let's hear it."

"You have to think about the big picture. The entertainment value in the anti-defamation suit alone is priceless and we'd have the inside track on the scoop of the century. We write the tell-all book. Hit the talk show circuit. And then – ta da – we produce the feature."

The whole thing is so crazy, I can't help laughing. And once it starts, I can't stop. When Nolan realizes that I'm helpless, he can't resist feeding the fire.

"George Clooney puts on 200 pounds to play the Bossman. DeNiro plays Poppi. Aaron Paul bleaches his hair blond to play me. We give Amanda Seyfried copper highlights and freckles to play you. Pepé Le Pew plays the skunk. We win an Oscar. Buy an island. Live in luxury."

My side are aching.

"My only concern is finding someone we can hire to protect *us*. You got any pull with retired Basque terrorists back in Boise?"

"Stop!" I manage to gasp.

"I'll take that as a 'No'," he grins.

Back inside, it takes me a good half hour to recover and get back to work. For the rest of the morning, I find myself giggling every now and then. I'm relieved that the Bossman doesn't try to follow up with us. They'd have to call 911 and carry me out on a stretcher.

With Sam, our researcher doing what he does best, looking into the military angle and a few other details, Nolan and I make pretty good headway on our next steps. By quitting time, we've confirmed a meeting with Ethan first thing in the morning and after that, we'll be doing key interviews with the Muckers.

By seven o'clock I'm ready for my date with Tad the Cad's plumber friend, Jason. I'm wearing a sage green tank, a chocolate brown skirt and gladiator sandals with 2-inch heels. I've brought a jacket in case he wants to walk. The plan is to meet for drinks at a cozy Irish bar and play things by ear after that.

When I walk in, the place is pretty quiet. It's a Monday night and the happy hour crowd has headed for home. There's a handsome guy in a baseball cap sitting alone at the horseshoe shaped bar. He's wearing a blue shirt that accents his eyes perfectly. I'm a sucker for guys who know how to play up their best features. It's one of the things I love about Nolan. He always finds a way to make women take notice of his green eyes, thick blonde hair and lazy smile.

I smile at this guy, but keep it neutral because I'm still kicking myself for my coffee shop gaffe on Saturday night. I grab a seat across the bar and signal the bartender. Before he reaches me, the guy sitting across makes the first move.

"Bartender, will you ask the gorgeous redhead if I can buy her a drink and call her Lana?"

My grin makes it clear that he's picked the right girl, so he brings his drink and sits beside me.

"What would you like to drink?"

"White wine spritzer."

"You heard the lady, bartender. She will have a glass of your best white wine."

As I watch the bartender pour the wine Jason ordered instead of the spritzer I'd asked for, I have one of those moments. What is it with men?

"Soda water on the side, please," I smile as the bartender delivers the wine. "Slice of lime if you have it," I add.

"Sure thing," the bartender says and then walks away, ignoring my request. Arrgh.

Jason raises his glass and taps mine. After I take a sip and he has a deep swallow, he puts his glass down on the bar and sits back in his chair. At least it's not going to be a chugging contest.

"So I want to know all about you, lady. Tad tells me that you work in TV. Somehow I don't think you do repairs, so fill me in. What do you do and where do you come from?"

I start with Boise and mention that my big brother is in law enforcement. Then I tell him about the move to LA with the plan to do serious documentaries and fill him in on the random kinds of craziness that make up a typical day in the life of a reality TV producer. After that, I switch the focus to his career and him.

"I'm not nearly as glamorous. I've worked for other guys. It sucks. For the last couple of years I put money aside and now I have my own company. It's a little risky to be on your own, but I like the freedom. When I find the perfect lady I want to have control over my time so I can be with her. When we have kids, I want to be the Dad who never misses a soccer game or a dance recital."

My heart skips a beat. This guy is perfect!

Jason signals the bartender for another round.

"I'd really like soda water instead please." I tell him. "All this talk is making me thirsty."

The bartender pays no attention to me and places another glass of wine beside the first, which is still half-full. Frustrated, I'm about to get into it with him when Jason steps in.

"The lady has a powerful thirst, man. Give her that soda water like she asked, okay?"

And just like that, the bartender's tragic hearing loss is reversed. When the soda water with lime arrives, Jason winks and taps my glass with his.

"Anyway," he continues, "I managed to put enough money aside for a small house about eight months ago and I just finished installing a hot tub. My next big project is putting up a fence so I can get a dog."

My frustration is a thing of the past. My imagination shifts into high gear as I see myself in front of a cute house with two kids, two dogs and my gorgeous electrician husband.

"What kind of dogs do you like?" I ask.

"I've always had German Shepherds, but the only kind of dog I want is the one my lady wants."

A warm glow spreads over me as I recall growing up with German Shepherds. I feel like I've known this man forever. My natural nervousness melts and we talk like old friends. He tells me how hard it is to find a woman who doesn't have a crazy make-over plan for every guy she meets. I tell him how long I've been trying to find someone who wants me to be me. I even tell him some of my best 'worst date' stories and he keeps shaking his head, laughing at the crazy stunts I've put up with.

We're just hitting our stride, it seems, when the bartender rings a bell. Last call? How is that possible? We both check our watches simultaneously, totally shocked to find that we've been talking non-stop for four hours. After he settles the bill, Jason walks me to my car, leans in and gives me a kiss on the cheek.

"Will you have dinner with me on Friday?"

"Definitely!" I exclaim with a bit too much enthusiasm. His face lights up with his gorgeous smile and my heart melts again.

I'm pulling into my parking spot when the phone rings. I check the caller ID and smile when I see that it's Jason. My heart starts pounding.

"I forgot to say goodnight, beautiful. I hope you'll think of me tonight, 'cause I'll be thinking of you. See you Friday."

Wow. I'm still on Cloud Nine when I hear the phone ringing. I fumble with my keys and manage to grab it before it goes to voice mail. It's Jonah.

"Hey, what's up?"

"I'm betting you had more fun tonight than I did."

I toss my bag on the table and settle on the couch. "...because you were...?"

"Holding Mitzi's hand for most of the evening. Again."

"Oh no! What did Tad do this time?"

"He took her to dinner to make up for the fat remarks the other day. When the check came, he told her he didn't have enough to cover it, so she paid. When they got home, he told her she wasn't giving him enough money, can you believe it? Amazingly, Mitzi turned the tables on him. She told him he could have more money than she could really afford to give him if he accepted a job at her company. I guess the idea that he should work sent him over the edge. He threw his drink into the fireplace and then he knocked a Tiffany vase onto the floor. When she heard all the yelling and crashing, the dog came running and stepped on the broken glass. Barks turned to yelps of pain. Mitzi threw Tad out and rushed Ginny to the vet. While she was waiting, she tried to reach you and then Kat. I was the only one who hadn't turned my cell phone off, so I went to her rescue. I just got home."

"Wow!"

"She says injuring Ginny was the last straw."

"D'you think she means it?"

"Nope."

I sit there, wondering what it's going to take to get Mitzi to see Tad for the worthless piece of shit he truly is. Then, one of Jonah's remarks hits me.

"Wait. You had your cell phone on? On a date? What's up with that?"

I hear him laugh. "Oh, honey, you have NO idea."

"Tell me, tell me!"

Big sigh. "Remember that big deal developer I met at the mixer last month?"

"Sure. And?"

Another sigh. "Okay, here goes. The thing is, the bar was dark and I might have been a little drunk, so…"

"…you had no idea what to expect. I get it."

"Right. And then this great looking guy walks in. The minute he sees me, he waves. But there's something odd about his hand. When he reaches me, I realize he's wearing green oven mitts."

"I'm sorry?"

"You heard me. Before I can say anything, this lunatic says, 'Aren't you wondering what the oven mitts are for?' I smile, because what else am I going to do, and he says – and I quote – 'Because youuuuuu are tooooooo hot to handle. RAWRRRRRRRRR.'"

I'm shocked into total silence for a second and then, I can't help it, the laughter explodes.

Jonah sighs heavily, but that only makes it worse. It takes several seconds before I've got myself under control. "Go on," I tell him, voice quivering.

"Okay, here's my dilemma. I've just ordered my drink. I can throw the money on the bar and leave, but running for the hills seems just as over-the-top as his oven mitt gag, so I decide to stay till my drink is gone and in the meantime, think up an excuse for cutting the date short. While he's taking the mitts off I turn my cell phone back on and pray that one of you will call."

"Smart move," I acknowledge. "Then what?"

"He orders a drink and while the bartender is building it, he tells me he reads palms."

"He reads palms. This is how he gets his big development deals?"

"Are you going to let me tell this ghastly tale, or not?"

"Sorry."

"I'm taking steady sips of my drink with my free hand while he traces lines on my palm and mutters 'Mmhmm' and 'Ahaaa'. Finally, he looks up, opens his eyes very wide and wiggles both his eyebrows. I'm about to tell him *'Never do that again with your face'* when he blows me away with the worst line I've ever heard in my entire life. I cannot believe he actually says, 'You need someone who is willing to take on the challenge of a fiery temptress.'"

"Did you say 'temptresses?'" I blurt it out.

"Shut up."

I cover my mouth but it doesn't help. A few seconds later I manage to whisper, "Sorry. Go on?"

"Fortunately, he says he needs to use the men's room, so while he's gone I signal the bartender and hand him enough to cover my drink and the tip. The bartender says, 'Was that guy wearing oven mitts?' When I nod, he grins and hands me my money back. 'It's on me.' Just as I'm about to thank him the bartender winks and says, 'See you around, Temptress.' I wanted to die."

"Oh, Jonah! So then what?"

"The developer comes back, tells me he's starving and wants to order dinner. That's when Mitzi calls and I'm saved from a fate worse than death."

"Wow."

Jonah sighs heavily. "So enough about my love life. How was your date?"

"I'm embarrassed to tell you."

"Why? Was your guy wearing, a tutu?"

"Nope. He was wonderful. Perfect. Handsome. Funny. Charming."

"No oven mitts?"

"None."

"Smug bitch."

"You know it," I laugh. "Better luck next time, Jonah."

"Easy for you to say," he mutters. "Sleep well, Lana."

And I do.

Tuesday, Day 6

I'm at work bright and early but Nolan is a no-show and his cell phone is off, so it's just me waiting in the conference room when Ethan shows up. His eyes light up when he sees me and we spend a few minutes talking about Sunday's skydiving adventure before I get back to business and take a look at his reel. His mix of gutsy hand held camera work, slick commercial teasers and dreamy outdoor sequences blows me away.

"Why do you need a job?" It's the only thing I can think to ask him. If he'd been working for me, I wouldn't let him go without a fight.

"I figured you'd ask me something like that. Nolan has been talking my ear off about coming to work with you guys, because he knows what it's like to work solo, waiting for the phone to ring. I'm ready for something a little more structured, as long as it challenges me and keeps me on my toes, but I've been reluctant to take Nolan up on his offer because great teams with no egos are rare. Even when he told me how the two of you operate, I had a hard time believing him. Then I met you and I got to see the kind of person you are. That's when I decided to give it a shot." He shrugs, "And here I am."

Here's the thing about shooting reality content... You get roughly 400 hours of raw footage to piece together a decent 40-minute show. So what you're looking for in a cameraman is much more than a guy who knows how to point, focus and shoot. You need someone who blends in anywhere at any time, because your cast is entirely made up of quirky amateur actor wanna-bees and they're easily spooked. Then you need someone with the patience of a saint, because the show is essentially unscripted and tends to wander all over the place. And by no means least, you need someone with an instinct for those perfect moments that never come this way twice.

I barely knew Ethan, but his demo reel really did blow me away and I'd had a good feeling about him on Sunday. So I decide this is one of those times when you go with your gut instinct. I give Nolan's cell phone one last try. When it goes to voice mail, my next step is easy.

"Okay, here's my deal. Nolan was supposed to take one of the staffers to shoot some interviews today, but I can't find him. If you're available, I'll pay your day rate. You bring your camera and we'll make it up as we go along. Think of it as a trial run. If you like the work and I think you'll mesh with us, we'll talk about a contract. How does that sound?"

Ethan grins. "I keep my gear in the car, just in case something comes up, so count me in!"

After a quick lunch, we head over to The Muckers. Gina gives us a tiny office and tells us she has four people, including her, to talk to. When Ethan has the interview shot all set up and we begin to roll, I start off with the kind of chatter that puts people at ease, asking what the work is like, how they got into it, slowly letting them get comfortable with me before I start with the harder questions. The room fills with laughter more than once as we get into some crazy stories and, at one point, Ethan throws in a comment that totally cracks me up and instantly transforms the interview – and the interviewee. If I wasn't sold on Ethan before, I am now. The man is seriously good.

Gina gives us a clear view of the big picture. *What made them use the name Muckers?* I ask. Two reasons: A mucker is someone who works in concrete and, her eyes twinkle, with an essentially English name, people are less likely to ask if they specialize in cement shoes. I feel my cheeks burn a little.

As she tells us how her Grandfather planned his business and I begin to see how many pies he has his fingers in, I'm wondering how much power this guy really has. Cement shoe jokes aside, could the Bossman be right? I shove that thought out of my head as soon as I think it and focus on the questions we need answers for: like, how do we get these people to give us insider details, and how do we get away with airing what they've said? I'm loving the stories but wondering what I'll have to do to get them to open up and share the seriously good stuff and once we get that, how we'll actually capture it on camera without turning the show into something that looks like a staged pile of crap.

The next person we talk to is Gina's cousin, Johnny. He turns out to be one of the beautiful musclemen whose work was holding up traffic last week. When he sees me, his eyebrows go up and he smiles. Johnny tells us he's like an apprentice. Wherever he's needed, he has to be able to fit in. Commercial, residential, public access areas, job quotes, crew supervision, training, past due collections, he does a little of everything. And oh boy, has he seen some crazy stuff.

At *past due collections* I get a tingle. "Any chance we'd be able to shadow you?" I ask casually.

He smiles and shrugs. "If Gina gives the okay, I'm okay."

I nod excitedly as I make a note about needing to get additional resources in case we come across potentially hostile clients.

When Johnny leaves, we meet Johnny's dad, Uncle Mike. This is the older guy who gave me his card on the jobsite. Mike is Gina's uncle and, by extension, Poppi's son. He grins when I ask him if he has stories.

"Missy, I've got stories that'll make your hair curl."

I can't help laughing. "Curly hair is great as long as we don't get sued."

"Listen," he says, turning serious for a moment, "if Poppi likes this idea, he'll make sure you get what you need and nobody's gonna give you any trouble."

I'm still smiling at the curly hair comment. "Really?"

Mike nods, still serious. "Loyalty isn't something you see much anymore, you know? With Poppi, it's like a code of honor. When you got a friend in Giovanni Vitale, you got a friend for life."

I'm suddenly stuck for words. Before I put my foot in it, Mike is all smiles again. "Don't get me wrong. You piss him off, you'll hear about it. He's gonna be a friend, not some kinda fool."

And that's when Poppi enters. "I'm-a too soon for you?" His smile is gracious and he moves like a dancer, yet there's something quietly menacing just beneath the surface. Dark eyes penetrating, hair greying at the temples and teeth sparkling, he's the most interesting person in the room from the moment he enters and he knows it.

Mike happily gives up his seat to his father and, as they exchange greetings, it's easy to see that the bond between them is strong. Mike may not be calling the shots from behind a desk, but it's clear that his father is still very proud of him.

"So, you're gonna tell-a me how this-a business is-a work?" Poppi begins as soon as Mike has left us. I realize that I'm going to have to bring my A game if I want to be calling the shots.

"When a show like this is done right, the people watching feel like they're developing new friends," I tell him. "The only difference is that they get to hear the stories and watch the lives unfold all from the comfort of their couch."

"An' instead of-a lookin' at-a nice, normal family, they get to watch a bunch-a craziness should be better off in-a zoo," Poppi adds with a twinkle in his eye.

I'm so surprised, I can't help myself. I laugh right out loud. Ethan does too.

"What?" Poppi says with a straight face. "Just-a because I'm-a talk like-a this, it's-a don't mean I'm-a no dumb guy."

"Poppi," I tell him when I get myself under control, "dumb is the last word I would ever use to describe you."

"That's-a good thing," he says. "It means you gonna say 'Yes' when I invite-a you to have-a dinner with-a me this-a Saturday. So we can take-a time an-a talk about this-a show."

"I- - my- - what?" I stammer and then stop. "Dinner? This Saturday? Well… yes! Thank you. That would be great."

"'at's-a good," he smiles and gets to his feet. "We talk-a then. Six o'clock. Nice-a to meet you," he says to Ethan just before he leaves. "I like a quiet guy, pays attention."

When the door closes behind him, my mouth is still open. I turn to speak to Ethan, who surprises me by shaking his head and, subtle as all hell, putting a finger to his lips.

"Can't wait to get these interviews back and start taking notes on all the great ideas," he says briskly. "Can we stop for a coffee on the way back, d'you think?"

"Uh, sure," I reply. *What the hell?*

The closest drive thru coffee joint is less than a block away. I pull in and park.

"Okay, spill it," I tell him.

"That room they gave us is wired for sound," Ethan tells me. "Didn't you notice me moving all over the place, adjusting my headset when I was setting up? I was fighting feedback."

"Why would they do that?"

He shrugs. "A recording eliminates any of that 'he said/she said' stuff."

Wow.

"So everything they volunteered…"

"All that stuff about 'we'll give you great stories' you mean? They're willing to back it up."

Cool.

"It also means that whatever he wants to tell you on Saturday will be off the record."

"Wait. What?"

"He wants to tell you something without anyone listening in."

"Why? What could that be?"

"How would I know? I just met him."

"Huh. Interesting."

"I wonder if you could somehow record it without him knowing."

"WHAT?"

"I'm just thinking out loud. It would be great if you could get him on tape. Given that whole loyalty speech from Mike, though, it wouldn't be good if you recorded him and he found out."

I'm ready to kiss this man. As we head back to Slum Central, Nolan calls. He can't talk now. When he says he'll call tonight and explain what happened, I remind him that I'm going out for dinner. Given that Ethan represents a direct line to Van, I keep the details to a minimum. This isn't hard to do, since I barely know anything about the guy I'm meeting, other than that he's a DJ, his name is Doug and we're dining at one of my favorite upscale bistros.

Back at Slum Central, I give Sam some follow-up instructions and introduce Ethan to the crew. He's excited to take a look at his footage, so I give him the guided tour and tell Sam to take care of anything Ethan needs. My plan is to duck out before the Bossman thinks of a reason to ruin my mood. I take it as a sign of good things to come that I manage to hit the road ahead of the rush-hour gridlock.

Given the upscale venue tonight, I decide on a flirty tan skirt with matching tank top and a mossy green jacket. My wobbly moments in high boots at Nolan's bash make me choose wedge heels.

As I stroll up the sidewalk, I hear this amazing voice calling my name. I turn, expecting a lonesome cowboy type to match the deep, sexy drawl and have to stop myself from staring. If the skinny little guy coming up behind me is over five feet tall, I'll eat my invisible hat. I'm only five two, but the shoes I'm wearing bring me up a few inches.

"Lana? Hey, I'm Doug. Wow, statuesque or what!"

"Uh, thanks!" What do I say, I'm thinking. *Good things in small packages?*

Doug doesn't seem to notice or care. He stops just before the door and takes a look around, noticing the high end cars pulling into the lot. "I've heard about this place, but I've never been. Great choice for our first face-to-face, Lana."

He grabs the door, smiles at the hostess, admires the décor and, as soon as we're seated, he asks the waiter to bring us the wine menu first. I'm impressed – and once we're seated, the height problem resolves itself. The minute we start talking, any fleeting concerns fade away. He's witty. He's fun. He's courteous and complimentary without being creepy. And, a big plus for a DJ, he doesn't hog the conversation. I've really hit the jackpot here.

"So, tell me," he asks, once the wine is presented, tasted, approved and poured, "are you looking for a rock star romance or could you be happy with a regular guy who wants to spend quality time with a smart, creative, independent woman?"

Wow. In a blink I'm picturing lively debates around the table, our kids eager to get into journalism, the Ivy League schools calling, and big family reunions.

Doug excuses himself when the waiter has taken our orders and I take the opportunity to check out the other diners. So many couples end up with nothing to say. This will never happen with us, I'm thinking. We'll be the envy of all our friends.

I'm still daydreaming when our appetizers arrive and I suddenly realize that Doug's been gone a long time. I ask the waiter if he'd mind checking the men's room to make sure everything's okay and he gives me the thumbs up. That's one of the things I like about places where they know you: no one thinks you're strange.

Several more minutes pass and I'm beginning to wonder if a sink hole has opened under the men's room when the waiter returns, the look on his face surprisingly grim.

"Jerry wants to see you his office," he says.

Jerry is the owner. Bewildered, I grab my jacket and purse and head for the long hallway at the back of the restaurant. I've only made this trip once or twice. Both times it was to plan a special party. This is the first time I've gone in search of a missing person.

I tap on the door and hear him say, 'If that's you, Lana, come on in.'

Inside his cramped office, there's barely room for a desk and a couple of chairs.

"Have a seat, hon." Jerry points to a chair. "I want to talk to you about your dinner date. I've never seen him before tonight and I don't want to pry, but how well do you know him?'

"It's a first date. Why?"

Jerry fidgets a little, looking very uncomfortable. "We caught him stealing."

"WHAT?" For a second, I wonder if I'm being pranked and this is one of those candid camera moments. I glance around the room hoping someone bursts through the door followed by a camera because this is crazy. Sadly the seconds tick by and the cameraman and host never show up. The more Jerry talks the more real it gets.

"On her way back from seating some people, my hostess actually sees your guy lift someone's wallet, so she automatically calls 911. Then she rings my office, tells me he came in with you and I tell our security guy to hold him instead of letting him go back to your table. When the cops arrive, they lift six wallets from his jacket and a dozen more from a box in the trunk of his car. Adding it all up, he had over two grand in cash, a bunch of credit cards and a zip-bag full of watches and rings in his glove compartment. That's a Grand Theft charge. Then they ran his ID and he's a repeat offender."

I'm stunned. "Are you sure it's the same guy?"

"Five foot tall, curly brown hair, deep voice, goes by the name Doug."

I feel my face getting hot as I nod. I bring a lousy thief to one of my favorite spots and he does his best to ruin their reputation and mine. How am I ever going to make this right?

Jerry continues. "It's going to be on our security camera, but it's so much easier to deal with the problem if the guy is still here when the cops come. Do you want to see him?"

"See him? I want to kill him!" I say with my face burning.

"Calm down, hon. I had to ask. And listen, this isn't your fault. You wouldn't believe the stories I could tell about people who've done a lot worse. Do you need a ride home?"

I shake my head, wishing I could just melt into the floor and disappear.

"Seriously, Lana. Are you okay to drive?"

I stare at him.

"Not for booze. I just want to be sure the shock hasn't been too much for you."

I suddenly realize how embarrassed *he* is and it makes me smile. "Thanks, Jerry. I'm fine."

There's a tap on the door. "Lana's take-out, Jerry."

Now I'm totally confused. "What take-out?"

"When you get home and the adrenalin wears off, you're gonna be hungry."

This is my cue to make a polite exit. "I wish I'd never agreed to have dinner with that guy in the first place and I'm even sorrier that I let him bring me here. Thanks for being so good to me."

Jerry comes around the desk and gives me a hug. "Come on. Let me walk you to your car."

Fifteen minutes later, I'm home. I can't look at the food or the wine, so I put them in the fridge and call Jonah. When I get his machine, I leave a message.

"I'll see you your silly-ass oven mitts and raise you a light-fingered DJ."

Then I shut off the phone and crawl into bed. I'm right on the edge of sleep when the phone rings. It's Nolan.

"So do you want the update?" He asks.

"What the heck happened to you today?"

"Okay. So Amy and I were having drinks the other night and we bump into Stephanie."

"Stephanie of the orange grove fortune and the temper?" I'd met this one a couple of times.

"The very same. And why didn't I remember about the temper?"

"She's a fabulously rich knock-out?"

"I knew there was a reason. Anyway, Steph was on her own so I invited her to join us and everything seemed fine. We hit a few clubs, grabbed some food and wound up back at my place. Amy suggested a swim, so the girls went to change and that's when everything went to hell."

"What happened?"

"I have no idea. One minute I hear giggles; the next minute they're yelling. I went to investigate and made the mistake of stepping into a full-on cat fight. What a disaster. I was the only one sober enough to drive everyone to Emergency. The girls look like hell. As for me, except for a broken nose, two black eyes, and maybe a broken rib, I'm fine."

"Wow. Are you sure you're okay?"

"Positive. See you tomorrow."

Just when you think yours is the saddest story in town, you get a glimpse of something worse. My disaster date was nothing compared to this!

Wednesday, Day 7

As soon as I check my phone in the morning, I find two new GRAND Plan replies waiting and, in spite of last night's disaster, I'm excited. I figure you have to go through some frogs to find the prince, right? Grabbing my calendar, I add a realtor named Gale and a teacher named Phil. That makes twelve dates, counting Van, Jason and Skylar asking for seconds. If I don't find my Mr. Right after this, I'm throwing in the towel and joining a nunnery.

Nolan and I manage to pull into the parking lot at Slum Central at the same time. Ethan is already there, leaning on his car. His jaw drops when he sees Nolan's war wounds.

"What the hell?" Ethan clearly can't believe it.

Nolan smiles. "It doesn't hurt much, but it makes me look tough, huh?"

"Nice man, real nice." Ethan replies with a chuckle. "What are you doing here?"

Nolan whispers, "I figure it's safer here. My attackers know where I live."

Ethan looks at me confused.

I shake my head. "Jealous women. What's a Romeo to do, you know?"

Ethan laughs. "Tough life there, buddy. Have you thought of making a reality series about the struggles of being a heart throb?"

I can't help grinning.

Nolan shakes his head. "Keep it up, Ethan, and you'll be out of a job before you start."

"Too late," I tell him. "He's already on the team. While you were duking it out with the girls, Ethan and I had a great day with the Muckers."

Ethan grins. "Wait till you see what we got."

With our researcher, Sam, joining in, we spend the morning reviewing Ethan's footage and brainstorming ideas. What we're looking for is a show that has the essential elements that make a great reality series – sex, violence, addiction, and/or stupidity – and that magical something extra that sets it apart and gives us an edge. What we have, thanks to our subjects and Ethan's uncanny ability to capture great/funny moments, is a better than average chance of pulling it off.

Just before lunch, Jonah calls. With Nolan and Ethan listening in, I share the details of my pick pocket date. As the laughter subsides, Ethan says, "You need to be more careful. After all these crazy reality shows you've worked on, hasn't it struck you how crazy people are? It takes a special kind of jackass to invite a woman to dinner and then slip away to boost a wallet, but there are guys capable of doing much worse. Look at Nolan. You could get seriously hurt."

It's a sobering thought and I feel like an idiot, a) because somehow safety hadn't occurred to me, and b) because my brother had already tried to pound this concern into my brain. I decide to play it smarter and, before we get back to our brainstorming, I put together a list of the men on my GRAND Plan calendar and email it to Trent. My other safety precaution will be to give Jonah and Nolan the same list and let them know where I'm going with each guy.

Tonight is probably okay, I'm thinking. What can possibly go wrong on a dinner date with the son of a French diplomat? Back home, I shower and fuss with my hair before slipping into a little black dress that seems just right, add classic pumps and crystal tear drop earrings and find my way to the patio at a quaint little French restaurant.

An elegant dark-haired man in a gray V-neck cashmere sweater, dark designer jeans and tasseled loafers in the same charcoal tone turns out to be Henri. He stands when I appear at in the doorway and hands me a long-stemmed red rose as he kisses my other hand in greeting. When we're seated, he lifts a finger and the waiter promptly sets an ice bucket by our table, holding up a bottle of champagne for Henri's inspection. When the ceremony is complete and we have our champagne flutes in hand, Henri's toast – To Love – sends a flash of heat and excitement through my whole body. The waiter returns with menus and, while I'm deciding what to order, Henri asks my permission before reaching into his pocket for his cigarettes.

I'm not a smoker and I'm not a fan of the habit or the smell, but everything about this man is so elegant, I'm certain his brand of tobacco will be as deliciously exotic as the fancy cigarette box he flips out of his pocket.

I'm wrong. My daydream of life strolling hand-in-hand on the Champs-Élysées goes up in smoke as he lights one foul-smelling cheroot after another, all through our meal.

"Do you always smoke?" I ask, eyes watering.

"But of course," he shrugs with a world-weary smile that shows stained yellow-brown teeth.

I'm so put off by the smell of his cigarettes and his stained teeth, I decide to cut our date short. When the waiter returns to take our order, I tell him I only have time for an appetizer because I must get back to work. The waiter nods and turns to Henri. To my astonishment, he proceeds to order everything from soup to nuts.

"Henri, I won't be able to stay for the meal," I remind him.

He just pats my hand and waves the waiter off. "This ethic of work, it is America's curse."

"Don't you work?" I can't help myself.

"Why should I?" he seems amazed, even offended. "My father married someone rich and I, too, will do the same. I will find an heiress. A movie star. Perhaps a Hollywood producer like you." He attempts to give me a sexy grin. It doesn't work.

Our appetizers arrive and as I begin to eat, Henri tells the waiter to bring the check.

"Have you decided to cancel the rest of the meal you ordered?" I ask.

He laughs. "Why would I do that?"

The waiter returns with the check. Henri nods in my direction with an amused look. "Mais, non. This is for mademoiselle. I am, how do you say it, her treat."

Excuse me? If this French freeloader thinks he's just scammed me for a seven-course meal *and* a bottle of champagne, he's in for a surprise. After my humiliation with Doug the Dip, I'm done with this kind of crap. I abandon Henri as I grab the leather folder in one hand and my purse in the other and, with the waiter trotting behind me I make a bee-line for the hostess station.

"I will pay for my appetizer," I tell him when we're standing at the register, "and nothing more. The champagne was clearly ordered and before I arrived and you were there when I told the gentleman that I had to leave directly after the appetizer. You took his order for an entire meal, knowing I would not be there while he ate it. The bottom line is that his portion of the bill has nothing to do with me."

I'd chosen a modestly priced appetizer but I want this over, so I pull two twenties out of my wallet. "You can keep the change when you give me my receipt."

The waiter hesitates. I'm pretty sure he knows this is the only tip he'll see off this meal, but just to be sure I win, Lonely Girl Looking For Love steps aside and Producer Girl Who Never Sleeps locks eyes with him. In a couple of seconds, he caves.

"Very good, madam." He punches in the cash transaction and I hand him the twenties. When the register spits out the receipt, he passes it to me.

On my way home, I look back on the last seven days: A hippy with B.O., a sky-diver dreamboat, an office prankster, a hunky electrician, a kleptomaniac, a hot TV show and a chain-smoking gigolo. What a week!

Week Two

Thursday, Day 8

As I head in to work, I realize that last night's fiasco has given me an idea. The trigger was Henri's high-handed remark about the American work ethic. What if we use *Meet the Muckers* to show what you get when the modern-day American work ethic and "old world" customs meet? We've got three generations working at a family business; we've got a woman running the show instead of hiding in a kitchen somewhere, barefoot and pregnant; and we've got a father figure pulling the strings behind the scenes. Granted, he's a Sicilian, but we can point to the same trend in any multi-generational family with European roots. The more I think about it, the more I like it: It gets us past the gangster stereotype that's making me crazy and, when we add the women in the military angle, it gives us the magic ingredient that sets our show apart.

Today being the morning after Nolan's run-in with his women, he's hurting so bad and hobbling around like such an old man, he can barely focus on what I'm saying. Fortunately, Ethan is ready to step in so I send Nolan home and call The Muckers to see if Poppi can come in for a chat. He agrees to join us that afternoon, and while we wait, we take a second look at the footage Ethan shot. I'm excited when I see the screen flicker with magic. Poppi is a natural and the camera loves him. Now I know for certain that Meet The Muckers can be a reality show with depth: it can entertain the simple, distracted viewer and at the same time explore the tensions and prejudices that surface when cultures collide.

When we break for lunch, I make a mad dash for my date with the personal trainer. We're meeting at a vegan place, which isn't my thing, but I start thinking it might be worth a try when I pull into the parking lot in time to see this total hunk walk inside. If this is my date, I may kiss my beloved red meat good-bye.

I flip my visor down to check my hair and teeth, rub on some shiny gloss and step out of the car. I'm glad I opted for boots, skinny jeans and a stretchy t-shirt that show off my trim shape. Once inside, he's easy to find. I wave and smile, expecting a similar response. Instead, to my surprise, this guy actually frowns and turns away. Confused, I look behind me to see if something upsetting is happening. Nope. There's no one back there.

Thinking maybe he's not my date, I grab a seat and signal the waitress. When she comes by, I ask her to find out if his name is Frank and if it is, to tell him I'm waiting for him. I watch her approach him, speak politely and, when he nods his head yes, she points to me. Frank's frown grows deeper as he walks over. Given his size, I'm starting to worry. I can't quite decide whether I'm embarrassed or terrified.

Before I have a chance to speak, he crosses his muscle-packed arms and says in an accusing tone, "Is this supposed to be a joke?"

"Excuse me?" I say.

He unfolds his muscle laden arms so he can stick his finger in my face. "Listen to me carefully because I'm only going to say this once. I'm in the fitness business in a big way. I'm not just a personal trainer. I'm a personal trainer to the stars. To people who matter."

I can't believe the size of the veins popping along each side of his forehead. The conversation all around us grinds to a halt as the other patrons become spectators to my humiliation.

His voice takes on a really ugly tone. "Working with celebrities means that I have a reputation to uphold. Even if you were remotely attractive, there's no way I'd be seen with someone 'pudgy' like you. People who think it's okay to let themselves go the way you have make me sick."

And I'm still sitting there in my cute skinny jeans and stretchy t-shirt with my mouth hanging open when he turns on his heel and walks out. I give my head a shake. What just happened here? One or two patrons meet my gaze with looks of disbelief and sympathetic shrugs. Most of my fellow diners try to look anywhere else and I don't blame them. Anywhere else is where I'd rather be, too. Putting one foot in front of the other all the way to my car, all I can think of is how lucky I am that I'm not related to that guy. Then I drive directly to Taco Bell and order a take-out burrito slathered in salsa, with a quesadilla side. 'Pudgy' my size four ass, Jerk!

I'm back at work with my mood restored when Poppi arrives for our meeting. As I explain my cross-cultural concept, the women in the military angle and Nolan's idea of using him as the voice that opens and closes each episode, his smile wipes away any lingering traces of my lunch date disaster. When I give him something to read and send him into the recording booth, he turns out to be a natural. A totally unexpected bonus is his off-the-cuff commentary – a running editorial that mocks his accent and his awkwardness and has us all in stitches.

"So. In-a this episode," he says, veering off script almost immediately, "you gonna see somebody with-a way better accident than I'm-a got, tellin-a you what it's-a like to get-a tha road-a rage in-a you face all-a tha' time. Wait. That's-a no accident. That's-a accent! Santa Maria, I'm-a sound like-a *stunad*! We gonna do this-a voice-a thing again, no?"

As soon as I can talk without dissolving, I call Nolan so he can hear the tape. His howls of pain over his laughter – I'd forgotten about his broken ribs – set me off again and my attempts to apologize sound ridiculous through all the giggles. Ethan isn't any help either, so Poppi gets on the phone and the result is even more hysterical.

"You want I'm-a get-a you something it's-a stop-a tha laugh, or take-a tha pain?" he asks. Before Nolan can get a word in, Poppi places the cherry on the icing on the cake of my day. "You gotta choose-a one, because-a they's-a no cure for whaddaya you call a pain in-a tha laugh."

Things are going so well that when Poppi leaves, after confirming our dinner date for Saturday, I'm about to ask Ethan if he has plans for the evening – I'm thinking we grab a pizza, hang out with Nolan and talk about the show – when I suddenly realize that it's Girls Night. So I tell him I'll see him tomorrow instead.

I'm the first to reach our favorite watering hole – it's a dark bar, full of atmosphere, decorated with plush, semi-circular banquettes and cherry wood tables. I grab the coveted corner seat that puts me in the middle of things. Even though it's only been a week, so much has happened and I can't wait to share with my girls.

When Kat arrives, early for a change, she's all smiles. I can see from the gleam in her eyes and the bounce in her long-legged step that she's onto something good.

"You have amazing news," I say, grinning, as she settles in. "You're never early!"

"I'm in love, Lana! You met him at Nolan's party. I met him ten days ago, but it feels like I've known him my entire life!" She beams.

I'm trying to forget Nolan whispering 'We think he's gay' and focus on something positive about this man. "Wow! He's very cute. Was his name Tom? Timothy? Trevor?"

"Trevor," she sighs.

"So where did you meet him? I want all the details!" I'm hoping against hope that Nolan is wrong for once and Kat has simply found herself an elegant, metrosexual man.

"He sells dental equipment of all things. Last time I had a cleaning, I was telling the office manager I had tickets to the opera and no one to go with and the next thing I know, this dreamy guy says he's an opera fan and would love to go if I promised to have dinner with him!"

I shake my head in amazement. I can't stop my sarcasm from leaking out. "And all I get when I go to the dentist is a lecture on flossing and a whopping big bill."

Luckily she ignores me and continues. "So the opera was Wednesday. Nolan's party was Friday. We went to the symphony on Saturday. Dim Sum and the art gallery on Sunday. Monday and Tuesday he was on the road. The life of a salesman, you know. And yesterday, Trevor took me to dinner in his new luxury car."

"You did all that in just the past week? I'm totally jealous and so glad you're happy!" I hate all the secret second-guessing I'm doing, but I can't help it. I just don't want to see her hurt again.

Kat snaps out of her dream-boat reverie. "How can you possibly be jealous of me? How many dates have you had this week, thanks to your GRAND Plan? Ten? Twenty?"

"Have you forgotten that my full time job doesn't include dating as a paid activity?"

"Right," she snaps her fingers with a laugh. "How many?"

"Well, six. But I met the first one at Nolan's party and three of the other five were total losers."

"Wait: That's three new guys you liked in the first week! Why are you talking about jealousy?"

I can't help smiling because she's right. Why focus on the negative? In one week I've had more romantic fantasies and crazy loser dates than I've had in the past six months. Life has certainly not been dull.

As the waiter brings our standing order for munchies and drinks, I notice Jonah and Mitzi walk in and I wave. As they both wave back simultaneously, an odd idea occurs to me. Seeing them make their way through the regular crowd, stopping and chatting here and there, I can't help notice that they're moving in sync, matching their rhythms unconsciously. Though I'll admit that I've had the occasional fantasy, I've never seriously thought of Jonah as swinging both ways. Watching the two of them in step, though, I'm beginning to wonder.

When they reach our table, Kat is bursting to share her news, but it's clearly going to have to wait. Mitzi is not about to let anyone else go first.

"I know how much you all care about me," she begins, and every face at the table freezes. Her chin comes up and her voice takes on a slight edge. "And I know how hard it is for any of you to see Tad's better qualities, thanks to the way I keep putting him down."

In unison, we all reach for our drinks.

"I hope you'll respect and support my decision, because I've already done it and there's no turning back," she says defiantly.

"What is it, Mitz?" I try for a perky smile. If she says she's married the son-of-a-bitch, I won't be able to stand it.

"I've given Tad some money to start his own business," Mitzi says proudly, "so he can finally be completely independent and show everyone how smart he really is."

The collective sigh of relief I hear tells me Kat and Jonah had been sharing my thoughts. So, the good news is, no wedding. The bad news is, she's floated him another loan. Well, she's done it before and she'll probably do it again, I'm thinking, when a new wave of fear takes hold. She's making such a big deal of something she does all the time, so the question is... How much?

"What's the business?" Jonah asks in a strangled voice.

"Tad's calling it Wine Lovers. The way he explained it, it's an opportunity to help people open their own businesses as wine-tasting party hosts. They pay a fee to become one of his distributors and they make their money by taking orders for the wine that their guests like!" she says happily.

"I think it's such a great idea that I've already signed up as his first distributor. I'm hosting my first wine-tasting party next Friday and I want you all to come."

"What does it cost to be a distributor?" Kat asks.

Mitzi's chin goes up again. "It's $10,000."

"Wow!" It jumps out of my mouth before I can stop it.

"I know the fee seems a little steep," Mitzi says, "but the wines are top shelf, so that means you'll be able to make your investment back in no time."

"What's the distributor's commission?" This is from Jonah, whose voice still sounds strange.

"Five per cent," Mitzi replies. "And you make an additional five per cent on sales that come from your down line."

"From your down line?" Jonah says sharply. "You mean you gave Tad money to set up a pyramid scheme?"

"It's not a pyramid scheme. It's completely legitimate," Mitzi says hotly. "And besides, every business in the world is built on a pyramid."

Before anyone else can get a word in, she continues. "I'm not going to do twenty questions all night. All I'm asking is that you give Tad a chance. Promise me you'll come to my wine-tasting party next Friday and then let's change the subject. I want to hear all about Lana's dates and Kat's new man."

I love her like a sister, but I hate it when Mitzi puts on her bossy hat. It's like trying to kick back and relax with a drill sergeant. I have so many questions I'm not allowed to ask and now there are forbidden topics to avoid. I decide to give them a quick rundown on my adventures and then plead a headache – not a total lie at this point – and make my escape.

"In a nutshell, gang, I've had six dates so far – though one of them wasn't part of the Plan – and six more lined up. I'm going on second dates with three guys from the first group and I've crossed the other three firmly off my list. Now I've got to love you and leave you before this headache makes it impossible to even find my car. Kat, honey, you're up."

Sunday	Monday	Tuesday	Wednesday	Thursday	Friday	Saturday
				WEEK ONE[1] The Plan	Nolan's[2] Birthday	Tony?[3] Skylar
Skydive - Van[4]	Jason[5]	~~Doug~~[6]	~~Henri~~[7]	WEEK TWO[8] Frank The Girls	Jason #2[9]	Poppi[10]
Skydive - Van #2[11]	Jeremy[12]	Lotar[13]	Paavo[14]	WEEK THREE[15]	[16]	[17]
[18]	[19]	Gale[20]	Phil[21]	WEEK FOUR[22]	[23]	Oscar[24]
[25]	Michael[26]	[27]	[28]	DEADLINE[29]	RESULTS[30]	My Birthday[31]

Friday, Day 9

I wake up with that out-of-breath feeling you get when you've just run a marathon, but no memory of the dream that caused it. I grab a coffee to go, questions churning in my head from last night. What is *wrong* with Mitzi? Why is Jonah so bummed about her latest change of heart? How can a woman like Kat, who matches people for a living, not know a gay guy when she sees one? And what the heck am I going to wear for my second date with Jason?

Every one of these unknowns is shoved aside when I reach Slum Central to find the parking lot completely empty and one of those yellow police tapes blocking the entrance. What the hell? Where is everyone?

Suddenly, a booming voice fills the air. "Drive to the municipal lot around the corner."

For a crazy second, I think I'm hearing the voice of God on traffic duty. Then my grownup brain kicks in. *'Sanity calling Lana: It's a loud-speaker.'* I can feel the blush of embarrassment flood my cheeks as I shift gears and keep driving. When I get to the lot, everyone is there. Some are standing as if rooted to the spot, others are leaning on their cars, or wandering back with coffees from the cafe up the block. I catch sight of Ethan talking to a cop and I head in that direction.

"What's up?" I ask.

"Your crazy prankster, we think," Ethan says. "Roofing nails all over the parking lot and something sticky that burns the skin spread all over the door handles."

"Seriously?" I ask stunned.

The cop moves in, standing a little too close to me for comfort. "This man tells me you're a senior Producer, is that right?" His words blow hot coffee breath in my face.

I take a step back and nod.

"Okay. We've got a squad in the building, checking to make sure there aren't any booby-traps. Do you have an emergency contact number for your boss? We can't seem to locate him."

I reach for my cell phone and pull up the number. "Do you want me to call him?"

The cop nods. "Just ask him how soon he can get here. Don't give him any details." He stares until I nod my agreement and then he gives me the go-ahead to dial the number.

I turn aside to make the call. When it goes to voice mail I leave a *'Where are you, When will you be here'* message and avoid any details. Since I never do this kind of thing, the Bossman will know it's a priority of some kind. If he's in a meeting or on the highway, the last thing I want to do is send him into a panic.

Next, I call Nolan. When I get his voice mail, I don't pull any punches. "If you're driving, pull over. We need to talk. NOW."

When I see the cop give me a raised eyebrow and take a step closer, I tell him, "My partner. He's one of those guys who thinks on his feet. He'll find our boss if anyone can it's ...uh... team ....us." I finish weakly.

After a moment, he nods. The last thing I need is a cop with an attitude. Ethan nudges me as Nolan pulls into the lot. We excuse ourselves from the cop and walk over rather than make him hobble to us.

"What's going on?" Nolan says.

"Roofing nails in the parking lot. Something disgusting on the door handles."

Nolan stares. "What kind of disgusting?"

"Corrosive glue," Ethan says. "The cop told me 911 got a call from the janitor requesting an ambulance and someone to block off the parking lot. Showing up early earned the poor guy some nasty blisters and four flat tires."

As Nolan's eyes narrow, I can practically hear the mental gears meshing. "So last week we had fish and skunks. He starts by creating a stink and we think he's sending a message aimed at the Bossman. You wanna eat fish and garlic in the edit suite and stink up the joint, buddy?

Take this. You wanna brag all over the place about your ritzy car? Take that."

He looks at me. "Right?"

I nod.

"So this week he's got a new theme and expanded his reach. What's he saying? We do tacky work? He wants to get under our skin? What do you think?"

"I think the guy is a whack job." Ethan shakes his head.

"Why us?" I wonder.

"Good question," Nolan replies. "It has to be someone who knows the Bossman's habits, right?"

"Not necessarily," Ethan says. "It could just as easily be a protective boyfriend, a jealous husband or even a supplier who's heard the stories and wants to even the score."

"Oh great," I toss in. "A whack job on a crusade to defend the weak against the strong. Hey, maybe he'll start wearing a cape. He'd be much easier to spot if he did."

"Where *is* the Bossman?" Nolan asks, looking around.

"No idea," I reply. "The cop asked me if I had an emergency contact for him. When I called, it went straight to voice mail. Which is no reason to panic," I add. "The same thing happened with you a minute ago."

Nolan nods, distracted.

"What are you thinking?" I ask hesitantly, suspecting I may not like the answer.

"He may have had the right idea when he asked to you talk to Poppi," he says. "When are you seeing him next?"

"He's taking me to dinner tomorrow night," I tell him, lowering my voice to make sure the cop doesn't hear what I'm about to say. "You and I have been over this. I'm not bringing up the subject of hit men with Poppi and that's final."

"I know, I know. But if he brings it up, I'm just saying keep an open mind. Wait... did you say dinner? Isn't the man of a thousand suits a little old for you?"

"Easy there, mister. It's business," I tell him.

Nolan wiggles his eyebrows. "Don't be too sure."

The idea is so far-fetched that we all start to laugh, earning a curious glance from the cop.

"You people find this funny?" he asks in a 'stern cop' voice.

"No sir," Nolan says, getting out of the car and introducing himself. "It was my fault. I was trying to relieve the nervous energy. Think of it as one of those laugh-in-church moments."

The cop frowns and starts to speak when my phone rings. "Bossman," I tell them, checking the caller ID before I answer "Yes sir."

I can barely get a word in, he's so angry. Someone's been sending him on wild goose chases all over town, texting urgent instructions to go to meetings that don't exist. When he got my message, he decided to call it quits. I manage to jump in while he's catching his breath, telling him a cop wants to talk to him. As I'm handing the phone to the cop, we all get to hear the Bossman's startled *'What the f***?'*

Giving the cop some room to speak in confidence, the three of us take several steps back. As Nolan leans against his car to take the pressure off his ribs, we exchange curious looks.

"Okay, how does giving the Bossman the runaround fit in?" I ask.

This time it's Ethan who puts it together. "It's got to be an outsider," he says. "Someone who has no idea that you guys are independent. Someone who thinks it has to be your Bossman who makes all the decisions. Isolate him, the guy figures, and you end up with a studio with no leader. Without the Bossman, everyone panics and nothing gets done."

Nolan nods. "And the rest of it still works. The Bossman's a stinker, a real skunk. Take him down a notch, deflate his ego, get under his skin, give him the runaround and panic his flunkies. Before you know it, he's out of business. The question is, who'd be carrying a grudge that big against Bossman without knowing how his business works?"

"A, someone who doesn't work in entertainment," I throw my two cents in. "B, It can't be someone we know. That makes it C, an outsider with an axe to grind."

"With break-and-enter skills and a lot of nerve," Nolan adds. "Don't forget the cans of tuna."

I'm nodding. "That's right. He did that right under our noses."

"Twice in one day," Nolan says. "So what kind of person can wander around a building they don't work in, carrying all kinds of crap, with no one asking any questions?"

"Electricians," Ethan offers, ticking off his fingers. "Guys who service the furnace and air conditioners. A handyman working on windows and doors. Painters. Equipment repair guys. Computer geeks. Phone, cable, internet. Oh, and plumbers. On the crime shows, those guys are always scoping out a place right under people's noses."

Nolan looks at me. I give him a very small head shake. A plumber with a questionable friend named Tad is not something I want to discuss in front of Ethan. Nolan gives me an equally small nod in return. Thank God for small mercies and perceptive men.

I'm trying to remember the number of times I've complained to Mitzi and the gang about the crap I put up with at work and how much of that would have filtered back to Tad. The thing is, so what? Like the old saying goes, *'Cui bono?'* Who benefits? What's in it for Tad or Jason if the Bossman goes under and I'm out of a job? If Jason is anything like The Cad, that's the last thing he'd want. The whole thing's too crazy.

"Not to shrug this whole thing off," Ethan says, "but what's our plan for today?"

I love this guy! I turn to Nolan. "He's right. Bossman's a big boy. We've got work to do."

I head over to the cop to let him know we're adjourning the meeting and give him our contact numbers. The cop hands me back my cell phone, telling me the Bossman is filing a complaint and they'll be talking to the landlord. Not for the first time, I'm glad I made the decision to work freelance. Like gypsies, we can choose to pack up and move any time we want to. It's an ultimate freedom I appreciate.

When I get back, Nolan says, "Ethan and I want to keep you in sight for the next little while."

"What, I've got body guards all of a sudden?"

"How about humoring me until you talk to Poppi?" he says. "One day is no big deal, right?"

After a couple of seconds, I nod. If Jason had something intimate in mind, it'll just have to wait.

"So we're joined at the hip for the next twenty-four hours. How can we put that to good use?"

"Let's be secret shoppers today and cruise the construction sites. Ethan's got his camera. We can get some candid shots if we see anything good. You and I can chat people up. After work, you've got a date, but you don't have to worry. Ethan and I will be super sly. You won't even know we're there."

He turns to Ethan. "An old-friend dinner will be a nice distraction for Lana."

Thinking I'd like to kiss Nolan for that, I remind him, "I'm going hiking with Jonah tomorrow. Your broken rib won't like that."

Ethan says, "I'll take hiking duty. I can grab some shots."

"And I'll be your back-up en route to your dinner with Poppi," Nolan adds.

With that out of the way, we head off on our excellent adventure. The afternoon turns into a great bonding exercise and Ethan gets some terrific footage: A mother duck and her ducklings leaving footprints across a fresh patch of concrete. A toddler grabbing her mom's keys and flinging them into a portable hopper. Two guys squaring off in full-on road rage diverting the crew's attention while their accomplice makes off with one of their power tools. It's going to be a pleasure turning that last piece over to Gina and watching the sparks fly.

In no time at all, it's quitting time. We head back to the municipal lot and Nolan volunteers to tag along while I go home to change for my date. As Ethan drives off, Nolan says, "I get it that you want me to keep Ethan in the dark on your GRAND Plan. You like Van and there's no reason he needs to know about it. What worries me is the number of guys you're planning to meet that *you* know nothing about."

I try to cut in, but he holds up one finger.

"Hear me out. I know you're stubborn, but no romance is worth putting your safety at risk. I'm not going to let you skate on this."

"Does it help to know that Trent has their names and he's running background checks?"

"Not much. Your brother's great, but there's no way to know if these guys are giving you their real names or if they've done things they never got charged with. My point is, I don't want you getting all clever and giving me the slip. Are we clear?"

His tone is one I know better than to fight. "Yes, Dad," I say, partly teasing to lighten the moment.

Nolan follows me back to my apartment and comes in to make sure no intruders have taken up residence. After I change, we head out with Nolan trailing my Cabrio by several car lengths.

Jason's plan was a pub crawl along Manhattan Beach. When I meet up with him, I'm going to tell him I'd rather find one place where we can relax, get to know each other and eat. He should like that.

We're meeting at one of his favorite haunts and I like the idea that he wants me to get to know his turf. I also like the fact that Manhattan Beach is an upscale waterfront community. The locals are mostly young and successful and this is a good sign that Jason is doing well on his own, unlike Tad the Cad.

The bar has old worn wooden floors and license plates nailed to the unfinished wood walls. I'm scanning the room looking for Jason when he taps me on the shoulder and I jump. With my heart pounding like crazy, his *'Hey, beautiful'* falls flat.

He searches my expression and steps back. "What's wrong?"

"Totally crazy, stressful day," I shrug. "Lots of pressure and bad juju at the office. I'm really glad to see you; I just need time to relax."

"Then let's make that a priority," he says. "Why don't we have that drink we'd planned and you can tell me all about your lousy day. We'll think of a nice, relaxing place to eat and leave the pub crawl for another night."

My smile says it all. How lucky can a girl get to find a man who's willing to listen to her rant after just one date? I've no intention of telling him what's really going on, so as soon as we get our drinks I change the subject and ask him to tell me more about him.

For the next hour or so, he describes a couple of projects he's working on, using them as a way to explain why he wants what he wants in the home he designs for the woman of his dreams. A big bathroom with lots of natural light and plenty of mirrors. Tons of closet space. A cozy home theatre. An open concept kitchen for big family gatherings. A fenced back yard. A tree fort. The more he talks, the clearer the picture becomes. I can see myself lounging on the wrap-around porch, sipping a nice chilled *Arnold Palmer* while Jason and the kids play tag in the yard.

When we decide to eat at a beach front bistro close by, I notice Nolan and Ethan strolling along on the opposite side of the street. To have such great guys who care about me... how lucky am I?

The hostess seats us at a fabulous table and tells us the waiter will be along very soon. I take the opportunity to ask Jason a question that's been bothering me since I met him.

"How do you know Tad?" I ask, trying to piece together the idea of this wonderful man having any time for such a jerk.

He actually blushes! "I've been waiting for you to ask. Tad was my dorm neighbor in college. We don't have a lot in common, but as roommates we spent so much time together and have so many memories that we tend to keep in touch even though we don't hang out a lot. He's a nice enough guy, but he has this dumb habit: He thinks it's smart to keep a woman guessing, so he does things to make them jealous. You know, making it obvious he's checking other women out; pretending he's seeing someone on the side; leaving napkins with phone numbers lying around. That kind of thing. I think it's juvenile, but what can I do? I'm not his keeper."

He leans forward and gently caresses my hand. "I'm not like that. Any time I do something that bothers you, you just have to say the word and that's it. Any question you want to ask, fire away. You can't offend me. Just be sure you want the answer, because I won't pull any punches. You'll always get the truth. Okay?"

His intense stare catches me off guard, but I like the message he's sending, so I smile. "Okay."

I see the waiter coming, so I change the subject. "I can see why this is a local favorite."

In between ordering and eating and enjoying the waves crashing on the beach, we talk. Jason is leaning forward totally engaged with me, so I find myself telling him stories about life back in Boise I'd almost forgotten I knew.

"Would you like to go to a cozy lounge just a block from here?"

His sexy smile and husky voice make me melt.

"Yes!" I sigh. Then I remember my agreement with Nolan. "Uhh, I mean no," I add lamely.

"Which is it?" He looks confused.

Looking at his sweet face, I feel like a traitor. "I'd love to, Jason, but I can't. Not tonight."

He pulls back, a hurt look on his face. "I didn't figure you for someone who plays games, Lana."

His hurt look and comment make my heart sink. I do my best to explain. "Jason, it's not a game. I'd love to keep going and getting to know you, but... I'm sorry, it just won't work tonight. Please bear with me. It's got nothing to do with you. It's all related to work."

He stares at me for a long, silent moment and I feel like a total jerk. Suddenly he grins and it feels like the sun coming out after a storm. "Okay, dear. You win."

As he signals for the check, I tell him I need to visit the ladies room. Once inside, I send Nolan a text: *'Need some privacy to say good-night. Meet me at my car.'* Seconds later, I get his *'OK'*. Maybe now I'll be able to relax!

As Jason and I walk back up the street, he suddenly grabs my hand and pulls me into a doorway. My heart skips a beat. He's going to kiss me! How romantic!

How wrong! The next thing I know, his hands are all over me, grabbing, pulling and prodding, kneading my breasts, fumbling with the buckle on my belt. His lips are fastened on mine and his tongue is so far down my throat, I'm afraid I'm going to choke.

His sudden transition is frightening. I'm pushing him away, but he's much too strong. I finally manage to turn my head and yell at him to stop, but it seems to make him even crazier. Suddenly, I feel strong hands pulling us apart. Nolan, I'm thinking. Salvation! But I'm wrong again. It's not Nolan. It's some disgusting drunk who wants to get in on the act.

"Heyyyy, baby," the guy slurs. "Save some for me." He burps and the smell is deadly.

As the drunk grabs me roughly by the arm, Jason springs into action, attacking him from behind, kicking him where it hurts. When the drunk staggers to his knees, Jason takes aim and kicks him twice in the ribs. Jason grabs my hand and hurries me back out into the street. His strong grip feels like he's crushing every bone in my hand. I struggle, but I can't break free.

"Stop!" I finally yell at him. "Let go of me!"

And just like that, he stops and drops my hand. As I stare at his face, backing away to a safe distance, I see the adrenalin anger fade and the soft, kind look return to his piercing blue eyes.

"I'm sorry," he says quietly.

"What the hell is wrong with you?"

"Nothing. Everything." He takes a deep breath and lets it out, running his fingers through his hair as he turns his back on me for a couple of seconds. Then he turns back to face me again.

"Look, what I did to you back there was unforgivable. If you never want to see me again, I'll completely understand." He shakes his head. "I don't know what came over me. There was nothing you did that triggered what I did. It just came over me. And then when that drunk jumped you, I saw what I'd been doing, what it must have felt like for you. I wanted to kill him for thinking he could do that. When I kicked him, I was kicking me for being such a jerk."

"Okay. Thanks for the apology." I'm still in shock and don't really know what to say. "We all do things we regret," I tell him. "Let's leave it at that."

"Will you see me again?"

"Let me think about it, okay?" I try to smile, but it's a struggle.

He nods dejectedly. "Okay. I'll call you next week. Let me know then."

We're silent as we walk to my car. How did he go from so perfect to so scary so quickly? Was there something I should have seen earlier? Was I too focused on my problems not to notice his?

"Thanks," I tell him when we reach the parking lot.

He brushes his hand across my cheek. "I hope I get another chance, Lana." He steps forward to kiss me, but I flinch. Fortunately he takes the hint and steps back and lightly pats my shoulder before turning to leave. As I get in my car I see that he's watching and I hope he's making sure I'm in safely. He waves one last time and walks off with his head down. The sight of this confident man so dejected makes me feel terrible.

Before I start the car, I text Nolan. "Heading home." As I drive, I run over the evening in my head. The whole episode makes me feel so sad that tears well up in my eyes and spill down my cheeks. What is wrong with people? Why did he have to ruin such a perfect night? If he thought so much of me, why was it suddenly okay to maul me in an alley? Is that the kind of guy I want for a husband? Is that the kind of behavior I want him teaching our kids? In my mirror, I see Nolan's car coming up to pass, so I quickly dry my eyes and slap on a smile. I'm not ready for an "I told you so" lecture.

By the time I get home, there are three messages waiting. The first is from Jonah, confirming our climbing date. The second is from Nolan, telling me Ethan will be picking me up at seven. The third is from Jason. I'm tempted to delete it without listening, but I can't.

"Hi Lana: Just a quick call. I want you to know that I meant every word I said earlier. I know that there's nothing I can do or say to erase the pain I caused. But I give you my solemn promise that if you're willing to give me another chance, nothing like tonight will ever happen again. All I want to do is make you happy. I really think we were meant for each other. Good night."

He sounds sincere, but – and it's a big but – I can't forget how frightened I was and how stupid I felt for sending my bodyguards on ahead. For what? So I could neck with a guy I barely know? When am I going to grow the hell up? I grab my warmest pj's and climb into bed, taking comfort in the knowledge that I'm going hiking with Jonah tomorrow. Even if Ethan is a no show and dinner with Poppi is a bust, my day will be fabulous.

Saturday, Day 10

*E*than is on time and, yay, he's brought coffee! I may suck at picking boyfriends, but I clearly rock when it comes to work partners. When Jonah greets Ethan with a big smile, I'm happy as a clam. There's nothing better than time spent in the great outdoors with people who get what friendship is all about. The only thing I'm regretting is that there's no way to pull Jonah aside and ask what was going on the other night with Mitzi. When we stop for brunch, Jonah wants to hear the latest updates on The Muckers.

"I've told Miss Lana from Montana, here, that I want to be at every casting session," Jonah tells Ethan. "I mean, seriously, where else am I going to get access like that?"

Ethan looks at me with a puzzled frown. "I thought you were from Boise, Idaho," he says.

"Oh, she is," Jonah jumps in.

"But…?" Ethan's confused look grows.

"We gave her that nickname 'cause we don't want no one callin' her a 'Ho'," Jonah grins.

To my relief, Ethan cracks up. Every now and then, Jonah gets a little crass. If you're not expecting it, things can get awkward. But Ethan is having no problem. Even better, Ethan seems to be enjoying Jonah. He's so interested in everything that he's quizzing him about opportunities to shoot other climbing locations too. By the time our meal is over, they've made plans to go hiking again the following Saturday and I'm feeling as pleased as if I'd matched them up.

Later, after Ethan drops me at home, I take it easy before my dinner with Poppi. Ethan's idea of recording our conversation has a certain appeal, but I've decided to pass. I want to protect the good feeling I've established with Poppi and I need to focus my full attention on everything that's been happening so I can organize what I want to say.

I decide to run a bath and I'm just about to step in when the phone rings. Still nervous from last night, I hesitate even going to grab the phone. I'm not ready to talk to Jason yet. I decide to grab my phone and get a pleasant surprise when I see Skylar's name. With everything that's happened, I'd almost forgotten him!

"Hey, Skylar! How are ya?" I say with a grin.

"I'm great, Lana. I just aced an audition and I'd like to take you to dinner to celebrate. Are you busy Wednesday evening?"

"Let me just check my calendar," I tell him and dash into the living room and wake up my computer. At quick glance tells me I'm free and clear.

"Wednesday's perfect. Where and when?" I can't wait to hear what kind of place he thinks is a celebration spot.

"Let's do it right," he says. "How about Pinot Bistro at eight?"

"That must have been some audition," I laugh. "I'll see you then."

Writing his name in the Wednesday slot after we hang up, I start to feel a flutter of excitement. Why was I getting so worked up over Jason when I've got all these new men lining up to meet me and great guys like Van and Skylar that I've already met? As I climb into the bath, I'm grinning from ear to ear. I wouldn't have thought it was possible to top the great day I'd just spent with Ethan and Jonah, but Skylar has taken it to glorious. An hour later, things go from glorious to grandissimo when Poppi calls to tell me that he's sending a car for me.

"Why should-a you drive, Bella? My car, she's-a sit all-a day long. Johnny's gonna be there at six. He's-a nice boy. I'm-a not send no speedy guy for you, drive like a maniac."

I give Nolan a quick call to let him know the change of plans and he promises to hang back so he gets a chance to see where I'm meeting Poppi without anyone knowing I have an escort.

In Poppi's honor, I choose a pretty blue tank top, charcoal pencil skirt and matching shrug. I pull my hair up into a soft chignon. The only jewelry I wear is a simple gold chain and diamond drop earrings. I decide to go with classic pumps and a matching clutch in charcoal leather. Oh the girls would be proud of me matching an outfit like this, I think as finish applying lip gloss.

When my doorbell rings, I glance outside to make sure it's not a pizza delivery guy buzzing the wrong apartment. When I see a black limousine waiting by the curb, I grin. Now this, a girl could get used to. Too bad Poppi's old enough to be my grandfather – he's quite the charmer.

The driver, Johnny, and I are old friends by now. When I interviewed him for the show, he turned out to be as funny and charming as he is handsome. When he sees me, he smiles.

"Miss Fray," he smiles broadly as he opens the limousine door and gestures for me to enter.

"Johnny," I smile, "what happened to first names? It's Lana."

"Poppi's orders," he explains. "When I drive for him, I follow his rules."

"I understand," I forgive him and settle back with a sigh against the buttery leather seats.

Thirty minutes later, Johnny pulls up outside a quaint Italian eatery. Two of the other gorgeous hunks I remember from that first day at the construction site are waiting to escort me from the limo to the restaurant. All three of them (Johnny included) are dressed alike, in black pants and crisp white dress shirts.

"Johnny, I didn't get to meet these men at your offices. What are their names?" I ask.

"Pietro will be opening your door. Vincenzo will take you to Poppi."

"So, do their friends call them Pete and Vince?" I tease.

"Not if Poppi is listening," Johnny grins.

"Got it," I wink. "Thanks for the lovely drive."

"My pleasure, Miss Fray. Enjoy your dinner."

And I do. What I'm treated to over the next several hours couldn't be more different from my everyday life if I'd been shuttled to a distant galaxy instead of this tiny perfect oasis where Poppi holds court.

I am *La Signorina*. Poppi is *Il Patron*. Everyone is charming. Nothing is rushed. The food is incredible. The wine, to die for. And Poppi is an attentive and witty host.

When the last morsels are gone, I visit the ladies room where I find an attendant waiting to hand me freshly laundered hand-towels, still warm. When I look for the tip jar, I find nothing but a tasteful selection of hand creams, tissues and tiny sample bottles of mouthwash, per-fumes and hair spray tastefully displayed. I'm reminded all over again of the gap between modern day America and old world customs.

Back at our table, beautifully decorated pastries have been served while I was away. Coffee is poured. A waiter arrives with a bottle of cognac and two glasses. Vincenzo appears from nowhere, nodding to me as he leaves a leather-bound folder by Poppi's elbow. Poppi nods his thanks and we are left alone. I sense a shift of purpose. The meal was the ice-breaker. *This* is why we're here.

"Lana," Poppi speaks softly, "I have been very successful. This is not by accident. I am successful because I listen. Because I do my home-work. Because I demand respect. Because I settle for nothing less than excellence."

It suddenly hits me with full impact how much more there is to this man than meets the eye.

"May I ask a question?" I say it very carefully.

He smiles. "But of course."

"What happened to your accent?"

His smile widens. "You like my camouflage? My *'Who's a-gonna worry 'bout some-a guy don't gotta da English?'* An accent can be a most effective tool, you know. It sets helpful boundaries. Sometimes it charms. Always it isolates trouble-makers and fools."

"I interrupted you just now. Forgive me."

"Not at all, Bella. It is your nature to ask questions. I am pleased that you care." He sips at his coffee. "Even if you have little room, I urge you to try a pastry. The woman who makes them is very talented" – he pauses with a smile –"and very proud."

He watches closely as I choose a tiny golden confection with a deli-cate pink flower adorning the top. When I take the first bite, I'm amazed:

the cake is light as a feather. The filling is rich without being heavy. The raspberry flavor is so fresh, I'm sure the berries were hand-picked today. Poppi smiles with pleasure when I can't stop a small moan of ecstasy.

"She will be pleased. So. Back to this." He taps the folder by his elbow.

"If you permit, I have three things to discuss. The first is this Bossman, as you call him. In my time, I have met many like him. I know that he will wish to make a mockery of my family and my business, because it is his nature to bring others down to his level. I want you to know that it is my intention to prevent him from doing this and I would like to do it with your help."

When I start to comment, he raises his hand. "Permit me. It has been my experience that men like this do not care what it takes to get what they want. A Bossman will only help those who can help him. When they can offer nothing more, Bossman drops them and moves on. He has done it before. And, by the way, he will do it to you unless you realize that you offer something he does not have without you. Do you understand?"

"I think so. He needs my production savvy. But lots of people can do what I do. I kind of need him, too."

"It is more than savvy, what you have, Bella," Poppi smiles. "He needs your integrity. Busy people will make the time for you because they respect your integrity. Talented people will take risks for you for the same reason. He knows from experience that they will not do these things for him because he is not a man who earns respect."

I'm at a loss for words. I mean, I barely know this man. "Well, thank you. I'm sorry, that sounds so lame after your kind compliments."

"These are not compliments, Lana. These are facts. In business, integrity is a rare thing. The doors it can open, the trust it can promote, these are priceless. Even your Bossman knows this. It is time you knew it and recognized its power."

"I'm not sure how it qualifies as integrity if you manipulate it," I reply cautiously.

"But this is not what I have said," he smiles gently. "I have said that you must recognize respect for what it is and understand where it comes from. It is not something you can buy, as example."

This suddenly makes me think of Mitzi and Tad. I nod my head.

"And when someone does not respect you there is only one thing you can do to change the way you are treated." He pauses. "You must be willing to step back, disengage and walk away."

"Can't you teach them to respect you?" I ask.

Poppi spreads his arms. "How, if they do not respect you, will they respect your teaching?"

I'm confused. "Okay. So if Bossman doesn't respect me, how do I make him do the right thing?"

"Lana, you do not need to make him do anything. He will do it himself as soon as he understands that you are willing to walk away."

"Now that would be a show stopper. He doesn't think I have the guts to do that."

"And this is because?" Poppi nudges me along.

"Because I…" I'm at a loss for words.

"Because you want the best for everyone," Poppi offers.

"I was going to say it's because I'm a push-over," I confess. "I hate the idea of hurting people."

"So you will compromise your best interests to save someone's feelings and deliver a diminished product instead of standing up for the thing you know is right?"

I suddenly hear the question he's really asking and I smile. "I probably do compromise my own best interests more often than I should, but it stops there. I've never delivered anything less than my best. It may not look like I stand up to Bossman when he puts his foot down, but I'm pretty good at finding round-about ways to get the product I want."

"That is comforting to hear, given our situation, but did you not move to Los Angeles to make documentaries that matter?" Poppi asks gently. When did that goal disappear?"

Somehow it doesn't surprise me that Poppi knows about my career goals. "That's a very good question. I don't think I know the answer."

"Would you like to change this round-about thing you feel you must do to protect these people who do not deserve your protection? Are you not tired of being pushed over?"

As I think of the last few deadly dates, I grin. "More than you know."

"So, I can help you, and when you are strong, you can help me. It is a very good arrangement."

He raises his cognac glass and we touch glasses.

"It will not be easy at first," he cautions. "What you will gain will change your life in every area, including work. But the Bossman, he is skillful. He will play to your fear."

I'm nodding. "I know what you mean. I've heard him tell all kinds of people they'll never work in this town again if they don't do what he wants."

"And are they still working?" He smiles.

"The good ones are." I smile back.

"There you are," he says. "And now let us talk about the second thing on my list: these pranks you are dealing with. I am in a position to help."

I'm stunned. How could he possibly know about the prankster or about Bossman urging me to reach out? Who would have told him?

"I make it my business to know what is happening, Bella."

"You're not kidding."

When he grins, I'm horrified. I hadn't realized that I've said the words out loud.

His expression turns serious. "Tell your Bossman I will look into the matter, but only if he calls me directly and asks me to do so."

Wow. The man is a master. "And when he does call you, he will owe you. I like it."

Poppi shakes his finger. "That is only one thing. He will also owe you when I tell him my terms: that this TV project will only go forward if *you* are in charge."

"But I am in charge."

"No, Bella, you are not. Your Bossman is allowing you to call the shots because it pleases him. When it pleases him to take your power away from you he will do so... unless there is something that matters to him even more."

"His safety."

"What is on the table is much bigger than his safety, Bella. My bargaining chip is his fear. Fear is the greatest motivator of all."

"I love the idea of not having him over my shoulder, but this sounds a bit shady." I say curious to hear his thoughts.

"Ah, Bella, there is that integrity. I will not create fear for him, only show him that he must be ethical and follow through with his promises to have others do the same."

I shake my head. "I see." Then the freedom becomes clear to me and I can't help but grin as I picture life without my name being screeched over the loud speaker. I look at Poppi. "That's amazing! How will I ever be able to thank you?" I ask smiling.

"I hope you continue to feel so positive," Poppi smiles, "because the final thing I wish to discuss is this dating plan you are following."

I feel my cheeks getting hot. "I guess it doesn't matter how you know about that."

"You are right. What matters is that you understand why I wish to discuss it with you. Those who are helping you care for you, but they cannot protect you. It is one of the reasons to look at the choices you are making."

I'm feeling a little defensive. "Which choices do you think are wrong?"

"I did not say they were wrong. What I wish you to consider is that they may not be right… for you. I am making no demands. This is not a deal I am proposing in which you are forced to choose. All I ask is that you take some time to think of the purpose behind this plan you have made. What fear it is you are trying to overcome. And what role it is you are seeking to fill. When that is done, I would ask you to think of the men you are meeting and how they behave. Think of the compromises you may be making to spare feelings you imagine them to have at the expense of your own. And when you have done all of that, I would ask that you look deep inside and ask yourself why you would entrust your future to a man who is not worthy of you."

"What do you mean, not worthy of me?"

Poppi smiles again. "I leave it to you, Bella, to discover for yourself."

And with that remark, he closes the folder and business is over. Vincenzo materializes and whisks it away and Poppi once again becomes the gracious old world host. In a gentle flurry of handshakes and beaming smiles, we say good-night to the talented family who saw to our every need. Out on the sidewalk, Johnny stands waiting by the car. Poppi kisses my cheeks and thanks me for a lovely evening. Johnny opens my door and, feeling like Cinderella, I sink into the buttery back seat with a smile.

I'm so pre-occupied by Poppi's words on the drive home that I almost forget to thank Johnny when he drops me at my door. I totally forget about Nolan trailing me until he sends me a text: *Unless it's urgent, see you Monday.*

My head churning with a million thoughts, I toss a few flakes into Fish's bowl and head for bed without giving a thought to my emails or my answering machine.

Sunday, Day 11

I'm up early. Out of the jumble of questions spinning round my brain, the ones I'm most curious about concern Poppi. I mean, last night could have been a scene straight from The Godfather. How does a retired cement finisher get to know so much about me? And why does he care? Like the man said, *'Cui Bono?'* What's in it for him?

The other thing I don't get is his final remark. If I'm the one who came up with my GRAND Plan, how am I letting anyone but me decide my fate? Okay, suppose I am less than impressed with most of the guys so far. How am I supposed to find a gem without sifting through the dirt? And really, how is the GRAND Plan much different than some dating website? Isn't it better since I'm asking people I know to help me out? Hmmm....

I check the clock. Ethan should be here any minute. At least the only dirt I'll be dealing with today is the stuff I land on after my dive with Van. I send Ethan a text confirming his arrival. When I see *I'm downstairs, Boss*, I'm all smiles. I'll give more thought to Poppi's proposition later. Right now, I'm giving myself a day of flat-out fun.

I'm looking forward to this Sunday's jump way more than last week. In the first place, I'm not heading off into the desert with two complete strangers. And when the crew welcomes me like an old friend, I feel right at home. I'm still nervous and my knees are still a bit wobbly but my heart is beating fast this time because I'm imagining myself flying in Van's arms again.

We sign up to jump on the second load and this gives me time to watch everyone prep and then watch while they land. Seeing them fall through the sky is incredible. The colorful parachutes popping open and floating through the air is pure beauty. Van's chute is black and green and I scan the sky anxiously until I suddenly find him swooping and turning, coming closer and closer to the ground. He lands perfectly within feet of where I stand. When he turns to me and grins, my heart melts.

"You ready?" He asks and I nod.

Ten minutes later, we're taking off. My stomach is in knots, but I'm so excited that the flutter in my heart covers up the crunch in my gut. When the door is flung open, Van hooks me in and snuggles me close. My nerves calm as a warm feeling fills my whole body. With each cinch on the cord I am one millimeter closer to this man I adore. When he says, "Ready for more tricks this time?" I nod.

We follow the skydiver tradition of the good luck fist bump and point, which I've been told means 'don't forget to pull'. It sounds crazy that you'd forget a thing like that, but all it takes is one jump to see how easy it is to lose track of time and leave it until it's too late.

After almost everyone has thrown themselves out of the plane, we shuffle from our places on the bench to the open door. I start to drop to my knees, but Van says "no" in my ear and turns us around so our backs are to the opening. I feel him step back onto a small bar on the outside of the plane, then reach out and grab the bar above the door. Before I know it, we're clinging to the outside of the aircraft. I look down and almost throw up when I realize that I'm hanging out the side of an airplane at fifteen thousand feet.

Van yells, "Here we go!" He jumps off the bar and suddenly we're dropping backwards, looking up at the plane as it flies away. He rolls us over and we begin our descent. When he pushes my knees down, we start to fly backwards. Then he grabs my hand, twists it ever so slightly and we start to turn that direction. After that, he maneuvers my hands from one direction to the other, and the next thing I know we're weaving through the sky. It's like being in Superman's arms and I'm filled with wonder.

When he puts his finger out in front of my face, giving me the sign to pull the cord, it almost seems too soon. This time, I reach back with confidence and pull, bracing myself for the jerk as the chute opens and catches our fall.

At this slower pace, we cruise. The loud flapping of the wind on the parachute adds a rhythmic beat to the tranquil silence of our flight through the sky. Van points off to the side where another jumper swirls down to the earth. I know he's asking if I would like to do this, I nod and snuggle into his chest. He leans forward and kisses my cheek before pulling the right-hand toggle down, sending us into a quick moving spiral. We swirl and swirl as the ground reaches up toward us. Just as I start to get dizzy, we level out and head toward the orange flag that lets us know the wind direction.

Moments later we near the ground where the others wait, smiling. I feel Van's knees behind me pushing my legs up, so I follow directions and we manage to land on our feet this time. The other jumpers applaud, telling me later that landing a tandem on their feet is hard, but my Superman Van has done it! He unhooks me from him and takes a step forward so he can see my face. He is beaming. I look up at him and smile. As he leans in for a quick peck on the lips, the others groan and laugh, "Get a room!"

I grin and watch as Van leans down and begins loop up the cords so he can carry the parachute back to the hanger. I'm so happy I feel like my heart may burst. And I know there's more. The icing on the cake is that we're all heading back to Van's place to watch my skydiving DVD.

As Ethan turns off the highway and we head for Van's house, he murmurs in my ear, "Wanna stick around after the video, have a beer and a burger on the BBQ, maybe watch a movie? I'll drive you back when you're ready."

My "Yeah, sure, why not?" is a thin disguise for "Of course I'll marry you!"

Ethan is pulling into his driveway when Van's phone rings. I try not to listen, but his "Hey babe, what's up?" makes that impossible. What I hear next makes me cringe.

"I'm on it, babe. No worries. Love you."

As he hangs up, he's already turning to me and I brace myself.

"Lana, I'm sorry. Sarah's got a big problem. We'll have to reschedule."

My cheeks are burning. It's obvious that I'm nothing but a fill-in until this Sarah, whoever she is, whistles and he comes running. It's all I can do to smile like it's no big thing.

Van touches my shoulder briefly and then he's gone. Ethan grabs his gear while I get my stuff together and wait by the truck. I'm trying not to let my feelings show, but I know my face is red. Poppi's words are ringing in my ears right now. Why AM I letting men treat me like this? Ethan gives me a hug. When we're back on the highway he clears things up.

"It's gotta suck, being a single parent," he says.

I've no idea where this random comment comes from, but I nod, "Yeah. My brother's divorced. Even when you get along with your ex, he says shared custody is really tough."

"I hope it never happens to me," Ethan says. "Every time Sarah's world turns upside down, it drives Van crazy."

At the sound of this name I've grown to hate, my ears perk up.

"What?" I screech as my jaw hits the floor.

"Sarah," he says. "Van's daughter. Every week she's with her mother, he waits for the call."

"Oh." That's all I say out loud. Inside my head, I'm singing *Poppi's wrong! Van is a prince! Sarah's his DAUGHTER!*

"Sometimes I think Van made a big mistake when he hooked up with his ex, but if he hadn't, there'd be no Sarah," Ethan shrugs. "Nothing's simple when it comes to love, I guess."

It suddenly dawns on me that I don't know the first thing about this cool, creative guy. Like how did I not know he was a parent? When did I suddenly get to be so wrapped up in my own little world?

"What about you, Ethan?" I ask. "How many hearts have you stolen?"

He smiles. "Just one... that I know of. The first girl I ever kissed, which probably sounds lame. Her name is Bonnie. Full name, Bonita Iverson. Currently deployed with the 11th Marine Regiment in a third-world hell-hole. She's due back in a month."

I'm speechless. Why, I don't know. I mean, practically everyone knows someone who's serving somewhere. Then I realize that, except for Gina Vitale, who gave up her military career to run Muckers Cement, I don't know any women on active duty. Maybe that's it.

Riiight... Because I'm not remotely stung by the reality that women are putting their lives on the line for their country while my current roster of noble deeds includes schoolgirl obsessions and schlock TV. When did this crap become my priority? And how did it get to be all about me again? Geez, enough already!

"Ethan! You must be worried sick!"

He shrugs. "Goes with the territory, right? Fall in love with a girl in uniform, pay the price. She's been offered a job state-side, but I don't think she's ready and I'm not going to push her."

"How long has she been gone?"

"Long enough to miss everything she has back home... creature comforts, creative outlets, me." He flashes me a boyish grin.

"What's she into, creatively?"

"She designs clothing. Casual stuff... jeans... painted shirts... funky purses. You'd love it. In fact, now that I think of it, the two of you could be a seriously dangerous duo." He grins. "She's a redhead, too."

I grin back. "I can't wait to meet her!" I'm feeling super-charged by a woman I've never met and it feels great. For the first time in a long time, I've been shoved out of my stagnant self-pity pool.

And then another thought pops into my head. "I wonder if any of The Muckers have family serving overseas. I mean, Gina can't be the only one, right?"

"Wow, good idea," Ethan says. "What a great way to take them from hunks to heroes."

"You know, beyond the typical drama threads you look for in a reality show, I haven't given Thought One to their personal lives," I tell him. "Let's focus on that tomorrow."

"You got it, boss." he winks.

All the way home, we're brainstorming. I'm so focused on the ideas we're tossing around, there's no room for my schoolgirl crush on Van or any of the other contestants in my crazy GRAND Plan.

It's not until I play back my messages that Ethan's girl and our brain-storming session get nudged aside. The first call is from Van and I feel my skin tingle at the sound of his voice.

Lana? Hey, doll, sorry about this afternoon. I just wanted to update you. Sarah was in a car accident. She was hitching a ride home with one of her friends from school when some jerk came out of nowhere and T-boned them. Sarah's got a couple of broken ribs and a bad bump on the head, but the doctors say it's nothing life-threatening. They're keeping her for a few days to make sure the head injury isn't serious and that's fine by me. I'll need the time to buy a few things to make her comfy and re-arrange my bachelor pad to feel more like a home. I should have weekends free to go jumping again in a month or so. Okay, I guess that's about it. Hope you understand. Later.

How sweet, is my first thought. *What's sweet about it?*, comes next. Other than letting me know he's out of circulation, what does any of this have to do with me? Where's the wistful *Just when we were going to spend quality time together* apology? I'm ramping up for another pity party when Ethan's comment about commitment comes back and I come to earth with a thump.

Are my feelings for Van deep enough to commit to a 'goes with the territory' daddy-daughter-rescue scenario? For heaven's sake, how could they be? We've met three times – the first was Nolan's birthday bash where we rocked the dance floor and the other two were skydiving adventures. We've never been alone when the music wasn't pumping or my heart wasn't thumping and we've never said more than a dozen words to each other. Sure, it feels like there's great chemistry between us, but that could easily be the adrenalin rush. And I don't know the first thing about him. Other than the fact that he has a business, I have no idea what he actually does for a living. I mean, what if he runs a Ponzi operation? What if he fences stolen goods? And other than sky diving and his daughter, I don't know any of his likes or dislikes. What if he's into polygamy? What if he's a compulsive gambler or a secret hoarder? What if he loves cats and hates fish? I may be willing to compromise on some things in life, but I draw the line at my fish.

Shaking my head, I hit the button to hear the next message. I seriously need to get a grip.

The second call is from Mom.

Lana? Are you there, dear? It's your mother… Shirley. Listen, dear, Dad and I were thinking about your birthday. I know you're busy, but we'd love to see you and I just know you're going to fall in love with the newest member of the family. Do you remember the horse your father wanted me to see? Well, one look and I knew we wouldn't be going home without her. Her name is Dixie and – Lana? I swear she's got your coloring. We'd love to see you if you can make it. Trent says he'll feel better when you get fed up with Hollywood and come home and I can't say that I blame him. Oh, goodness, there's the doorbell. If it's not the repairman, I hope it's the insurance adjuster. It's nothing for you to worry about. Your dad says we're covered and I was tired of those window coverings anyway. Yes, I'm coming! Bye for now, hon.

Panicked, I'm about to call her when I catch myself. If it was anything serious, Dad would have called. I'm betting it was the dishwasher again. Why they don't just get a new one is beyond me.

I hit the button to hear the final message. It's from Jason and I brace myself.

Hey Lana, I hope this isn't intruding, but I had to call. After telling you all the ways I want to make a life with the woman of my dreams, I had to go and act like a jerk. You must have thought I was some kind of Jekyll and Hyde character, all chivalry one minute and mauling you the next. Then I go and beat some lame-ass drunk to a pulp. That's not the kind of guy any woman should have to put up with, so why would it be okay to act that way with someone special like you? I'm sure you've been asking yourself questions like that. And that's why I want you to know that if you're the one who's having me followed, I'm okay with it. The way I see it, if you didn't care about me a little, you wouldn't bother. No need for explanations, either. You're going to a lot of trouble to find the guy who's exactly right for you, so why wouldn't you do your homework? I like seeing that side of you. It shows character and that's what I'm looking for in a wife. Anyway, that's all I wanted to say. I hope I get to see you again.

Wait… what??? I'm about to hit Trent's speed dial code when I stop dead, thanks to a little voice inside my head. *Whaddayou think, Bella? Maybe we go grab a coffee someplace?* I shove my keys and wallet in my jacket pocket and walk up to Café Aroma, where I ask to borrow their phone for a long distance call. After the usual greetings, I get down to business.

"Hey. Listen, I have three questions. First, why did Mom and Dad call the insurance adjuster?"

"The dishwasher dumped all over the kitchen floor."

"How did that ruin the curtains?"

"Mom used them to mop up the water."

I start to laugh and it's a huge relief. "Good old Mom. Okay, question two: Have you been looking into an electrician named Jason? Friend of Mitzi's Tad the Cad?"

"Just a sec. I've got the names right here. Jason, Jason… yeah, but it was just a quick search. We checked his license, looked for any priors. He's clear. Why? Should we be digging deeper?"

I feel cold all of a sudden. "So you haven't had anyone follow him?"

"FOLLOW him? You think I work for the FBI?"

"Okay, next question: What kind of connections would someone have to have to know that you're doing background checks on these guys I've made dates with?"

"Listen, this may not be as bad as it might seem. Here's why: To get access to my inquiries, they'd have to have an inside contact letting them know when any names are checked. Each search has an authorization code, so they'd automatically know who initiated the search. It wouldn't take a rocket scientist to trace me back to you because we have the same last name. But that's going about it the hard way. They'd have to know why you had the names in the first place for any of it to make any sense. And the easiest way to know that is if you told them. So this could be coming from someone you know."

"One more question. How difficult is it to tap a person's phone?"

There's a long silence. "Okay, that's it. What is going on?"

"I'm not sure," I tell him. "I had a rotten dinner date with Jason on Friday and I've been thinking of crossing him off my list. I just retrieved a voice message from him saying he's okay if I'm the one having him followed because it shows that I care. Saturday night, I had dinner with one of the people we're doing a show on. He's an older gentleman who seems like a great guy. He thinks Bossman is a jerk and that I can do better."

"So far, I like this older guy and want to strangle this Jason creep. What felt squirrelly about this old guy to you?" Trent says.

"He's a retired Sicilian cement finisher. His business is supposed to be totally on the up and up. But he had a limo pick me up and bring me to this Italian restaurant where they waited on him like he was a king. He knew a lot about Bossman. He knew all about some pranks we're experiencing at work. He knew about my dating plan and warned me about settling for guys who aren't worthy of me. And although he was subtle about it, I'm pretty sure he knows that you're checking the guys out. When he said that the people protecting me were limited by so many rules, that's when I thought he could have someone with serious connections or--"

"—he could be bugging your phone," Trent finishes. "Where are you calling from now?"

"Café Aroma. The coffee shop on the corner."

"Good girl. So the question is, why is he going to all this trouble?" He asks.

"Exactly. The last thing he said before he sent me home was I should ask myself why I'm letting the wrong kind of men decide my fate."

"Well, I've been asking you that for years, just not in so many words. Maybe he's got a candidate he wants you to choose and telling you all this other stuff is a way to distract you."

"You can't be serious." I laugh.

"Yeah, you're right. Either way, I don't like the idea that he might have had someone invade your space," he remarks. "That kind of stuff is a first step down a slippery slope."

"He said he's successful because he makes it his business to know who he's dealing with. He's willing to let us do the show, but he's not about to let a guy like Bossman drag their name through the mud for the sake of ratings."

"You know what?" Trent says abruptly. "Why don't I come for a visit? Spend a few days, bond with your fish, hang out with your gang. I'm slammed this week, but next week is clear and they owe me some vacation time. I can be there on the Wednesday and fly back on the Sunday. What do you think?"

I'm so relieved, I feel tears filling my eyes. "That would be amazing."

"Okay, I'm on it." He states with certainty. "In the meantime, don't change anything. Use your phone. Do everything you normally do. And don't forget to tell your buddies that I'm coming. The perfect reason is that it's your thirtieth birthday and I'm bringing presents. Okay?"

"Okay."

"And don't worry, kiddo. We'll get you through this crazy plan of yours."

When I hang up I realize that I'm suddenly starving. I'm about to ask Penny to fix me something to take home when I think of Nolan. I grab the phone again and give him a call.

"Why the hell are you calling from Aroma? Never mind, where have you been?" he says.

"Are you interested in getting together to talk? I'm just about to order some food. I can get double and bring it over, if you're free." I offer wanting to be sure I get a yes.

"Brilliant. I'm starving. Order triples," he says and I sigh with relief.

Thirty minutes later I'm at Nolan's, ready to faint from hunger, anxious to tell him my news. When I'm done, Nolan is less concerned about Jason than he is about Poppi. Ethan's comment that our interview room at Muckers Cement was wired for sound made him choke on his food. He sees eye-to-eye with Trent. On top of that, because he's seen every side of show business, he has plenty to say about the sneaky ways people can acquire creative rights.

"I don't get it, Nolan. Why would Poppi try to steal our stuff? What's in it for him?"

"Who knows, and more to the point, who cares. People get all kinds of crazy ideas and if you don't have a sharp lawyer, you can lose your shirt. Not only could we find ourselves out of a job if Poppi stole our concept, since we're under contract to Bossman, he could sue us for every dime we ever had. When is Trent getting here?"

"A week from Wednesday. What do you suggest?"

"I'll call a couple of lawyer friends who owe me favors. First we'll get them to take us through the learning curve; then we'll get one of them to put some quiet protections in place. Even if Poppi is totally innocent, this may be a timely wake-up call to take better care of our business. What if one of these jerks you're dating tries to sue you for breach of promise? What if one of my crazy girlfriends tries to cut herself in and cut you out? What if Ethan tries to sell our footage behind our backs?"

My cousin may get blind-sided by his flaky Fashionistas and he may look every inch the surfer dude, but he's no dummy. He knows when it's time to get serious.

When we finish our food, I'm suddenly exhausted. I give Nolan a gentle hug in consideration for his ribs and head for home. Thankfully, there are no messages from anyone so I feed Fish, grab a book and spend the day doing nothing that requires any kind of mental gymnastics.

Monday, Day 12

I'm pulling into my parking spot at Slum Central, wondering if our prankster has anything new up his sleeve when the side door next to Bossman's parking spot bangs open. He comes rushing out, throws something on the ground and starts jumping on it.

"What's going on?" I ask.

Eyes wide, face flushed, he yells "That goddam son-of-a-bitch!" and then he jumps into his rental car and drives off.

Inside, I get the update. The prankster has been blitzing the Bossman's cell phone again. Whoever it is has managed to hack into Amy's account (she's Bossman's assistant) so the bogus texts and calls appeared to be legit. When he finally realized what was happening, Bossman totally lost it. He's gone to get a new phone with an unlisted number.

"But as soon as he starts using it to call everyone--" I protest.

"Don't waste your breath," Amy shakes her head. "Believe me, I've already tried."

I give my team the gist of the brainstorming session Ethan and I had on Saturday and give everyone directions to investigate military connections in the Muckers' enterprise. I'm going to call Gina and get her feedback while Sam, our researcher, does some digging on immigrants and their military service trends after they make America their new home. Nolan and Ethan start working on concepts of shoots, looking at ways to tie-in the military theme. When I reach Gina, she's instantly excited by the direction we're taking. She wants to set up a time to do a follow up interview with us as soon as she's had a chance to clear it with Poppi and those directly involved.

With everyone busy, I jump back into the technical details. Before we can sell a concept to a network, we need a pitch packet and a budget on top of the awesome sizzle reel designed to introduce the concept, characters and hooks that will make the show a hit.

My role in process is a lot like profiling and demands serious concentration. By five o'clock, my brain is numb and I'm ready to pack it in. I'm also looking forward to my date tonight with a guy named Jeremy, who just moved here from New Orleans. He seemed really nice when we spoke on the phone and, since he's chosen one of LA's famously laid-back restaurants for our date, I can't wait to meet him in person and enjoy an excellent, stress-free meal.

I send Nolan a quick text, letting him know my plans. He texts back that Ethan will be my shadow tonight and follows with *p.s....war vets rock.* I've solved enough puzzles for today, so I let it go. Tomorrow I'll be ready to hear all about it. Right now, all I can think about is a soak in the tub and dinner with no demands.

Two hours later, I'm sitting at a table with a view of the water, sipping an ice cold Arnold Palmer when I see a gorgeous blonde guy in a polo shirt and khakis anxiously scanning the room. When he sees me, he rushes over.

"Ah'm so sorry to keep you waitin'," he drawls. "Ah had no inkling LA was so crowded!" He shakes my hand and gives me a gorgeous smile. "I'm Jeremy an' ah'm pleased to make your acquaintance."

"And I'm Lana!" I reply with a happy grin.

"You are so much prettier than June Anne said. Ah'd reckon you'd have dates all the time an' not be lookin' to spend an evenin' with a suth'n hick like myself."

Polite, cute and funny is good, I'm thinking. And the accent is adorable.

"Why did you make the move from New Orleans?" I inquire. He seems so sweetly suited for the south, I worry that Los Angeles will eat him up.

"For a change." He flashes a smile that melts my heart.

"And June says you work in video? What do you do exactly?" I ask.

"Ah'd rather not talk about it. It ain't real meal time conversation." His eyes dart nervously around the room.

"Now you have me intrigued." I smile, hoping this convinces him to share.

"Tell me about your favorite spots in LA first," he says.

I'm beginning to wonder what is so wrong with his job that he can't – or won't – talk about it at dinner. Is he into porn? Something worse? I'm trying to think what the 'something worse' might be – human sacrifices, alien possession, exorcism, cross-dressing – when he suddenly says that he wants to be completely open and honest with me.

"Ah'm a computer video technician for Funeral Homes."

"That's it?" Too late, I realize I've been rude, but computer video tech? It sounds pretty tame.

"There's more to it than y'all might think," he says defensively. "One time a website crashed an' ah had to go in at midnight. Ah'm stumblin' around, lookin' for the light switch 'cause the place is darker than a tomb, pardon the pun, an' the next thing ah know, a coffin opens up all by itself an' ah hit the ground runnin'. Next mornin' they're makin' all kinds of fun of me."

"Putting up with idiots is par for the course," I agree. "You wouldn't believe the stuff I have to deal with every day."

"Ah'm bettin' it's nuthin' like the stress on my job," he says, and jumps into another story that takes us nowhere close to getting to know each other.

As he talks, I find myself hearing Poppi's words and I start to realize that, on our first date – when impressions count – it's more important to this guy to top me than sympathize with me. What will it take to make him care what happens to me if I'm in his life?

After our meal, Jeremy suggests a walk along the water. I'm thinking that the ocean air might change his mood and give us a chance to get to know each other better. Turns out I'm wrong.

He talks nonstop, telling me his favorite sports and favorite foods – I'm wondering if my grilled cheese and tomato sandwiches qualify as *suthu'n cookin'* – and how much his mother will like me (If y'all don't tell her your middle name right up front, she'll call you Lana Ann). *Okay then.*

When we circle back to the parking lot, I shake his hand to avoid anything more personal.

"So when can ah see y'all again?"

"Let's get in touch next week. I'll have a better idea of my schedule by Wednesday."

Out of the blue he grabs me and snuggles me in a huge bear hug. "Y'all take care."

You bet. As I drive away I'm thinking, *Was it something I said that made you think a first date should be all about you?*

I pull into my parking space and head for my apartment building. As I'm about to unlock the front door, a set of headlights flashes behind me. What the hell? I'm starting to panic when the car cruises past and I see Ethan at the wheel, giving me a smile and two-fingered salute. Weak at the knees with relief, I smile and wave back. Safe inside my apartment a minute later, I check my messages. The first one is from Jeremy.

"Hi Lana, this is Jeremy. Ah had a great time. Can't wait to see y'all again."

Message number two, five minutes later, Jeremy again.

"Lana, ah'd love to take you to dinner and a movie tomorrow. Call me back."

Message number three, five minutes after message number two.

"Lana Ann, ah'm making ma favorite dessert right now. You need to get over here, girl, and see how good ah can cook for you. Call me the minute you get home."

Twenty minutes ago, I'd said 'Call me Wednesday', hoping he'd get the hint. Clearly, this guy needs the direct approach. I decide to send him an email, saying Thanks, but no thanks. When I log in, I find message number four.

Lana Ann, it's amazin' when two people come together an' their hearts join as one. I'm cookin' your favorite dessert, darlin', just like mama makes. You need to get over here. Call me as soon as you get this. PS. Better pack your overnight case, Babe. Love, Jeremy.

The first thing I do is shut down my computer. I'm about to turn off my phone when it rings. The caller ID says Jason. I take a deep breath and decide to get it over with. I'm going to have to deal with him sooner or later, so it might as well be now.

"Hi Jason."

"Lana, I want to make it up to you. Can I buy you dinner next Friday?"

"Jason, I still need to think about it. You seriously freaked me out. I asked for time and you just called me." I can't believe I'm saying this stuff, but I like how it feels.

"I know I can't help myself. Will you please give me a chance to prove that I've learned my lesson? I promise you won't regret it."

"Let me think about it. Call me tomorrow."

"Count on it." He says with hope in his voice.

As I hang up, I'm impressed with this new me. Even though the sound of his low raspy voice turned me on, I'd managed to make it sound like he didn't matter to me.

After a long, hot shower, I climb into bed and drift into a peaceful, dreamless sleep. Looking back, I'm glad I grabbed a few solid hours. The next thing I know, I'm wide awake. It takes me several seconds to realize that the phone is the culprit. Before I answer it, I squint at the clock. Who phones at 3 AM unless someone has died? With panic clutching at my heart, I answer it.

"Is this how it's gonna be?" an accented voice asks.

"What?" I say rubbing my eyes.

"Ah thought we had somethin' special."

"Who is this?" I say struggling to turn my lamp on.

"Ah thought we had the kinda somethin' that other people only dream of. Well, let me tell you, missy, you ain't that special. Mama warned me 'bout girls like you, but ah wouldn't listen. Ah believed in you an' me an' the promise of forever. Ah reached out to you when you acted like you was reachin' out to me. Ah gave you the best of me an' you threw it away. You turned somethin' innocent an' beautiful into somethin' ugly an' now ah know. You may be alright lookin' on the outside, but inside you're rotten to the core. Don't you never call me again, y'hear?" And with that he abruptly hangs up before I say another word.

I stare at the phone for a few moments before I quietly hang up. I shake my head and laugh, thinking... *You got it, bubba.*

Tuesday, Day 13

*T*here's nothing like a lunatic calling at 3 AM to take the bounce out of a girl's stride. On top of the weirdness with Poppi, Jason's comment about being followed and the roller coaster dates I've had, I'm tempted to tell the remaining guys on my calendar thanks, but no thanks. When I get to the office, Nolan gives me the boost I need to get back in the game.

"Gina called. Sam hit pay dirt. And Ethan and I have some pretty good stuff too."

"Excellent! I can't wait to hear all the details. Just let me grab a coffee."

"Got it covered, Boss," Ethan appears in the doorway carrying three coffees and a bag of donuts.

"Pinch me, someone," I grin at him. "I must be dreaming."

Nolan hangs up and grabs his coffee. "Ethan, let's update Lana in the editing suite."

With Ethan leading the way and Nolan bringing up the rear, we weave through the bull pen. "Meet the Muckers has a whole new layer, thanks to this idea of yours," Nolan begins. "For a lot of people who come to America in search of a better life, the opportunity to serve turns them into passionate defenders of everything this country stands for."

Ethan nods. "Nolan barely got a word in when Gina called him back. Next thing we knew, she had interviews lined up back-to-back. They were practically crawling out of the woodwork."

Nolan grins. "We called a halt when we reached third cousins twice removed. In fact she was so crazy about the idea she took it upon herself to ask them to video themselves talking about their military experience. It's genius. Check this out!"

For the next 2 hours, I can't take my eyes off the screen. Even with crappy lighting, shaky cameras and audio that's hard to hear, I know we've struck pay dirt. With some audio mixing, color correction and editing I think we're going to set the bar higher than any other reality show in production. In a blink, we've turned *The Godfather* meets *Greensburg* and *Jersey Shore* meets *Magic Mike* into something with serious legs.

Our show is going to do a lot more than follow a Sicilian Mafia family that went straight and opened a cement finishing business. With this angle, we're going to give the viewers heartbreak and courage on top of road rage, graft, greed and corruption. We're going to have a chance to thank our military brothers and sisters for their work and we're going to do it by showcasing the hottest bodies in town... in AND out of uniform.

I sit up in my chair. *Meet the Muckers* is going to be a whole lot more than a hit series. It hits me like a brick that it's going to be my ticket to the kind of stuff I've always wanted to make. The thing is, I can't let anyone know my long range plan. This means that my number one priority is to keep the project on track. If we lose sight of the kind of thing Bossman likes, we lose his support. And even if Poppi does turn out to be the guy I want and need in my corner in the future, in the immediate present, Bossman is my connection to the network. And because Bossman is a pig, it's going to take fancy footwork and tight editing to keep him interested when the show begins to show signs of intelligence and heart. How the hell are we going to distract him enough to buy into the show?

"Ask Poppi," Nolan says from the doorway, reading my mind and jolting me out of my seat.

"What?" I ask.

"I didn't mean to startle you. I figured you were wondering what we all are. How do we make something high quality work for the King of Sleaze? I've been sitting here struggling with it too. The only thing I've come up with is that we ask Poppi and then let him explain it – to us and the audience."

I stare at him, slack-jawed. It's so perfect, I can hardly stand it. "And if comes from Poppi, and the Bossman needs Poppi, how can he refuse? It's brilliant! Now, who are you and what have you done with my cousin?"

We spend the rest of the afternoon brainstorming story lines and clips that would be a natural fit for Poppi and come up with a shortlist of images we want Ethan to grab. We're so focused that it isn't until Amy pops her head in to say thanks and good-night that we notice the time. I give Nolan directions to the restaurant where I'm meeting my date and hit the road.

Relaxing in the tub, I start thinking about my evening. Tonight I'm meeting a German art critic named Lotar whose reference told me he's handsome, sexy and smart. Whether he's a dream walking or has one eye in the middle of his forehead, I know one thing for certain: I'm done with the nonsense of taking off to happy-ever-after fantasy land the minute we meet.

So much for good intentions: I'm sipping a glass of wine at the bar when this tall, handsome blond guy in a perfectly fitted suit walks in. When he moves directly to me and introduces himself, I let out the breath I'm holding. Two – not one – gorgeous blue eyes, a killer smile and this accent that makes my knees go weak. In a flash, I start picturing the two of us in one of those sleek, uber-modern condos, entertaining the Who's Who in the art world.

Lotar charmingly orders what I'm having and while we wait for the server to come back, we use the art on exhibit to break the ice. This bistro supports local artists by showcasing their work in a revolving art collection. Its regular patrons get to enjoy something new every week and it's not uncommon to find an art critic on the hunt for an emerging talent rubbing shoulders with artists and potential buyers.

When Lotar suggested the place as a meet-up, I thought it was perfect. My minor in college was art history and I love to look at paintings and discuss their meaning. As we tour the collection, I'm realizing how much I've missed looking at art.

At a painting of a butterfly floating above a big red carnation, Lotar says, "Vat do you sink?"

"I don't care for this style," I begin, "but I think the butterfly represents beauty. The carnation looks gorgeous at first glance, but the edges are turning brown and there's some kind of bug in the center. I think the artist is showing us how age changes us."

He nods. "Ya. Das ist a goot interpretation. It is ze vork off mein freund."

Ouch. What else can I put my foot in?

"Do not vorry, Lana," he smiles. "I like your honesty. You haf a good eye... among other sings."

I like the sound of this!

"I sink ve should haf dinner visout zese artistic distractions. Do you agree?"

When I nod, Lotar takes care of our tab. He suggests that we leave our cars and walk over to the restaurant he has in mind. I glance casually over one shoulder as we stroll and see Nolan half a block behind. I'm in good hands.

Our destination turns out to be a nearly invisible hole-in-the-wall where the aroma of authentic Mexican food makes my mouth water. When we walk in, it's obvious that Lotar is a very popular customer. From the hostess to the server to the owner, who hurries out of the kitchen to greet us, I can tell that we're going to get the red carpet treatment tonight.

The only jarring note comes when I see Mitzi and Tad seated at a table in the corner. If we weren't being treated like royalty, we might have escaped their notice, but Tad the Cad isn't the kind of guy who misses out on an opportunity.

"Lana!" he calls. "Come and join us!"

I give Mitzi a hug and avoid a kiss from Tad by introducing Lotar.

"So where's Jason?" Tad says as he and Lotar shake hands.

I opt for smiling brightly instead of smacking him in the head. "I've no idea," I reply, turning to Lotar. "Jason is a friend of Tad's. You might say that Tad is getting his feet wet in a new wine tasting business. And my friend Mitzi is in stocks and bonds. How's the start-up going, Tad?" At this point, I don't care if my remark upsets Mitzi. I want the subject of Jason off the table.

Tad pulls Mitzi in and gives her a kiss. "I'm lucky to have a hot sugar mama taking care of me." He grins at Lotar. "So are you the next contestant?"

When Lotar gives me a puzzled look, I echo his expression, hoping he gets the message that Tad is an idiot. "Great seeing you, Mitzi. They're holding our table, so we'll see you later."

As we walk away, I hear Mitzi begin the familiar wind up to one of their arguments. She has lots of ammunition, thanks to Tad's 'sugar mama' comment and I'm glad we're not sitting near them.

Instead, we're whisked away to a cozy table with a shared, padded bench. Lotar recommends their margaritas and I happily tell him to go ahead and order for both of us. When our food and drinks arrive, I'm glad I trusted his judgment. The margaritas are chilled to perfection and the food is hot, spicy and delicious.

With so much going on – the great food, my gorgeous date, our amazing connection – I don't notice how many times my margarita glass is refilled. The other thing I don't notice is that he has steered our conversation away from art to more intimate subjects and he's quizzing me about my highly personal preferences.

Feeling the effects of the wine earlier and the tequila now, I'm enjoying the unfamiliar buzz and getting turned on by his questions. I hear myself say things I've never admitted to a living soul. The fact that he takes it all in stride, like this is completely natural, is soothing. Blaming the spicy food for the heat I'm feeling, his suggestion that we go somewhere to get some air seems like the most sensible idea I've heard all year.

How do we end up at my place? I've no idea. Why doesn't Nolan make his presence known? That's a puzzler too. The door hasn't even closed before Lotar has me up against the wall. And instead of fighting him off, the way I did with Jason, I'm loving every minute of his slow motion assault. From his soft and sensual kisses, to the lazy yet insistent fondling, to the heat he's building, he's making me feel blissfully sexy and happily helpless to resist anything he wants. Even though this isn't who I am; even though this isn't the way I want my perfect romance to begin; nothing he's doing triggers any alarms.

Somehow we move from hallway to bedroom and from vertical to horizontal. He has me floating, weightless, spineless, totally open, and totally ready. And then, suddenly, he laughs. It's not a sexy, throaty chuckle. What I hear is almost boyish and full of surprise and so completely different from the sweet nothings he's been whispering that it breaks the rhythm and brings me out of my daze. When I open my eyes, I realize that he's been caught off guard by my boy-cut cotton panties with their *"I'm cuter than the cheerleaders"* slogan.

Laugh all you like at the idea that I wore them on a dinner date, but they have saved me from making a really stupid mistake. Before he gets back to business, I gently pull away.

"Vat has happened?"

"I... Lotar, I'm sorry. I'm not ready for this."

"I see zis. And yet, so ready haf a moment ago."

"I know." I gently ease a blanket between us. "I'm confused. So I'd like to stop until I'm sure that this is what I want. Can we come back to this another time?"

Lotar's smile is fond, almost like a big brother with a foolish child. "For me, zere is no confusion. Sex is part of knowing somevon. It is natural. It feels good. Zere is no reason to wait."

He's waiting for me to get over myself and what am I doing? I'm ruining my chance with this guy because I'm not ready to have sex on my first date with him. Am I an idiot? A total prude? Is he the one who's right? I mean, he seems to like me a lot and he's totally gorgeous. What the hell is holding me back? I take a deep breath and shake my head. He nods graciously and dresses quickly with no embarrassment. When he's ready to go, he gives me a sweet kiss.

"I haff enjoyed our evening, Lana. Zis vas not how I hoped it vould end, but some sings are not meant to be. Gute Nacht."

When I hear the door open and close, I punch my pillow. Grumbling at my lame seductress act, I pull the blanket over my head and eventually fall asleep.

Wednesday, Day 14

*T*he next morning, I wake up with a killer hangover. *How did I let last night happen?*

As I hunt through my medicine cabinet for relief, I come up with the answer I couldn't find last night. *By drinking wine and chasing it with all the tequila in Los Angeles, you idiot.*

When I check my calendar, I grumble a bit. I'm having lunch with a guy named Paavo and dinner with Skylar. I know I need to rally, so I grab a nice greasy breakfast burrito on the way in, loading up on carbs and protein to stop the hangover in its tracks.

Luckily there are no surprises waiting for me at Slum Central and with Nolan and Ethan off on scouting missions, I'm get to sit quietly and read over the transcripts for the sizzle video with no ugly surprises. I sneak out a little early to make it to my lunch date ahead of the noon traffic and that gets me to the parking lot ahead of the rush. I find a great parking spot and walk through the door right on time. The greeter takes me over to a table where a darkly handsome Greek jumps to his feet to hold out my chair. Now this is my kind of style! My morning grumpiness fades and I sit back to enjoy this date.

Paavo turns out to be a genuinely funny guy with lots of stories about the world of used car sales. I suddenly realize that he may be the inspiration for my next reality show, so I share some of my horror stories with him. We're getting along famously and I'm very happy that he's not putting any moves on me.

When I introduce the subject of TV, Paavo asks if it's true that the camera adds pounds. He tells me how he's been fighting the battle of the bulge and proudly announces that he's lost over 140 pounds in one year. I make the mistake of telling him I can't imagine it.

The next thing I know, he leaps to his feet and lifts up his shirt and there I am, staring at this slab of loose, hanging flesh. Now, I'm the first to commend someone on reaching a goal, especially one as challenging as massive weight loss. But pulling up your shirt at a restaurant is not something I was hoping to see.

But he doesn't stop there. He grabs a fold of flesh and smiles. "Lana, check this out, when I go in they'll cut here" he says pulling the flesh up and down "and here before they cut if off and sow me back up. Then they'll go after these." He shows flapping his arms so the skin under his arms sways like a pendulum.

I smile as best I can. "Wow that's a great accomplishment." Thankfully, just at that moment my phone buzzes and its Nolan saying another tape arrived.

With that I explain to Paavo that I have to head back into work and I think him for a tasty lunch. Then I quickly head back to work. I already know I'll be spending the rest of the afternoon pulling my interview sound bites together while nibbling my left over salad I picked up after leaving Paavo.

For the second time, I duck out a little early and head for home. Ethan texts that he'll be on duty tonight and, not for the first time, I find myself envying his girlfriend, Bonnie, for having such an amazing guy in her life. Then I smile. I mean, technically, I have him in my life, too... without the fringe benefits.

Back at the apartment, I take extra care choosing my outfit for my date tonight with Skylar. He's not only picked one of the most expensive places in town, I'm feeling guilty for the way I judged him on our first date. After a long soak, I take my time getting ready and the effort pays off the minute I arrive. When I hand my keys to the valet, I catch his admiring glance and I smile. There's nothing like a little black dress, shiny hair and strappy shoes to make a girl feel great.

Sadly, my feel great moment fades when I find Skylar lounging at the bar in grubby jeans and a faded rock concert T-shirt. His hair is a greasy mess and it looks like he hasn't shaved in a few weeks. When I see clumps of sleep in the corners of his eyes, I want to turn and run but before I can make a move, he spots me.

"Wow! You look great!" he glows.

"Thanks." I indicate his get-up. "I guess I got the message wrong. I didn't realize you were coming straight from a session and we were dressing casual."

He stares at me with a puzzled look and then shakes his head and laughs. "You are such a funny girl. Come on, our table is ready."

As I follow the hostess, I'm trying to talk myself into being okay with his grime, but it's not working. I just want out. When we get to the table, he reaches out to grab my chair and his body odor is so bad that I almost keel over. I pull my chair in quickly, leaning away from him. As he moves to the other side of the table, I get another whiff and I feel sick.

When Skylar takes his seat, I can tell that the older woman at the next table has caught wind of his body odor too. She turns pale and gets an awful look on her face. At the same time, her husband lifts up his head, blinks and says, "My God!" A second later, he's signaling the waiter, who is by his side immediately.

"My wife and I wish to complain," the man says firmly. "There is a foul odor and we have no intention of putting up with it."

To my total shame, all three of them turn and look pointedly at Skylar. Incredibly, he doesn't seem to notice. And for some reason that's what does it. In that moment, the light dawns and I finally get what everyone has been trying to tell me for years.

These disaster dates aren't getting worse because there's something wrong with me nor are the men are getting crazier. The madness is escalating because I'm not learning the lesson. It's not up to *them* to transform themselves into my 50's era fantasy prince. It's up to *me* to get a grip, set a standard and stand firm when it isn't met. If I don't do that, I deserve what I get. In this case, total humiliation. Because let's face it, the only reason I'm sitting in an elegant dining room with this smelly, self-centered loser is that I didn't cancel our date the minute I saw him in the bar.

"I'll take care of it immediately," the waiter tells our neighbors and rushes off. Less than a minute later, I see the manager heading our way. Skylar is still completely unaware.

"Excuse me, sir," the manager says to him. "May I have a word with you?"

Skylar looks confused. "Sure," he says. "What's up?"

"My office is more private," the manager adds gesturing to the back hallway of the restaurant. "If you will be so kind?"

Skylar shrugs and gets up to follow him. As he passes by, his stench hits me again and I get the irony of the situation. If I haven't been able to see the writing on the wall, I can certainly smell it.

Once they're out of sight the older woman at the next table leans over.

"I don't care how much money he has, dear. You deserve better. My nephew Earl is quite a catch and he's newly single."

Her husband nods. "He may be sixty, but he's a young sixty and full of fire."

The woman rummages through her oversized purse to find a pen and a piece of paper. "Here you go, dear," she says as she writes down his number. He smells wonderful and has a lot of money. Just tell him you met Dotty and Gene. I'll tell him to expect your call."

Can this nightmare get any worse? I smile politely and take the paper.

"Thank you." I hope the earth opens up and swallows one of us. "He's a blind date," I add.

As they nod sympathetically, I look down at the paper and realize that she's written her nephew's number on the flip side of a gynecologist's appointment card. Now that's a nice touch.

I see the waiter heading our way on a mission. When our eyes meet, he beckons me to follow him. When we reach the entrance, the manager is waiting and takes me to one side.

"Madame, I am very sorry to say that we are unable to serve your date this evening. We have a strict policy about personal hygiene and dinner attire. You look lovely, but unfortunately your friend does not meet our standards."

"He's a blind date." As the words leave my mouth, I wonder why I bothered. It's not as if I'm ever coming back here again.

The manager nods sympathetically. "Quite so. This must be very awkward for you. You are most welcome to remain with us and dine this evening and to return at any time, but your friend is not. He is outside waiting for you."

"Thank you," I say because *Kill Me Now* won't help. The fact that I finally get it doesn't help either and I can feel the color rushing to my face as I turn to leave, counting the seconds until I'm out of there forever. Just when I think the ordeal is over, I'm stopped at the door by the bartender.

"I'm sorry, ma'am. Your date left an open bar tab."

Numbly, I turn and follow him. "How much is it?"

"Twenty dollars."

As I pay Skylar's tab and add a tip, I suddenly find myself wondering how Mitzi does it. Granted, Tad looks great and smells fine, but he's constantly putting her in awkward situations like this and leaving her with the bill. I'm planning to ask her, first chance I get. Outside, I find Skylar leaning against a car parked on the street. He's laughing.

"Before I ask what you find so amusing, you owe me twenty dollars for your bar tab," I tell him with a fair amount of frost in my voice.

"That shouldn't be a problem for you," he replies.

"Excuse me?"

"If you can afford five grand to buy a man, the least you can do is buy a few drinks."

Even with my new-found wisdom, I'm unprepared for this.

"You're no better than the rest of them," he laughs. "You think you can buy people and they think their place is too good for a guy like me. Like none of your shit stinks."

And with that remark, my red-headed temper explodes. "Everyone's shit stinks, Skylar. The difference is that we have the common decency to wipe." I turn on my heel and walk away.

I'm so furious that I get halfway up the block before I remember that my car is parked at the restaurant. I take a deep breath and turn around to find the sidewalk empty. I have a few blessed seconds of relief as I walk back to the restaurant, but it's short lived. Just as I get there Dotty comes rushing through the door, waving my cell phone.

"You left this on the table, dear," she calls to me. "If you'd like to join us, we could call Earl and ask him to meet us. I'm sure he'd love to have a date with a lovely young lady."

I take a second to stifle the scream I feel rising in my throat. "That's nice of you, really, but this whole evening has been so embarrassing, I just want to go home. You understand, I hope."

I manage to pay the valet and retrieve my car. I pull out of the parking lot onto the side street where I spot Ethan waiting for me. Instead of giving him the usual two-fingered wave, I pull up next to him and roll my window down.

"Is everything okay?" he asks.

I take a big breath and let it out with a smile. "It is now. Thanks for being there for me."

He shakes his head. "I have to tell you, I didn't like the look of that guy."

I start to laugh. "Yeah. You and me both mister." And suddenly, the whole thing is very funny. The two of us have a good chuckle and say good night. By the time I get to my apartment, I've revised my plan to toss my little black dress in the garbage and burn my calendar. Instead, I crawl into my snuggly pajamas and climb into bed. I'm drifting off to sleep when a stray thought floats by: Jason didn't call me back yesterday. Before I can begin to wonder why, I'm asleep.

Week Three

Thursday, Day 15

J'm up at the crack of dawn. Coffee, calendar and pen in hand, I'm taking charge of this train wreck before it goes completely off the rails. Since I launched my GRAND Plan two weeks ago, I've had eight referral dates and booked eight more. I've also had two spectacular sky diving adventures with Nathan's friend, Van, and one of those ships-that-pass-in-the-night encounters at Café Aroma with a guy named Tony. I look at the date. That was the night I met Skylar.

I blink when I see that it was only two weeks ago. If I wasn't kicking myself about losing track of him *before* last night, I am now. If I'd followed my gut and talked to him instead of worrying about Skylar, things could be very different. Huh... *I wonder where he is...*

I shake off the might-have-beens and get back to work. I need to give some serious thought to Van, who I've decided to file under 'It's Complicated' due to his daughter. He's also got a difficult ex, apparently. On the other hand, we've definitely got chemistry, he does own his own business and he loves to skydive. Since there's no guarantee that I'll even hear from him again, I realize that I'm pretty much wasting time again. Come on, girl: Focus!

Okay, so two wild cards I shouldn't be wasting my time on. Wild card number three is Poppi. Even though I don't count him as a romantic possibility, the jury is still out until Trent has a chance to take a look. I'm really hoping he turns out to be a good guy because he's quickly become someone I'd like to add to my inner circle. I have to smile when I think of his game with the phony accent and sigh with gratitude for the wake-up call on the way I've been mishandling the losers in my life.

Now for the GRAND Plan Gang: Skylar, the stinky rock star, rocks a big, fat zero. The same goes for Doug, the klepto DJ; Henri, the wannabe gigolo; Frank, the arrogant trainer; Jeremy, the New Orleans whack job; Lotar, the German sex machine; and Paavo, the flap-of-flab car guy.

That leaves Jekyll/Hyde Jason. He asked me to give him another chance and then after he said 'count on it' he didn't call. That's bizarre. And so are his mood swings. And Tad the Cad's interest in Jason's success is equally alarming. So why isn't that enough to cross him off my list? Well, he has his own business and Trent said there were no red flags. No, wait. Jason *says* he has his own business. Okay, so Trent needs to verify that. But on the plus side, I feel like I can tell him anything and that has to count for something. Wait, I felt the same way about Lotar and look where that went. Dammit! I get up and start pacing.

Why does it feel like I'm making excuses? Why am I fighting this lesson instead of learning it? A sudden thought stops me in my tracks: This is how Mitzi acts when she's making her endless excuses for Tad. I'm so creeped out that I grab the calendar. Am I seeing Jason or not? I take a deep breath and let it out. If I'm uncertain, it's No. He is finished. I text him immediately to get him off my plate. If he calls back, I'll tell him in person.

Sunday	Monday	Tuesday	Wednesday	Thursday	Friday	Saturday
				WEEK ONE[1] The Plan	Nolan's[2] Birthday	Tony?[3] Skylar
Skydive - Van[4]	~~Jason~~[5]	~~Doug~~[6]	Henri[7]	WEEK TWO[8] ~~Frank~~ The Girls	~~Jason #2~~[9]	Hiking Ethan[10] Poppi
Skydive -Van #2[11]	Jeremy[12]	Lotar[13]	~~Paavo~~[14] ~~Skylar #2~~	WEEK THREE[15] The Girls	Wine[16] Tasting	~~Jason #3~~[17]
Stewart[18]	Barry[19] Greg	Joey[20] Gale	Richard[21] Trent Arrives	WEEK FOUR[22] Girls/Trent	Trent[23]	Oscar[24] Trent
Poppi[25]	Michael[26]	[27]	[28]	DEADLINE[29] Girls/Note	RESULTS[30]	My[31] Birthday

Wow. Eight out of eight guys on the plan suck and the one eligible guy I find on my own has put himself on dating hiatus. I'm beginning to wonder if I'll ever find Mr. Right. Then again, it's only been two weeks and I only need one good one, right? So what if the others are incredible creeps?

That probably sounds a little crazy until you remember that I work in Reality TV, which is the original breeding ground for craziness. I do live in that world five days out of seven, year after year, and it's amazing if you can still recognize crazy when the proverbial shit hits the fan.

As I head to work I think about my life. I start each day in a sweet little apartment in Studio City. The madness begins when I willingly choose to fight my way through LA gridlock for the privilege of descending into the dump where I work. Because no one wastes money on reality TV, my personal corner of Hell is a repurposed warehouse that lists several degrees off plumb in the shadow of the I-10 off-ramp. No matter the weather on any given day, at Slum Central the skies are always grey.

As a producer, I get my own office – formerly a cramped supply closet – that I share with Nolan. In addition to our desks, chairs and file cabinets, we wrestle on a daily basis with a ceiling fan whose high speed sounds like the helicopter assault at the opening of *Apocalypse Now* and whose low speed sounds like three cats in a blender.

We have a moth-eaten carpet that traps chair legs, shoe heels and remnants of food but refuses to stick to the floor – the other day I nearly killed myself tripping over the huddled body of some repair guy using with a murderous-looking nail gun to try to get the carpet under control.

Was he replacing or patching said carpet? Nope. He simply nailed the scummy shreds to the floor. And when I saw the roll of duct tape on his belt, I made a bet with myself that he'd be using it to tape over the nail heads when he was done with his gun.

The one ray of light in our cramped quarters shines feebly through a grime-pitted window that offers an unobstructed view of, 1) the el under the off-ramp where a small troupe of homeless people eat, sleep, store their begging-for-free-stuff signs, fight for territory and get stoned; and, 2) the stop sign (surprise!) that marks the intersection of the off ramp with a four lane boulevard filled with manic depressives frantically going nowhere. This intersection is where the homeless troupe takes turns holding up their weather-beaten, hand-lettered signs.

The windows in the edit bay would offer the same scenic view if the editors hadn't been so opposed to the light interrupting their work that they covered each and every window with a thick black cloth. To be fair, with everyone watching, timing, notating or editing footage, the last thing they need is the headache-inducing distraction of light reflecting off screens and monitors.

By default, this makes my office the place to be when the homeless troupe – consisting of three scruffy bearded guys in baggy pants and torn shirts and one ratty blonde in skin tight jeans and a cropped top – gets motivated to do something more challenging than lie around under the el and we get to watch a new episode of what we lovingly call Bum Theater.

Normally, the guys take turns holding up the begging signs and asking drivers for money while the ratty blonde sits on the curb or leans against the stop sign. If she's totally out of it, and the walk from the el takes all the energy and focus she's got, she lies flat on her back with one of their begging signs covering her head.

Every now and then, for no particular reason, she'll take it into her head to get up and stagger out of her comfort zone and into the boulevard full of cars, pickup trucks, delivery vans, SUVs, boat-trailers, scrap haulers, tour buses, refrigerated transport trucks, motorcycles, RV's, SWAT teams, ambulances, parade floats, cop cars and getaway vehicles.

When that happens, we get a full-on symphony of horns, bells, whistles, screams, screeching tires, whump-thumps of sudden impact and approaching sirens while one of the guys throws down his sign and dusts off his broken field running skills to snatch her out of the jaws of death and bring her back.

Sometimes they're joined by a younger guy who still looks pretty good for someone living on the streets. Since he never gets involved in the money-earning activities, we think he may be their dealer. When they can afford it, they party. How crazy the party gets and how long it lasts depends on the *stash du jour.*

While these shows can be colorful, they're nothing compared to the action we get when the troupe is attacked by this older, bald guy we call Skull because of the skull tattoo he's got on the top of his head. Skull appears out of nowhere every now and then, intent on stealing their signs and jumping their claim to the corner begging spot.

Though the troupe members drift in and out of that state we call reality, other than a little bickering and babbling and the occasional fit brought on by the demons they alone can see, they're relatively harmless. Skull, on the other hand, is completely out of his mind.

The first time I saw Skull on the attack, he was yelling, waving his arms and giving the others an occasional shove. It looked to us like his plan was to scare them into running away so he could steal their stuff and take their begging spot without having to keep watching his back. The thing is, stealing a sign is easy. Getting a bunch of dazed stoners to run is tough.

When he saw that yelling wasn't working – and when you consider the voices they're already hearing, his rant probably rated as little more than white noise – Skull just stood there for a minute, doing nothing. Or so it seemed.

What's he doing?

Why's he just standing there?

We couldn't figure it out.

Then Skull shoved one hand down into the back of his baggy pants. A few seconds later, when he pulled his hand back out, he was holding something. We couldn't see what it was. Then he started yelling again and began throwing whatever it was at the others. When he let go of it, it broke into pieces. When it landed on his targets, it stuck wherever it landed.

For some reason, whatever that stuff was did the trick. Yelling and waving their arms, the others managed to get up and stagger off. When they were gone, Skull casually wiped his hand on his pant leg, picked up the sign and walked to the corner, where he started to beg. We just stood there, in silence. And then...

Shit!

Yeah.

No, no. I mean it literally. That's what he just threw at them.

It took the rest of us a few seconds before we got it.

What?

Yup.

He did what he did and then he threw it.

And we saw him do it.

And then, because we work in reality TV, we shook our heads and went back to work.

Work, at the time, was an extreme make-over show with the all-inclusive make-over prize to be awarded to the lucky contestant who was willing to show America what it was like to live in his or her wretched, genetically-challenged world. My job was to use their stories to create the right combination of train wreck fascination and pity to keep the viewers coming back for more. Was it a tough job? Please. When you've got the real thing unfolding right outside your window as a guideline, coming up with a winning 'Freaks-R-Us' formula each week is hardly a stretch.

Hmmm...

Is my idea of 'business as usual' the reason I'm struggling with this whole dating thing? Am I so far out of touch with 'normal' that I can't recognize a whacko like Doug the Klepto or Jeremy the Clinger when I see one? Did I really need to go out with Skylar more than once to make sure he smelled like death in dirty gym socks? Was I planning to go out with Jason a third time just to confirm that his Jekyll and Hyde mood swings really do scare the crap out of me?

Is this whole game the last desperate act of a soon-to-be spinster with too many cats? Or worse... Will I wind up as the mutilated victim of some wild-eyed serial killer who finally got me alone when I ignored my better judgment and gave him a forty-third chance? Fortunately, I'm saved from swirling in a downward spiral of crappy thoughts and turning around to head home and directly into the bathtub when the phone rings.

It's Nolan. "Hey, have you got a spare key to the men's bathroom?"

"Um. Why?"

"Amy just called me. The Bossman is locked in."

"Nolan, the door opens from the inside. He doesn't need a key."

"Amy says he called her. There's a catch." I hear a strain in Nolan's voice. This must be serious.

"Have you called him?" I ask.

"Nope. Amy told me he won't take any calls."

"Well, why can't Amy unlock the door?"

"Apparently her keys are missing. If you don't have a spare, they're going to have to call someone to take the door off at the hinges. Boss-man would rather avoid that."

"Okay. I'm already on my way'."

"Thanks, Lan. See you soon." The relief spills through the phone.

As I cruise down the 405, I crack a small smile. I've got a boss who can't find his way out of a bathroom, a partner who gets beaten up by his girlfriends and three best friends whose social lives are a mess. Somehow this makes me feel better about myself.

A few minutes later I'm stuck at a traffic light, wondering if I should call Poppi and fill him in on the latest prank when my phone rings. It's Poppi calling me!

"Good morning, Miss Lana, will you have time to see me today?"

I notice that his voice remains accent free. "Poppi, I will make time! When and where?"

"Perhaps you will let me buy you lunch."

"At that restaurant?"

"If it is not too much trouble."

"Poppi, my mouth is watering already." I'm remembering the meal and those tasty pastries.

"I will have Johnny pick you up at your office at 11:30."

"I can't wait."

My curiosity about Poppi and his invitation is set aside when I reach Slum Central and get caught up in the general hysteria surrounding the prankster's latest stunt. Even though there's no end of butt jokes being traded, I find Amy looking grim.

"Here's my key," I tell her. "What's the story?"

She looks around nervously. "You won't breathe a word of this?"

"Not a word." I solemnly promise.

"If you do, I could lose my job. Seriously, Lana, he'll kill me if he finds out." Her face is pink.

"I get it Amy. Don't tell me if you're that worried," I reply.

She sighs. "I have to tell someone or I'll burst. Okay, here it is: He didn't call me. When I got here this morning, I found this note on my desk." She opens a file folder. "Don't touch it. I called the cops and they told me to keep it like this till they can get here."

The only thing written on the page is... *The big shit is where he belongs.*

"How did you know he was in the bathroom?"

"I looked all over for him. When I couldn't open the bathroom door, I knocked and called his name. I think he's been gagged, or something. I couldn't understand a word he said. When I went looking for the key, I saw that it was gone."

She's heading for the hall as she speaks. When it suddenly occurs to me that this weirdo may not have left the building, I put out a hand to stop her. "Maybe you'd better wait for the cops."

When she folds her arms across her chest and gives me the 'Amy' look, I give up. "Okay, then at least take Nolan with you."

She looks alarmed.

"Amy, you don't know what you'll find. Nolan's smart. He's good at figuring things out."

I'm very relieved when she gives in and lets me call Nolan. While the two of them head off on their rescue mission, I stand guard, sort of, at the end of the hall. Sure, the guy rubs me the wrong way. Sure, he's a pig. That's no reason to make this any worse for him than it already is.

My phone pings. Nolan has sent me a text...

Blanket, 1st aid kit, 911

What the hell? *Why 911*

Blood pressure

That's a relief. If Bossman's got blood pressure, he's alive. I call 911 as I grab the kit and the blanket from the bull pen. Amy meets me half-way. She looks pale.

"He's been duct taped to the toilet," she whispers. "His mouth is taped shut. He looks terrible."

We both hear the sirens at the same time. She heads for the men's room. I head for the door and bump into Ethan who is leading a cop and a first response guy toward me. Both men are carrying medical bags.

"A car caught fire a few blocks from here," Ethan says. "They were just wrapping up."

I recognize the bossy-voiced cop from the last prank. "We got a note this time," I tell him. "His assistant put it in a folder. No one's touched it but her."

He nods. "What's happened?"

"He's been locked in the men's room," I reply. "Just down there. My partner asked for a blanket and the first aid kit after he told me to call 911."

The first response guy's eyebrows go up.

"He's worried about blood pressure, I think," is all I add.

As they move down the hall, I take up my post. For a second, Ethan looks like he wants to follow the others. He's quick, though. When he sees the look on my face, he checks his steps.

"Now what?" he says.

"I'm meeting Poppi for lunch," I tell him quietly. "I don't know what he wants. All I know is, this is top priority. It has to stop."

Ethan nods. "I'm assuming you won't mention your lunch date to the cops?"

"I'll see what Poppi has to say. I can call them when I get back."

"I think I'll tag along for back-up," he says with a knit brow.

"Good idea."

It takes almost an hour before the cop is finished with his questions and things finally settle back to normal. The first response team takes Bossman out on a stretcher, completely covered in blankets. I'm sure his embarrassment is the reason he stays silent for once. The cops tell us the men's room and hallway are off limits until the crime scene techs can deal with it. When Nolan isn't needed any longer, I suggest that we go for a walk so we can talk.

"So, Bossman tells me he gets here ahead of the janitor," he starts. "I think he was planning on meeting someone, but he says he just wanted to get some work done. Anyway, his story is that before he even has time to flip the light switch, he gets knocked on the head. Not that I doubted him, but I checked and sure enough, he's got a bump and it's sore to the touch. The next thing he knows, he says he's in the men's room. Somebody's taped him to the toilet. Tape is wrapped around his head to close his mouth. His hands are taped to the front of his shirt. By the time Amy finds him, he's been in there a couple of hours. It's a good thing his mouth was taped shut. If he'd been able to shout, with his blood pressure, he'd have given himself a heart attack."

"Did Amy tell you about the note?" I ask.

Nolan nods.

"So what do you think?"

Nolan shrugs. "It's crazy, but I've got a feeling he's got a feeling he knows who it is."

"You think he figured that out today? Did he see them or...?"

"Not sure really, but something clued him in," Nolan says with a shrug.

"I'm having lunch with Poppi," I tell him.

"Good! Maybe he can get it sorted out."

"I hope so. Johnny is picking me up in a few minutes. Ethan's going to tag along."

Nolan's smile tells me he approves. "I'll stay here and wait for updates."

When Poppi greets me at the restaurant, he takes my hand and kisses each cheek. Immediately after that, we get down to business. The meal is served quickly and quietly. I say thanks but no to wine and ask for water instead.

"I know who your prankster is," he tells me.

"Did you know about the attack this morning?"

"Yes." Poppi's voice is calm.

"You knew and you didn't do anything?" I'm a little shocked that he just could let something like that happen, even to a slime bag like Bossman.

He looks at me with surprise. "I called you."

I close my eyes briefly. A second later, I get it. "You knew it wasn't life threatening."

"But of course."

"But of course." I close my eyes and take a breath. "Okay, who is it? What can we do?"

"This is the problem, Lana. I do not know if your Bossman wishes me to act."

"What? Why not?"

"You remember I told you that this Bossman is a man who does not care who is hurt?"

When I nod, he continues.

"I am told that your Bossman once cheated someone. I need to confirm the details, but it was someone who trusted him and helped him reach success. This person lost everything. He died after many long years in poverty. His family suffered. And now, his son has learned the story."

I close my eyes. "And he's the one. He's getting even and today Bossman found out."

Poppi nods.

"So even though you can help, you won't unless Bossman asks."

He nods again.

"And, uhh…" I choose my words carefully. "If he does ask for your help and you do agree to help him, it will be on your terms."

"Always."

I need to be sure. "So, no matter what kind of revenge he wants, you will do things your way."

Poppi's pats my hand. "No cement will be used and no harm will come to anyone."

I feel my cheeks starting to burn.

"And, as I have told you before, Lana, I wish to work with you to help your Bossman. I will not act until you tell me you are ready to proceed."

"Can I call you when I know what his condition is?"

When Poppi smiles, I can't help smiling. "What am I thinking? You already know."

"He is fine. They will watch him tonight and release him in the morning."

This seems like the perfect time to bring up my concern, so I take a breath and jump in.

"Poppi, do you realize that this is a little awkward? I know that you know this kind of stuff, but I don't know how you know it. It's somewhat... disconcerting."

He smiles. "An old man must be permitted to have a few secrets, no?"

I can help but laugh. "Okay, let me call you after I speak to him."

I'm quiet on the drive back. With everything that's happened, this wasn't the time to talk to Poppi about the military angle for the show. My purpose in meeting him was to find out what's been going on and I'm glad the mystery is solved. I hadn't realized how draining this whole prankster episode has been. It's a huge relief that Poppi really does seem to be one of the good guys. At the same time, it's good to know that Nolan isn't taking any chances, that Ethan is concerned and that my big brother Trent will be here soon. I've never been in a situation where I've actually had to worry about my safety, and I'm very glad these guys have my back.

Back at Slum Central, I sit down with Amy and my guys. When I tell them that I've met with an investigator who is on top of things, Amy is relieved and I can tell that Nolan and Ethan are reading between the lines. After that, with no access permitted to the central hallway and CSI techs still under foot, I give the team the day off. As soon as I get home, number one on my To Do list is a soothing bubble bath.

It's while I'm lazing in the tub that I realize how distracted I've been these last two weeks. On top of these crazy pranks, I've been up to my eyeballs with this new reality show. What little time I've had left has been booked solid with dates. Except for that first Saturday when we all went shopping to find me a new wardrobe, and the call from Jonah to tell me about his mad oven mitt date, I've been totally off the radar to my friends. I've no idea how Kat's new guy is working out and the last time I heard from Mitzi, it was a totally one-sided dropped call rant.

Since tonight is Girls Night, I decide to do something to make it up to them so I call Poppi. If anyone can make an evening special, it's Poppi. When I tell him my plan, he's delighted.

"Consider it done, Bella," he says.

And that's how the four of us end up at Poppi's Italian restaurant to celebrate Girls Night this week, with each us arriving in our own Italian-hunk, chauffeur-driven limo.

Jonah arrives first, his eyes shining. "Now THIS is more like it!"

I'm grinning at the look on his face. "So you approve?"

"Darlin', I'm signing up for Italian lessons first thing. Mama Mia, those boys are hot!"

Mitzi walks in on his remark. "I'll second that!" she laughs. "What a great way to get my mind off that what's-his-name jerk I've been wasting the best years of my life with."

And finally, Kat is escorted to the table by Poppi himself. "This-a beautiful woman, she's-a meant to be-a Queen," he says, full of accented charm. He kisses her hand and pulls out her chair. Before he turns to leave, he nods to me. "I'm-a speak-a with you in-a tha morning, Bella."

Kat stares after him and then turns on me, hands on hips. "THIS man is calling you Bella and you haven't said Word One?"

When the waiter has poured champagne, I raise my glass. "To friends," I suggest. They all agree.

I'm betting that the first person we'll hear from tonight is Mitzi, especially after I'd bumped into her and Tad on my date with Lotar. But I'm wrong. It's Kat!

"You see the way this lovely man treats Lana? The charm? The sophistication? The courtesy? THIS is how Trevor treats me. It's how we all deserve to be treated, girls!"

As the platters of to-die-for food arrive and their fragrant aromas fill the room, Kat gets no argument from us. We moan with delight as we dig into the Carpaccio with truffle oil and imported cheese, the bubbling chicken and eggplant parmesan, and the thin crust pesto and mushroom pizzas.

"So, what's been happening?" I ask Kat. "What have you and your lovely man been up to?"

Kat's face glows.

"Stop with the smiling kitty routine, Kat!" Jonah demands. "We want details!"

"Trevor is the single most considerate man I have ever met," she begins. "For starters, he really listens. He's there for me. And he has such great advice!" She sips her champagne. "It's more than the compliments and the little courtesies, like opening my door and automatically taking care of small details. We have so much in common. We talk about everything."

"I know you're going to freak that I'm asking, but seriously, what about sex?" Mitzi asks. "Do you talk about that with Trevor too?"

"I'm with Mitz," Jonah chimes in. "Enough with the Prince Charming resume. It's been two weeks, already. What's he like with the lights down low?"

"That's classified information, you awful voyeurs!" Kat turns three shades of red before she speaks again. "Let's move on. I want updates on Lana. Give us details on the GRAND Plan!"

"No way," I tell them. "My sorry tale comes last. Mitzi, you're next."

As I suspect, Mitzi is keyed up about tomorrow night's wine tasting. As she talks, I feel my attention drifting to Jonah. I'm wondering if he's going to let us know what's bugging him."

When our main course plates are whisked away, a dessert tray arrives filled with delicate pastries surrounding an amazing square of Tiramisu. I ignore the sweets for a moment and put him under the spotlight.

"Okay, so the burning question at the moment – other than how many calories these pastries have – is what's happening in oven mitt fashion circles these days. Jonah?"

While he chokes on a laugh, the girls demand answers. Over hugely theatrical sighs, he tells them about his crazy date. Their laughter is the perfect lead-up to me.

"Okay, so here's my story in a nutshell: I've met nine eligible men. I'm pretty sure eight of them couldn't be a worse match for me. Three seemed nice enough to see again at first, but two of them fizzled out on date two, hence no match. That leaves one guy worth thinking about and eight more to meet over the next two weeks."

"I want to hear about the crazy ones," Jonah announces.

"I figured as much," I laugh. "Let's start with the kleptomaniac who gets caught stealing wallets while we're on our date. How about the personal trainer who was too embarrassed to be seen with me? Or the son of the French diplomat who ordered one of the most expensive champagnes and then gave me the bill? And the whacko from New Orleans who went home after our date and baked dessert, then called at 3 AM to break up with me when I didn't answer his five emails or show up with my overnight bag and wedding dress. I met an art critic who expected after-dinner sex and walked away when he didn't get it. I got thrown out of one of my favorite bistros thanks to a guy who thinks Body Odor is a macho man quality. I got wined and dined by a man who said nothing was too good for me and then mauled me in the parking lot. And last but not least, I passed on lunch with the car salesman who lost 140 pounds and proved it by pulling a flab of skin out of his pants while lifting shirt up all right in the middle of a restaurant."

Three sets of eyes stare at me, unblinking.

"Wow," Mitzi breathes.

"Better you than me," Jonah grins.

"I think you deserve a medal," Kat says firmly. "Where do these people come from?"

"...and why were they referred to me?" I throw in.

"I told you this GRAND Plan of yours would cause trouble," Kat reminds me.

"Wait," Mitzi says. "They're not all bad, right? You said there's one you're willing to see again. That's one you wouldn't have met otherwise and one is all you need!"

"Amen to that," Jonah raises his glass and we all join him.

"Even more crazy than my social life is what's been happening at work. The crazy wonderful thing is the new reality show we're developing. The owner of the business we're following is the lovely man who arranged our dinner tonight!"

I pause while they cheer. "The super crazy thing is a mysterious prankster. In the last two weeks Bossman's been sent on pointless errands all over town. His unlisted number was blitzed by crank calls. A dead skunk was stuffed in the trunk of his $70,000 car. Cans of tuna fish were super glued to his hand-carved desk. Corrosive goo was smeared on the building's door handles. Roofing nails were spread across the parking lot and then, Bossman got mugged. His mouth was duct-taped shut, his hands stuck to his shirt and the seat of his pants taped to the lid of the toilet in the men's room. He sat there for two hours before his secretary heard his cries for help."

Out of the stunned silence, Mitzi says, "You're right. This is insane. What about the cops?"

I shrug. "They're doing what they can to try to find the guy. So far, it's not working."

Jonah clears his throat and gives a funny little sideways nod. "What about these guys?"

I grin. "The same lovely man hosting our evening is looking into it."

Jonah raises his glass. "I think we should drink to that, too!"

Friday, Day 16

riday turns out to be a day of decision-making. Nolan and I spend the morning reviewing Ethan's reel and discussing his work with us so far. We're so impressed that we decide to offer him a position on our team. Lucky for us, he decides to accept. We call a huddle and include Ethan and our researcher, Sam. We have lots to discuss.

Bossman rolls in just after lunch. I've asked Amy to let me know when he's free and, a few minutes later, she buzzes me. When I tap on the door and walk in, one look at him almost makes me think twice. I've never liked the guy, but that doesn't mean I'm happy to see him with dark circles under his eyes.

"So," I take a chair.

"So what?" He says, but his heart isn't in it. He runs his hands through his silly boot-black hair. Remembering Poppi's advice, I take a deep breath and hold nothing back.

"In the last two weeks, we've had the cops here more times than in the last ten years. Your car was destroyed. You've had to close down and send everyone home twice. The janitor got hurt. Given the lousy salary he makes, you're lucky he didn't sue you. Someone mugged you and you wound up in hospital. You're lucky you didn't have a heart attack. The bottom line is that no one is going to jump through hoops for you if it means working alone, after hours, in a place where who knows what could happen."

"What's your point?"

"In the three years I've worked here and I've never stood up to you. I've never told you where my line in the sand is. I'm doing it now: Whatever is going on with you is putting all of us at risk. And when I say 'all of us', I don't just mean the inmates here at the zoo. I'm including the people we're featuring on this new reality show. From what I can see, you don't give a rat's ass about them, or us, but I do. And I'm telling you that if you don't do what I ask, I'm ready to pull the plug on The Muckers and take my team and go."

Bossman blinks in surprise.

"Here's the deal: I've told Poppi that we will do the right thing by him and his family – meaning that I won't let you make them look like fools for the sake of ratings – if Poppi will sort out this prankster mess for you. Poppi said he needs to hear it from you, face-to-face, before he's willing to help. Once he gets your go-ahead, he'll take action. After the prankster is dealt with, you'll get your sizzle reel. Oh, and Poppi has told me they won't even let us pitch the show if I'm not fully in charge."

He nods and looks out his window. I give him a good 30 seconds.

I'm on a roll and feeling good. "So, yes or no" I demand. "Do you want Poppi's help? He's waiting for my call."

Bossman stays where he is, looking out the window. "Give me the weekend to think about it."

"If nothing changes by 9 AM Monday, you and I are done. Nolan and I are out of here and we're taking Ethan and Sam with us. You'll be starting a new team from scratch." I say with the authority hoping that Nolan doesn't kill me if we have to walk.

I shake that fear off and walk out feeling exhilarated. That not only felt good; it felt necessary. Bye-bye Doormat and Hello Control, I'm thinking as I strut down the hallway with a grin on my face.

Back in my office, I call Poppi and give him the news. Then after sharing the outcome of my meeting with Bossman, Nolan and I get back to work. Whether the Bossman's answer is yes or no, we've got a sizzle reel to finish and bills to pay.

Time passes quickly. For the first time, I'm working on my own agenda and it's exciting. Knowing I've got options is one thing. Taking action to explore them is something else. In spite of everything that concerns me about these pranks I'm excited by my new-found confidence.

As I head home to change for the wine tasting later that afternoon, I think about Mitzi and her latest "save Tad" venture. Whether the business amounts to much in the long run, I'm hoping it attracts some fun people tonight. If not, I plan to hijack Jonah and cut out early. I want to know what's going on with him and we always have a great time.

When Jonah swings by to pick me up, I'm ready. I've chosen a cute black top with a v-neck lined with lace, dark Paige jeans and sexy black sandals. My hair is swept off my neck into a loose knot and my ears sparkle with blue chandelier style earrings. As I head out the door I grab my blue wrap and call it done.

When Jonah and I reach Mitzi's, we realize we're the last ones to arrive. We find Kat and Trevor just inside the door. From Kat's expression, I can tell that she's planning a quick exit, too. I shoot her a wink and she grins.

Mitzi's spacious, open concept kitchen/dining/living area has been transformed since my last visit. She's replaced her dining table with two round tables. In the connecting space that leads to the living area, there's a raised platform with several stools. Her usual jumble of knick-knacks and cookware are gone from the kitchen bar. In their place, there's a pile of clipboards with judging sheets and a box of miniature disposable wine glasses. Tad is at one of the round tables, fussing over several bottles of wine while Mitzi is sitting on the platform with two couples. From the 'all business' tone in Mitzi's voice, I'm betting they've signed on as distributors. There are four more couples standing near the round tables. Add Kat and Trevor and Jonah and I, and that makes six couples serving as guinea pigs. Smiling my best break-the-ice producer's smile, I say hello to those I know and introduce myself to the others. Jonah is not far behind.

The first couple I meet is super serious about wine. Kassandra (with a K) and Victor (with an O) have a villa in Spain and shares in a winery in France. In three seconds flat, I get invited to subscribe to their blog, visit their winery and join a movement promoting Red for Heart Health. Next!

Toby and Taffy are couple number two. They're, like, totally into wine, right? And, um, cheese? And, um, everything that's, like, organic? Like my daddy's millions? Next!

Steven and Dimitri are couple number three. Theirs is a global success story, says Steven. He is a designer/decorator-slash-media darling, don't you know. And Poor Dimitri (and by that, he means Rich Dimitri) is apparently the Russian equivalent of Steve Jobs and/or Bill Gates. He knows very little English, Steven confides as he pats Dimitri in a proprietary way. Next!

And that brings us to couple number four. Carol and Dean are young/old outdoor types who know Mitzi professionally – Dean was a commodities trader and Carol is just about to retire. Their plan is to do whatever takes their fancy. When I mention that I'm from Boise, it turns out that Dean's brother has investments there. Jonah and I agree that, along with Kat and Trevor, these two are our best match-up for the wine tasting. Just then, Kat wanders over with Trevor in tow and we make the necessary introductions.

The rules as Tad explains them are simple. There are six couples who will be divided into two groups. There are ten different wines to sample on each table. One group will start with the Red wines. The other group will start with the Whites. When all ten wines at a table have been sampled, the groups will switch. As I suspected, the distributors will be observing. Mitzi will coach them, Tad will do the pouring and we will taste the wine, scoring by numbers because the labels are covered. As a thank you for playing the game, everyone will get a bottle of the red and white wines that score the most votes. Everyone in attendance will also get a small discount on the purchase of any wines they sample tonight.

Even though Tad rubs me the wrong way, I have to admit his plan is interesting. If the wines are decent, this thing might actually take off. All he has to do is find enough people willing to make a ten thousand dollar investment in a brand new start-up.

Since none of us wants to lock horns with the serious players, who clearly favor the red vintages, we opt to start with the white wines. An added bonus is that we'll get to avoid Tad, since he's already fussing over Kassandra and Victor and Steven and Dimitri in a big way.

Trevor volunteers to pour our tasting samples while Jonah heads for Mitzi's cupboard. With Kat beside me watching his back, he liberates her good stemware. Dean and Carol bring over our clipboards and Trevor pours out samples from bottle number one. The glasses are oversized and this prompts Trevor to pour generously. As we chat and sip, we nibble on chunks of crusty bread Mitzi has provided to clear our palates.

Though I do like a glass of wine now and then, I'm not much of a drinker. By the time I finish my sample from bottle number five, my back teeth are floating. When we finish bottle number ten, all six of us are pretty giddy. When it's time to switch places with the other group, we're ready to party.

I turn to see Victor scowling at our group and my tipsy-ness kicks into full gear. "Why so glum, Vic-TOR? Too much tannin giving you the puckers?" I giggle. When his reply is nothing but a frosty glare, I try to look serious but it only makes the giggles worse.

After the shift, Tad continues to fuss over his favorites while we drink our way through the Reds. We've long since given up on scoring. By now, we're a bunch of happy drunks who can barely see straight and it's at this point that Tad finally tears himself away from his new best friends to come and check on us. When he sees the condition we're in, he goes ballistic.

Watching his face is like watching one of those werewolf movies as the man turns into a crazed beast in seconds. One minute Tad is Mr. Charming and the next minute he's yelling so loud, we can barely understand what he's saying. We've seen it all before, of course, but the newcomers are mesmerized. As soon as the flailing around stops, he gets ice cold and his words are crystal clear. When he starts accusing us of deliberately sabotaging his new business, Mitzi comes running. As she steps in to defend us, he turns on her and that's when things get really ugly.

Whatever the smart move is at this point, we don't make it. Jonah tells Tad to back off. Tad gives Jonah a shove. Mitzi steps between them just as Tad takes a swing at Jonah and his fist connects with her eye.

Kat and Carol take charge of the other guests while I take Mitzi to the kitchen to put something cool on her eye. Dean and Trevor walk Tad out to the patio to cool off and that's when Jonah pushes Tad into the kiddie pool Mitzi uses to cool the dog off. When Mitzi sees Tad soaking in the dog hair filled water, she bursts into tears and runs upstairs.

While everyone muddles through awkward good-byes, I wander back to the kitchen. There isn't much of a mess, which is just as well, because I'm too drunk to clean up. I'm giving the counter a swipe when I realize I'm not alone. When I turn around, a soaking wet Tad is right behind me.

"Hey sexy," he says, sliding his arms around my waist as if this is standard operating procedure.

I back-pedal quickly and bump up against the counter. "Get away from me!"

He moves in, grinning. "Come on, baby. Give me a chance. I've seen how you look at me."

"Give YOU a chance? Are you insane?" I'm in total shock.

"Jason says you're a great kisser. Why don't you show me what you've got, babe?"

He's pressing me back against the counter and it's digging into my back.

"Let me go," I tell him firmly. "You're hurting me!"

He just laughs and presses his six foot frame more firmly into my body. "And you like it, don't you!" He says seductively.

"Get the hell off me, you idiot!" I'm really yelling now, because he's scaring me.

"I want you, Lana. We're a perfect match."

"Tad, there is no 'we'. Not now; not ever. Get away from me!" I bring my knee up straight into his groin. Tad howls in pain, stumbling backwards and I'm suddenly Cad free.

"And don't think I'll forget this, you son of a bitch!" I tell him as I grab my purse and turn away.

"What have you done to him?" Mitzi's standing in the doorway, staring at Tad on the floor.

"Seriously?" I stare in disbelief. "You're asking ME what I've done to HIM. Why not ask your deadbeat, loser boyfriend what the hell he just did to me? Why not ask him why he had me pinned against the counter? Why not ask why he wouldn't stop when I said he was hurting me? Why not ask what the hell you're doing with this dirt-bag, asshole jerkoff in the first place?"

To my astonishment, she runs to Tad and tries to help him. When he shoves her roughly aside, she turns on me. "This is all your fault!" She cries.

"He takes your money, he cheats on you, he punches you in the eye, he attacks me in your kitchen and it's MY fault?"

"He was probably kidding," she says hotly.

"And since when was groping a woman against her will remotely funny? This guy is a total pile of shit, Mitzi! He's making a fool of you and you're letting him."

"It's time you left, Lana," she says. "I don't have room for someone like you in my life."

"You got it, sweetheart!" I grab my purse and storm out of the kitchen, colliding with Jonah. One look on his face tells me he heard everything. He grabs my hand and drags me out of the house.

The next few hours are an angry, unhappy blur. Instead of sensibly grabbing a taxi and calling it a night, Jonah and I crawl through a dozen bars. After all the wine, the last thing we need is more liquor, but that doesn't stop us. When we finally run out of steam, we're in one of those padded booths at the kind of pub where everyone knows your name. Fortunately, the bartender is a friend who keeps an eye on us.

Since I'm still pissed at Mitzi and Tad, it's the perfect time to find out what Jonah's issue with her is. When he finally tells me, I'm stunned into silence.

"No one gets it," he slurs. "Our girl Mitzi is a real piece of work, you know that?"

I'm thinking about our kitchen confrontation and I nod my head. "No kidding."

Jonah shakes his head sadly. "You don't know the half of it. She's got this 'poor me' game she's running and we're all in it. She's loyal, Tad's an asshole. She's desperate, we come running. She swears it's over. Next thing we know, she's gone back to him. Every time she does it, she adds a new level to the game. This time she bought him a business. Last time it was a bachelor condo. The time before that it was a car. Every single thing she gives him attracts more women. And when the women appear, what's a guy like that gonna do? So he cheats on her. Again. And they fight. Again. And she throws him out. Again. And then she takes him back. Why? Cause that's where the action is."

"Yeah," I nod owlishly.

"The worst thing was sleeping with her," he mutters.

"What???" I say shocked beyond belief.

He looks disgusted. "I know. Hard to believe, right? Even I don't believe it and I did it.

"Uhhh... why?"

He shakes his head. "It was nuts. I keep wondering if the whole rescue me/rescue my dog scene wasn't a set up. But there was all that blood, Lana. And that poor dog and that broken glass everywhere." He shakes his head again. "For the life of me, I still can't figure out how we got from *I never want to see that bastard again* to the worst nightmare of my life."

Well, that explains everything. I'm saved from thinking of something to say when the bartender tells us our taxi is here. Neither one of us remembers ordering one, but that's okay. Jonah and I somehow manage to fall into the car. A short ride later, we stagger into his apartment.

"C'mon," he says muzzily. "S'go t'bed."

My 'OK' is the last thing I remember.

Saturday, Day 17

When I open my eyes the first time, I have no idea where I am. The only thing I know for certain is that I want to die. I close my eyes again, but the loud birds outside keep me from passing out.

When I force my eyes open a second time, the thing I know for certain is that I need a bathroom. Until I take care of that, nothing else matters. Death is going to have to wait.

As I plot the best steps to take care of this urgent matter while balancing my five hundred pound hangover, I suddenly realize that I can hear someone breathing. I'm not alone??? I turn my head – ouch! carefully! – and that's when I find Jonah's sleeping face just inches from my nose. I'm so surprised I almost fall out of the bed. The other thing I discover when I carefully pull the sheet back – because, no matter what, I really have to go – is that I'm naked. WHY???

I stare for a second at Jonah snoring away, and then I take peek at him under the sheet. Crap! He's naked too. I can't deal with any of this until I take care of my bursting bladder, so I pull a blanket around me and tip-toe to the bathroom. Seconds later, relief!

The way my head is pounding, I'm afraid to turn on the light, but I need pain killers. Squinting, I flip the switch. OW. When I reach to open the mirror cabinet, I catch sight of myself. Small wonder I want to die. My face is puffy and I have mascara smeared all over my face and on my arms. I've got lipstick on my ear and only one earring on. Good god, what the heck did we do!

Shaking the headache pills into my hand, I leave the bottle on the counter and head for the kitchen. I need coffee. As I walk through the living room, I come to an abrupt halt. I recognize my clothing, and

Jonah's, in a tangled heap on the floor. Couch pillows everywhere. When did that happen? And what did we do after that? My hangover is making it hard to think straight, but it doesn't stop me from being horrified at the possibilities. First Mitzi and now me? Dear. God. In. Heaven. How are we going to deal with this?

"We're not," a little voice mutters. "Not until I've had my coffee."

Jonah has one of those coffee makers that pours a perfect cup faster than you can get the cream out of the fridge. As I take that first awesome sip I think to myself, if I wasn't worried about our friendship, I could kiss him for his excellent taste in coffee. In the next second, I nearly choke to death. Like a kiss could make things worse at this point!

Back in the living room, I manage to get dressed without waking him and slip out after leaving him a note saying I'll call later. I walk to the corner and hail a cab. Ten minutes later, I'm back at my place. I grab a quick shower, close the curtains, shut off the phone and crawl into bed.

When I wake up, it's three hours later and I'm starving. The hangover cure that works for me is protein and lots of it. I throw on some clothes and head over to the local all-day breakfast diner and order eggs, bacon, more coffee and toast. When I finally push my plate away, I'm feeling more like a human and less like the walking dead. With things under control, it's time to think about last night.

First, because I can't bear to think about what we may have done, I want to focus on Mitzi. Even through the boozy haze, Jonah's assessment had the ring of truth. Mitzi's life IS a constant swirl. Every day it's a new crisis; a problem unfairly dumped in her lap; a long-overdue, well-earned celebration that fell flat. I think back. I can't remember a single time when things were just plain good in Mitzi World.

Even with the facts staring me in the face, it's hard to think of Mitzi as an adrenalin junkie pulling everyone's strings, but the more I think about it, it would be a heckova way to manage a control freak father. In spite of everything, I have to smile.

Next, because I'm still not ready to think about Jonah, I think about Kat. Last night I had plenty of time to get to know Trevor. If possible, he's even nicer than Kat said. The trouble is, there's no question that he's gay. And if I can see it, what is going on with my dear, sweet friend? Why – and come to think of it, how – is it remotely possible that this brilliant match-maker really can't see something so obvious? What on earth would possess her to latch onto a guy she will never have a future with? A guy who will never pop the question? A guy who will never leave her at the altar and break her heart?

Ohhh.

Now that's interesting. I wonder if she realizes she's doing it. And then I wonder if it matters, as long as she's happy.

Okay, I've got no distractions left. It's time to think about Jonah. Why is his life such a total train wreck when it doesn't have to be? He's gorgeous. Smart. Funny. Successful. You'd think great guys would be lining up to be with him. Instead, he's attracting the lunatic fringe. The way he takes on pointless exercises that are doomed to fail, it's like he's keeping happiness out of reach. As if he's rejecting the life he deserves before it rejects him. Wow. And each disaster he gets caught up in is worse than the last. I mean, look at Mitzi! Look at us!

Come to think of it, I still haven't done that. So I take a slow breath and think back. Was I so drunk that I can't remember *anything*? That's never happened to me. And when I think of Jonah and the kind of friendship we have, it doesn't seem remotely possible. But what about the clothing all over the living room? If that wasn't a make-out scene, what was it? Two people so falling down helpless they had to undress each other? As I picture it, I can't help the grin that sneaks up on me. Wouldn't that be a video to die for!

Okay, stop it. This is serious stuff. How do I sort this out? Do I call him? Do I wait? What do I say next time we meet? I shake my head. How do I make such a mess of everything when all I want for him and for me is happiness?

A sudden idea pops into my head. You know who'd be perfect for Jonah? Trevor. In the next second, I hit myself on the forehead. Talk about people trading up their disasters, here I am with two friendships teetering on the brink and now I'm thinking of breaking Kat's heart. Brilliant.

And that brings it back to me. It's my turn under the microscope and it's not a pretty sight. With my thirtieth birthday looming, instead of acting like a grown-up and giving my life a chance to unfold on its own terms, I convince myself that I'm nothing without a man. I cook up a silly ass plan and invite a bunch of semi-strangers to send me more jerks than I could find on my own to put me through all kinds of hell. And when they do, do I tell them where to get off? No! If I'm not suffering in silence, I'm giving second chances! Thanks to no one but me, I've let more men treat me like crap than anyone with an ounce of sense would have tolerated.

This is nothing like the girl who left Boise ten years ago. Instead of getting older and wiser, I seem to have lost the firm grip I used to have on common sense. So where did she disappear to, this sensible girl, and when? As I look back, I realize that it's been such a gradual transformation that I can't put my finger on anything I could call a turning point. All those dating site disasters definitely put me through the wringer, but if I'm going to be honest in this soul-searching, I was already thinking in terms of 'good enough' and 'not so bad' before that. It's not Bozmund, the Bossman's fault either. The bottom line is that it's me. As Poppi made me see so clearly, I'm the one letting me down. I'm the one opening the door to second-rate opportunities.

Funnily enough, even though last night was a set-back, I do think I'm on the right track. Crossing Jason off my list instead of seeing him a third time was a start. And laying it on the line with Bossman and telling Tad and Mitzi where to get off is the first time in a long time that I've caught a glimpse of the Boise Girl I used to be. And if I want her back permanently, I've got to keep that focus. I don't have time for pity parties or foolish teen queen fantasies and I definitely deserve better than one-night stands and morning-after agonies.

"More coffee?" The waitress raises the pot with a smile.

"No thanks," I reply. "Just the bill."

"It's all taken care of," she says. "That gentleman over there told me to put you on his tab."

I look around to find Van smiling at me from a stool at the counter. I take a deep breath and let it out, along with the butterflies. Here's my chance to stick with my good intentions.

"Can I join you?" he calls, looking nothing like the confident guy I've thought him to be.

"Inviting you to sit down is the least I can do," I smile at him. "Bring your coffee mug." As he slides into the booth seat opposite me, I ask, "How are you? How's Sarah?"

After the waitress tops up our mugs and leaves, I sit quietly, waiting to see what comes next.

He takes some time before he replies, filling the silence with the sound of his spoon stirring cream into his coffee mug.

"Sarah is spending the weekend with her mother," he says without looking up.

"Really? Isn't it a little soon for her to be traveling?"

Van finally looks up. "Look, here's the deal. I don't really want to talk about Sarah. I called your place last night and this morning and when there wasn't any answer, I called Ethan and asked him if he knew where I might find you. He gave me three places. If you hadn't walked in here an hour ago, I'd have staked out your apartment building and then your office building until I found you. I'm here because I want to see if you'll let me apologize for the shitty way I've treated you. And if we get that far, maybe we can talk about giving me a chance to show you that I'm a decent guy when I don't have my head up my ass."

I'm so surprised, I'm on the verge of interrupting his flow with forgiving remarks when I remember the first rule of interviewing: when your subject is on a roll, keep your mouth shut. But he's in such a funk that my silence backfires and he starts to get up.

"I'm sorry," he begins. "This was totally—"

"Stop," I tell him. "In the first place, a girl needs a minute to process a thing like that. You've been thinking about this for days, apparently, but this is the first time I've heard it. So sit down, please, and start from the beginning." My head is spinning. What the hell is going on?

Van leans back in the booth. "Did Ethan tell you what kind of business I run?"

"Uhhh, no." Now I'm worried he'll take that the wrong way too. "Not that I wouldn't have asked, eventually. It's just that things have been a little crazy at work lately, and--"

"I do security systems for celebrities. When I was eighteen, I joined the army. They put me through a bunch of tests and decided I was a natural to work in intelligence. I finished one tour of duty and came home, thinking I'd become a cop. I met a girl. We had lots of laughs and then the craziest thing happened."

"She got pregnant."

"Not so crazy, I guess. But she didn't tell me. She broke up with me instead. She said the clock was ticking and as far as she was concerned, cops were lousy husband material. I hadn't been discharged yet, so I signed up for another tour of duty. It was while I was over there that a buddy wrote and told me she was having my kid. I had some leave coming, so I grabbed the next plane home and convinced her to marry me. It wasn't because I was in love with her any more – or ever was, actually. I just didn't want my kid growing up without a dad. And if I didn't make it back for some reason, at least they'd have my pension and benefits."

"So you got married, finished your tour of duty, came home, had a couple of good years and then realized you couldn't spend the rest of your life with her, kid or no kid."

"That's about it. I gave her the house and half my pension and I had my brother – he's an accountant – put together a trust fund for Sarah. My ex isn't very good with money, and fortunately for Sarah, the judge liked the idea of an accountant being involved. Except for the times when my ex goes off the rails – I don't mean she's crazy. It's more like impulsive – the custody situation is pretty good for all of us. Sarah normally spends two weeks with her and then two weeks with me and I don't mind that at all. A girl needs quality time with her mom and I need time to run my business."

He takes a sip of his coffee. "So, it took less than a month back home to realize that a cop's life sucks. You work rotten hours, hang out with thugs and make just enough money to stay broke. Thanks, but no thanks. So I had another chat with my brother."

"The accountant."

"Yeah. You know, if he wasn't such a whiz in money matters, he'd have made a great profiler? What he came up with was a confidential security service for the kinds of people who can afford to pay the freight."

"Celebrities."

"...and a bunch of CEO's. I've got a partner who looks after scheduling and a team of guys that I served with who take the security details. Since I trusted them with my life, and that turned out okay, I've got no problem trusting them to look after my clients. I've also got a short-list of companies that provide alarm systems for home, office, car and whatnot."

He takes another sip of coffee. "So two weeks out of a month I'm a Single Dad and the rest of the time I'm Super Sales Guy and Carefree Bachelor." He looks away, fidgeting with his napkin. "I was feeling pretty good about everything. No commitments I couldn't handle. No demands I couldn't meet. And then you fell out of your car in front of me and I caught you and right after that, everything began to unravel. I always review the jobs my partner takes on because the buck stops with me. But I dropped the ball because I was mooning around like a schoolboy and that's why I didn't know what was going on." He finally looks at me. "That's why I needed to see you. I had to apologize for letting you down."

Whether it's the effects of last night's wine or this morning's soul-searching, I'm barely able to wrap my head around any of this. What ball did he drop? When did he let me down? And... wait! Did he just say he's crazy about me?

"Van, I—"

"You don't need to say another word. I get it. I had my chance and I blew it." To my everlasting astonishment, he's getting ready to leave the booth.

"Stop!"

I say it louder than I meant to and everyone in the diner turns and looks. For once, I'm too focused to be embarrassed.

I lean forward and speak more quietly. "Stop making decisions for me. If I want to tell you to take a hike, I'm perfectly capable of phrasing it my own way."

He blinks.

"Now what the hell are you talking about? What job didn't you know about and what does it have to do with me?"

He stares at me for a long moment and then shakes his head. "I clearly need professional help." He closes his eyes briefly and then nods. "Okay, this is a little tricky. When I said that I offer a confidential service, it means that I never tell anyone who my clients are. But if I don't make an exception now, none of this will ever make any sense. So..." he takes a deep breath and lets it out, "...it's my company Poppi Vitale uses to keep tabs on everyone."

WHAT???

Van rakes his fingers through his hair. "When Sarah decided to spend the weekend with her mother, I called my partner for an update. I'm thinking to myself, I've only been distracted for a couple of weeks. What kind of trouble could be brewing? Ten minutes into the briefing, he hits me with the brick. I was about to call you then and there when he told me you were spending the evening your buddies, so I let it go. When I tried to reach you this morning and couldn't find you anywhere, he told me he'd given our guy the night off since you were with your friends. Instead of killing my partner, I called Ethan. And here we are."

WOW.

"Uhhh... okay." I'm frantically trying to remember everything that's happened. "When did Poppi set the wheels in motion?"

"Right after you spoke to Gina, apparently."

"That was before I even met you."

"Actually, it was the same day. I met you at Nolan's birthday bash on the Friday, and we went skydiving Sunday. My partner and I do our briefings first thing Monday morning. By then, he had the report that we'd gone skydiving, so he figured we both knew about the contract."

"And from there, he assumed that you were in the loop on everything?" I ask

"That's what he says."

"Sounds like you need to rethink the way you run this business of yours."

"No kidding."

I'm stalling and I know it. I take the plunge. "So you know about my GRAND Plan."

He shakes his head, "Yeah. Speaking of rethinking ways of doing things…"

I hold up my hands in surrender. Mercifully, he says nothing and this gives me time to think. What I hear myself say next actually surprises me. Fortunately, it's in a good way.

"You know what's funny? You know what hit me a few minutes before we started talking?" I ask. "I've finally realized that my life is a complete train wreck and there's no one to blame but me. I've surrounded myself with people who either blame everyone else for their unhappy lives or give up on their opportunities before they have a chance to fail. And I'm no different, it turns out. The only long-term relationship I have is with my pet fish, but tossing a few flakes in a tank and changing water every week hardly qualifies as commitment. I can't even settle on a name for him, for heaven's sake, so I call him Fish. How pathetic is that?"

Fortunately, Van has the good sense to just sit there and let me rant.

"I used to tell myself that I came to L.A. to make great documentaries, but the fact is that I wasn't running toward a bright and shiny future. I was running from the worst boyfriend mistake I ever made. So, now that I'm here and that guy is behind me, am I making those documentaries? Nope. I've kept myself busy making crap TV about what kinds of people? More victims! How perfect is that? By the time my twenty-fifth birthday comes along, I've soaked up enough of their insecurities to convince myself that life is meaningless without a man. Do I make a list of the qualities I was looking for in a life partner? Do I widen my circle of friends? For heaven's sake, why do that when I can join every dating site known to man and wait for Mr. Right to sweep me off my feet. And when he doesn't materialize, that gives me permission to see myself as a woman unworthy of happiness. Poor, poor, pitiful me. And then, with my status unchanged and my thirtieth birthday a month away, I lose all touch with reality. When all else fails, I think frantically, why not try Bribery? We should meet all kinds of great people with a plan like that."

I take a sip of my coffee. Incredibly, it's still hot. "I think what must have happened next is that the Gods took pity on me. First, they hand me Poppi on a silver platter. Then, you and Ethan come along. What better way to show me the difference between nice guys with their lives in order and losers looking for a free ride? But just in case I fail to get the message, everything else I've come to think of as normal goes spinning out of control. My workplace is under attack. My partner gets beaten up. My best friend, Jonah, ends up sleeping with my friend, Mitzi. And last but not least, because I want these loser dates to like me, I put up with every kind of humiliation there is and end up getting attacked."

I smile a tired smile at the horrified look on Van's face. "So cut yourself a little slack there sir. You're not the only lunatic at the table." I finish.

"So where does that leave us?" he says.

"If you'd told me you were crazy about me two days ago, I'd have been sitting in your lap by now, planning our wedding," I tell him. "The thing is, this is the first time we've said more than a dozen words to each other. On our first encounter, the music was too loud for conversation. The other two times, I was incapable of coherent thought. I was too busy hanging onto you for dear life while jumping out of an airplane."

He nods.

"Does that mean there's no "us" to consider? To be honest, I think it's too early to know. But I'd be lying if I said there was no chemistry. And I like the way you wanted to make things right. So what do you think about making a plan to get to know each other? Is that good enough for now?"

Van's smile is an odd combination of exhaustion and relief. "That works for me."

"Great. Now I have to go home before I fall down. Any chance you can give me a lift?"

He grins and I grin back. When he drops me at my door, he has to nudge me awake. "Can you make it the rest of the way or should I carry you?"

"Nah, I got this one," I yawn hugely.

"I'll call you tomorrow," he says as I unlock the door. I give him two thumbs up.

Once inside my apartment, I walk over to my fish tank. "How do you feel about the name Roger?" Fish looks non-committal. "I know. It's all so sudden. Why don't you think on it while I get some sleep?"

Sunday, Day 18

 When the phone wakes me Sunday morning, I can barely open my eyes. I let the call go to voice mail and try to go back to sleep, but Nature calls. Afterwards, I think about getting dressed, but the combination of all that wine Friday night followed by all that coffee Saturday, plus the pizza I ordered late last night is too much. I go back to bed and the next time I look at my clock it's past noon.

I finally drag myself out of bed to deal with my day. After coffee and a hot, hot shower, I check my messages. Nolan wants to buy me breakfast. Kat wants to buy me lunch. Van says he has to go out of town tomorrow and he'll be gone for ten days. He'll call me before he leaves. Finally, Jonah. I take a deep breath and play his message. When I hear him telling me not to worry, he's not pregnant, I totally crack up. And just like that, even though I don't hear from Mitzi, I'm feeling more like my old self.

I'm not ready to talk to anyone, so I text my thanks to everyone. Then I grab my purse and walk over to Café Aroma. What I'm looking for is peace and tranquility and, with one of their signature salads and some cool jazz playing in the background, that's exactly what I get. While I'm sipping the last of my iced tea, I check my calendar. I'm supposed to have dinner with a guy named Stewart, but I'm just not up for it so I call and cancel. What I really need is 'me' time.

I decide to go for a drive, so I pop the top off my Cabrio and zip up Laurel Canyon Boulevard toward Hollywood, hugging the curves all the way to Mulholland. I pause at a great Mulholland view spot and enjoy the wind with the top down, taking in the gorgeous view of the Hollywood Hills all the way to the water.

A short while later, I'm ready to hit the road again. When I reach the 405, I decide to head for home. I'm almost there when I suddenly get a hankering for a Captain Morgan's martini the way my old friend, Donnie, makes them. Considering the fact that I've been a Sunday regular at his cozy pub for something like five years, and I haven't been to see him in almost three weeks, I'm long overdue. Then I think about the hot and spicy munchies he serves and my mouth waters. When I check the dashboard clock, I see that it's nearly five o'clock. Perfect.

Before I hit the pub, I swing by my apartment and change into something that feels more like me than the clothes I've been wearing the last couple of weeks. I throw on a pair of jeans, a cute navy tank with some silver sequins and a pair of kitten heels. I brush my hair into a low pony tail and walk out the door. Ten minutes later, Donnie greets me with a huge grin.

"Well, hey there, stranger. Where've you been?" he asks.

"When I haven't been locking horns with my asshole boss, I've been on a road to nowhere dating the kind of crazies only LA can supply."

"Wow," he laughs. "Sounds like you need some Captain Morgan's magic."

I give him the thumbs up and he goes to work. As I watch Donnie do his stuff, I realize I'm not alone. At the far end of the bar, there's a dark-haired guy with tattoo sleeves covering his muscular arms and he's smiling at me. It dawns on me that he just heard my 'road to nowhere' remark, so I give him a polite smile before giving my full attention to the final twist of orange rind being added to my drink. When it lands in front of me, I pick it up, take a slow delicious sip, and then I sigh with happiness.

Donnie gives me a wink as he places a tall soda water on a coaster in front of me and then turns his attention to a whole crowd of people who just walked in. As I sit back and enjoy the ebb and flow, I alternate sips of my martini with ice cold soda. A few minutes later, a platter of spicy munchies appears at my elbow. I'm in heaven. Just before I settle my tab, I remember the guy with the tattoo sleeves and shoot a look down the bar, but he's gone. Just as well.

When I get home, there's a new message from Kat. She sounds terrible, so I call her back.

"He's gay!" she sobs when she picks up the phone.

"How did you find out?"

"He told me this morning. He was so sad and so sweet," she wails. "What is wrong with me? Why didn't I know?" More sobs. "Friday night, I leaned in to kiss him on the cheek and he kissed my hand instead. I thought he was being romantic."

"Oh, honey, I'm so sorry."

"He said he wanted to be my friend," she cries. "I don't want a friend. I want a boyfriend!"

"Do you?" The words are out of my mouth before I can stop them.

"What?" Fresh sobs. "How could you say a thing like that? Of course I do!"

"Kat, honey, take a deep breath. In fact, take two. I'm on your side. You know that."

The sobbing subsides to hiccups.

"The thing is, Kat, you *are* smart. You *do* know when people are a good match. You have a real gift in being able to see that. So if that's true, and we know that it is, then what was it about Trevor that was so perfect for you? I think you should focus on that."

"What do you mean?"

It's too late to turn back now, so I plunge ahead. "Maybe you were overdue for a male friend in your life who showed you some respect for a change. What do you think the chances are that you saw this in Trevor and that's what attracted you to him? What if you knew he'd never be anything more than a friend... because you sensed he was gay?"

Calmer now, she says softly, "He was nice, wasn't he."

"Honey, he IS nice." I say knowing the silence is Kat realizing she will be okay.

"Yes." Her voice is a little stronger. "And so am I. Lana, I love you."

"I love you too." And I hang up. Whether my nudge helps her or destroys our friendship, it felt amazing to tell her the truth. I'm reaching for my calendar when the phone rings again. As I reach for it, I check who it is. It's Jonah.

"So here's why you didn't have to worry," he begins.

"I'm all ears," I reply.

"After that much wine, the Seventh Fleet couldn't have got a rise out of me."

"Now there's an image I won't soon forget," I tell him.

"Seriously, you were safer with me than at a nunnery."

"Now that's a little disturbing."

"And speaking of disturbed," Jonah shifts gears smoothly, "have you heard from Mitzi yet?"

"Not a word."

"I was sure she'd call one of us. I mean, sure, her wine tasting was a bust, but that wasn't our fault. Tad deserved everything he got. What was he thinking, coming onto you like that?"

"He gets away with murder with Mitzi, so maybe he thinks all women are the same."

Jonah laughs wickedly. "Wanna bet you gave him something new to think about?"

I find myself laughing too. "Yeah, the look on his face was pretty priceless."

Jonah's tone changes again. "So, what else is new?"

"Do you know that you'd make the worst spy in the world? What are you fishing for?"

"Well, Ethan called not long after you escaped from my lair yesterday. I was barely conscious, but I could tell something was seriously up so I told him where I thought you might be. Is everything okay?"

"Everything is absolutely fabulous," I tell him. "And speaking of fishing, I have two things to share with you. Are you sitting down?"

"I am now."

"Okay, first, Kat has learned that Trevor is gay."

"Oh dear. Is she okay?"

"Not yet, but she will be. Now here's the second thing: I know it's a bit soon, but brainstorming here but... I think he'd be perfect for you."

"Who, Trevor?"

"None other."

"First, it's ridiculous. And second, he and Kat just broke up."

"I'm not saying right now. And why is it so ridiculous? What's wrong with him?" I ask.

"Well, for heaven's sake, think about it: He's…"

As his voice trails off I have the good sense, for once in my life, to say nothing.

Jonah tries again. "Okay, but he's…"

I still say nothing.

"Good God. There's nothing wrong with the man. You may be on to something."

"I know! Wouldn't that be incredible?" I say "Kat is already working on moving on and she loves you. I'll bet with some time she's not only be okay she's be ecstatic."

"Do you remember when we were introducing Carol and Dean to Kat and Trevor at Mitzi's and everyone was exchanging business cards?"

"Sure. Why?"

"Trevor handed me his card too. I thought he was being polite."

"Really? Well, he didn't give me a card, so you can toss that idea out the window."

"Huh," is all he says for a second. "Imagine that."

"You hold on to that card, Mister. Maybe in a week or so…" I say with a grin.

"What? Oh yeah. Absolutely. Okay, I gotta go."

As I hang up, grinning, I realize that I haven't felt this free in years. What a transformation from the way I felt Friday night, when Tad was making his moves and Mitzi was ordering me out of her house. I'm heading for the kitchen when my cell rings and I make a dash for my purse.

"Hello Lovely Lady, is this Lana?"

"Yes."

"My name is Earl. I got your number from Dotty. You hadn't called so I took the initiative."

I'm so shocked, I can't think of a thing to say.

"Hello?"

"I'm sorry Earl. It's just that I don't remember giving Dotty my number."

"Dotty thought you might ask about that. When she saw that you'd left your phone on the table, she decided to take down your number just in case you lost mine. I hope it's not a problem."

"Actually, it is. Your friend was so insistent that I couldn't find a way to tell her I wasn't interested in meeting anyone. I'm sorry she pursued the matter and gave you my number."

After he apologizes one more time, we say goodbye and hang up. And as I stare at the phone, I realize how different that call was. For once, I didn't waste my time searching for a reason to let him down gently, or worse – I didn't give in to guilt and agree to meet him. The new Lana told him the truth without batting an eyelash.

My land line rings again. I'm beginning to feel like a switchboard operator. When I see that it's Van, I smile. "So you're leaving town?" I say by way of hello. "That's pretty shrewd, teaching me to miss you before I get a chance to grow tired of you."

He laughs. "Dammit. Why didn't I think of that? Look, I've been invited to fly to New York and then to Chicago. I'm meeting with a couple of security firms who want to pick my brain about the techniques we use and how we may potentially work together. I guess our clients have been saying good things about us. Anyway, I thought this was a perfect time to take them up on their offer. If this trip works out, it could take my business to a whole new level. It would mean a fair amount of travel, but as you just pointed out, that's not necessarily a bad thing."

"What a great opportunity! Congratulations, Van."

"Thanks. And Sarah's okay with it. She actually wants to recuperate at her mother's place."

"Perfect."

"I'm hoping I've saved the best reason for last. I want to be sure there's no hint of a conflict of interest that might ruin things between you and me. If I'm off the grid and my partner continues to be the point man handling things, you can finish up your GRAND Plan however you see fit."

"In other words…?"

"Dammit. This is harder than I thought it would be. Okay, here goes: In other words, I guess I'm saying that I like you and want to see where this goes, but I also know it's crazy to impose any limitations at this point. I think you're amazing, but that's my problem. You've got a bunch of guys you've just met and a few more to come. And while you're taking care of business, I'm about to hit the road. So it makes sense to agree that we're going to give each other the room we need to find out what we really want. What do you think?"

Wow. "I think you're a pretty smart guy."

He laughs. "I was feeling pretty good about it too, if you want to know the truth. Okay, doll. I've got to get packing. I'll call you from New York."

I'm hanging up when there's a knock on my door. When I peek outside, I find Jonah grinning from ear to ear.

"I can't stay," he says, "because I'm on my way to have drinks with Trevor."

"So much for waiting a week," I grin back at him.

"He called me, Miss Smarty Pants. He said he's been waiting for Mr. Right and after he'd cleared the air with Kat and asked for her blessing he felt good. He knew he didn't want to miss his chance to tell me he thinks it might be me."

I love seeing Jonah this happy and give him a huge hug before he rushes off. As I think about Jonah and consider the happy consequences of my call with Van, I stroll over to the fish tank and tap the glass. "Hey, Roger, guess what? Things are looking up!"

Monday, Day 19

*T*here's nothing like a wake-up call to give you a fresh perspective on things. First thing Monday, I tap on Bossman's door and walk in. I can tell he's been expecting me. His deflated look is gone. In its place, there's something new. Could it be that he grew a spine? I wonder.

"Two things," he says before I can get a word in. "Are we going to make money with The Muckers and can this guy Poppi really deliver?"

"Yes and Yes," I tell him.

"Okay," he nods. "Call him in. I need to deal with this crap. We need to get back on track."

As I head back to my office, I suddenly realize that that was the most productive, non-bullshit conversation I've ever had with Bossman. When I call Gina, she says Poppi will get back to me ASAP and, with Nolan, Ethan and Sam taking care of business, I take an early lunch. Today I'm meeting a guy named Barry, who apparently works in marketing.

My friends are wondering why I'm even bothering. The whole point of the exercise was to meet Mr. Right, and if Van isn't him, he's such a close second that it hardly matters. Or does it?

The thing is, it turns out that it does matter. Last week, I was ready to settle for Mr. Distant Third, but not now. The new Lana has a different agenda – one that places her interests first. If I settle for one person, just when this new chapter is beginning, I'm shutting myself off from an opportunity to find out who I really am. And how does that make any sense?

The first guy I see when I enter the restaurant could be the poster boy for tall, dark and handsome. His broad shoulders, well-muscled arms, and killer six-pack are loosely covered by a dark blue cashmere sweater. Long legs in perfectly faded jeans end at a dazzling pair of tasseled loafers. His killer smile, twinkling eyes and artfully tousled hair make my day. When he smiles back and stands up to greet me, I blink. THIS is my date? Wow! As I sit down I can't stop myself from telling him how gorgeous he is.

"So, with looks like yours, what kind of marketing do you do?" I ask him playfully.

"I make dreams come true," he grins.

"I'll just bet you do," I reply. "Who do you work for?"

"I'm self-employed," he says. "I guess you could say that I work for my clients."

"Something like a life coach?"

He laughs. "Let's say that what I coach them to achieve gives them a whole new lease on life." He finishes with a wink.

Slowly, my brain starts to compute the look with the words. I realize, oh My God. I'm having lunch with a real, honest-to-goodness Gigolo! I'm thinking what a winner THAT reality show would be and when I tell him the idea, he agrees. We have so much fun together that I'm amazed when the waitress brings the check and I see the time. As he gives the waitress his credit card and she heads off to process it, he pays me a charming compliment.

"My dates can be a little on the tedious side at times," he admits. "This one was pure fun for me."

How about that! When I get up to leave and he kisses me, I can see why he has his clients eating out of the palm of his hand. He's delicious in every way. As I walk out of the restaurant, there's no denying the spring in my step and when I look back and wave, I notice everyone staring, first at him and then at me. Talk about feeling great!

And the feeling continues with no interruptions from pranksters, stalkers, or anyone else with an axe to grind. When I tell Nolan about the gigolo show concept, he totally cracks up. Ethan does too, and we have so much fun brainstorming the idea that when my dinner date texts to cancel, I'm happy to spend a normal night at home for a change.

When I get home, Poppi has left a message. He is seeing Bossman on Friday and wants to know if I will have dinner with him on Saturday. His invitation couldn't come at a better time. With Trent in town, it's the perfect opportunity for them to meet. I send him a quick reply. *See you Friday. And Saturday is a Yes if I can bring my brother, Trent. He's going to be visiting for a few days to help me celebrate my birthday and I would love to have you meet him.*

I decide to raid the freezer and pull together a total comfort meal of left-overs. After that, I take a long hot bath and turn in early. I'm asleep as soon as my head hits the pillow.

Tuesday, Day 20

*B*efore I reach Slum Central, I've heard from Amy, Sam and Nolan. Our internet connection has crashed. The repair guy is on his way but Bossman is off the radar. Since no one seems to be able to make an executive decision, I step up to the plate.

"That coffee place past the municipal lot," I tell Amy.

"What about it?"

"They have Wi-Fi. Tell them we'll need a couple of tables all day. Ask them how much and I'll authorize it. If you can, take it out of Petty Cash. If not, I'll put it on my credit card. And if that works tell the editors to keep on working and to call us when a cut is ready."

"I'm on it," she says.

So screw you, prankster, I'm thinking. *Call us The Untouchables.*

We hear nothing from Bossman, even though Amy keeps trying his various numbers. By the time I break for my lunch date, I'm thinking we should work at the coffee shop every day, the place is so cheerful. Maybe we could set up an editing bay in a trailer parked outside.

Lunch today is with a guy named Joey, who works for a credit card company. Joey is such a gentleman that when I stand up to use the bathroom, he gets up too. The only setback is that we don't seem to have much in common and it's hard to find things to talk about. All through lunch, he's fidgeting and fumbling with his hands under the table and I feel really sorry for him. After a while, I ask him if he has any hobbies. To my relief he grins.

"I sure do," he says, and with a flourish he presents me with the thing he's been playing with under the table: a napkin he's folded into the shape of a penis.

Oh good. Origami Porn. When he suddenly giggles like a girl and reaches across the table to thump my forehead with the tip of his napkin penis, I'm at a loss for words. Luckily the bill arrives at that moment. He pays and we leave. Outside the restaurant, I'm trying to figure out a polite way to end this when Joey takes me by surprise again.

"It was a pleasure to meet you," he says, "but this isn't going to work."

Wow. Penis Napkin Guy dumping me after a productive morning at a bright and airy coffee shop? Maybe I should buy a lottery ticket!

Back at the café, the afternoon flies by and, even though we've had to make some compromises, the wait staff make up for it with their cheery smiles. More than once, I'm tempted to mention to Nolan how productive everyone is without the gloomy fog of Slum Central bearing down on them, but I hold back. I don't want to set something in motion that I can't deliver.

I'm supposed to have dinner with a realtor named Gale tonight, but when I get home I can't find his contact information anywhere. I flip back through my emails, but he's nowhere to be found. After a shower, I change into some dark skinny jeans and a striped sweater. This way, I'm ready if he calls and comfortable if he doesn't. When I hear nothing by six, I order a pizza and settle in with a good book.

At seven, the phone rings and I anxiously check for the number. I'm having such a peaceful evening that the last person I want to hear from is my lost date. What a relief…It's Kat!

"Hey pretty," I smile into the phone. "What's up?"

"You'll never guess."

"You've met someone fabulous?"

"YES!!!"

"What?" My feet hit the floor with a thump. "This is brilliant! Give me the details immediately!"

"He's one of my clients."

"That is awesome!"

"He's been on four dates, hasn't found anyone he likes, came in to tell me he was thinking of calling it quits and somehow, we started talking. The next thing I know, we're having dinner at The Ivy and he's asking me if I'd like to go to New York sometime."

"And does that sometime happen to be soon?"

"Wednesday!"

"Wow! So what's he like?"

"He's a little older but he's very fit and loves to travel. He's one of those economic analysts the government calls in to make forecasts and predictions, but he's got pots of money so he doesn't really need to work. His name is Peter. He's Italian. And I'm his first Nordic Goddess."

"And?"

"And what?"

"Kat, the man is taking you to New York. You won't be sleeping in separate beds."

She chuckles, and I hear something in her voice I haven't heard in a very long time.

"He's fabulous, Lana. I'm a totally pampered, purring Kat."

"So you're over Trevor?"

"Oh my God, you were so right! I *was* using him to hide. Losing him was the best thing that ever happened to me."

"So... you are totally cool with Jonah and Trevor talking" I ask cautiously.

"What?" She asks, her voice still peppy.

"Jonah talking to Trevor."

There's a long silence and I'm wondering if I've totally blown it. Then she laughs.

"Lana, you're a genius! They're a perfect match! And even though it sucked at the time, I gave my okay to Trevor a while ago, but now I'm over the moon about it." She says still cheery.

"Super! And as for you, young lady, I want all the details when you get back."

As soon as we hang up, I get up and make a cold Arnold Palmer to celebrate. I've barely taken a sip when the phone rings again. When I see Jonah's number, I smile.

"Now this is a conversation I can't wait to have," I say instead of hello.

"What do you have girl? Spill it."

"Kat's got a new man."

"YESSS!!!" he exclaims.

"Now you're truly and completely in the clear. I'd say 'Go get 'em'." I say laughing.

"It's On! You know it, girlfriend!" he exclaims.

Wednesday, Day 21

*I*t sounds crazy to say it, but with Trent arriving today, it feels a lot like Christmas. It's not about the presents. It's not even about the nosing around he was willing to do to figure out what's going on in my life. It's about Family. Nolan may be my cousin and The Girls may feel like sisters, but nothing says 'belonging' like a big brother coming to your rescue.

I arrive at the airport and get that big hug I've been waiting for. Trent's divorce was hard on him, but it looks like the year since it began has been good to him. As we drive up the 404, he tells me all the news from home. Next, he wants to hear mine, so I fill him in.

When I'm done, he's pretty much speechless for several miles. "The thing I can't wrap my head around is how someone so small and so smart finds a way to do something so big and so dumb and then, just when the shit is ready to hit the fan, you come out smelling like a rose. I mean, the email sounded crazy enough. And our talk on the phone had me losing sleep, I kid you not. But the whackos in this crazy town..." He shakes his head. "A guy hits you on the head with a napkin shaped like a penis? A guy with BO so bad they ask you to leave and another guy who's a kleptomaniac? A Jekyll and Hyde clown who can't keep his hands to himself and then... ta daa... a nice guy with a steady job who's so sure of himself that he leaves you alone for ten days to finish off your crazy-ass dating game? Jesus, Lana."

Since I totally agree with him, there's nothing I can add so I just keep driving.

"What I want to know is what sent you spinning off into space? You go to film school in Boise, Idaho of all places and a year later you land a job in Los Angeles with the King of Reality TV. You break away to build your own team and ever since then you've been cranking out shows with Cousin Nolan watching your back. You make great money. Your stuff is in demand. You're popular. By all accounts, you hang with great people. In your spare time you climb mountains. You're basically living the American Dream. And then - DING - this cosmic timer goes off and, at twenty-nine years of age with your entire life ahead of you, you turn into man chasing lunatic, chasing after the perfect mate. I mean, seriously: what are you thinking?"

He's so on the money, it's freaky. "You need to learn to use this mind reading power for good," I tell him.

Trent takes a deep breath and lets it out. "Okay, so you know you've been acting like crazy. Doesn't make it okay, but it's a start. Now tell me about the crap going on at the office and this Godfather guy you're hooked up with."

By the time I'm finished with that story, including the revelation that it's Van's company behind the spy games, we've reached my apartment. While I fix him a bite to eat, he tosses his bags into the spare bedroom and changes into a t-shirt and sweat pants. His plan is to grab a nap to make up for the sleep he missed all week working the night shift. When I tell him we're having dinner with Nolan tonight, he grins.

"That'll give me a chance to hear Nolan's take on all this," he says. "What worries me most is that you guys are as helpless as a couple of sitting ducks. You work for an asshole. Your shows feature weirdos. You've got an invisible psycho at your office acting like he's Casper the Not-So-Friendly Ghost. You never heard of this Giovanni Vitale character before three weeks ago and all of a sudden he's wormed his way into your confidence."

"When you're right, you're right," I tell him and that earns me a suspicious look.

"Okay," he folds his arms. "So who are you and what have you done with my sister? That's three times I've made comments you'd normally kill me for and I'm still standing."

"Any chance I could be growing up?" I smile.

"That'll be the day," he laughs. "One of the things I love about you is your all-or-nothing attitude, even when it gets you in trouble. It's not enough for you to work on something mindless. You want to change lives with your shows. You don't just want to meet a nice guy and hook up and maybe take in a ballgame – you want Prince Charming and the happy ever after ending. To get those things you'll go where most people won't. Crazy ass reality shows that risk your life, for God's sake. Jumping out of perfectly good airplanes. Dodging muggers and stalkers. What is that title you gave yourself?"

"Producer Girl Who Never Sleeps."

"Yeah. You know who you remind me of sometimes?"

"Who?" I ask not sure I want to know.

"Granny." He says decidedly.

"OUR Granny?" I say surprised.

"Yeah."

"The woman whose driver's license was taken away because she couldn't be trusted behind the wheel of a car? Gee, thanks."

"What the hell are you talking about? Gran never lost her license for bad driving."

"Sure she did. I wasn't very old, so the details are fuzzy, but I certainly remember a big hoopla when the citation came in the mail."

Trent stares at me as if I've lost my mind.

"What?"

"I am seriously starting to wonder about you. Granny was a great driver. It's what she did when she served with the Women's Army Corps in World War II. That's how she met Gramps. She was awarded a medal, in fact. She was Hell on Wheels. Don't you remember?"

"But... but... what about the citation?"

"From the War Office." He clarifies.

"Then why did she stop driving?"

"Because she broke her hip, skiing."

I shake my head in wonderment.

"For heaven's sake, how could you of all people forget her war stories?"

I sit down slowly. "What war stories?"

Trent shakes his head. "I can't believe you don't remember any of this. There were lots of women who enlisted in World War II. It was a big deal because the jobs they did freed up the men who were the only ones allowed at the Front. So most women served stateside pulling desk duty, but a lot of them went to Europe and North Africa. Granny's regiment landed on Normandy Beach just a few weeks after the initial invasion."

"So Hell on Wheels wasn't Gramp's way of saying she was a handful."

Trent grins. "The one doesn't actually cancel out the other, kiddo."

I'm stunned. I'm also beginning to wonder if I've underestimated Mom. "What about Mom?"

"Now THAT's a whole other story. Mom's the worst driver in the world."

"Well, that's a relief. Not that bad driving is good, but you know what I mean. Is there some other secret skill Mom has that I don't know about?"

"Not unless you deleted the fact that she's qualified as an expert marksman," he says casually.

"WHAT?"

Trent shakes his head. "Okay, you do know that Mom and Dad go to the rifle range from time to time, right?"

"Sure. But I thought she was just... I don't know... decoration, I guess." I feel like an idiot.

"Listen, kiddo, some of our best shooters at the prison are the female guards. Do you know why? They're easier to train and they're willing to practice. They don't think they're hotshots who don't have to work at it. Why not? Because they don't have the inflated egos a lot of men bring to law enforcement."

"Huh."

"Mom doesn't do as much shooting as she used to, but there was a time when she could have gone professional. She had a knack and that helped, but she also practiced all the time."

"So did she give it up when she married Dad?"

"What is wrong with you? She gave it up when she got interested in other things."

"Like what?"

"What do you want me to say? She couldn't tote a gun and change a diaper, so she made the ultimate sacrifice? Mom got interested in horses, for one thing. Sure, they were Dad's passion at first, but that's not why she likes them. And yes, she wanted kids. But she's still a force to be reckoned with. Raising a family hasn't taken that away."

"Okay, but when did she turn into Lady Indecisive?"

Trent stares at me. "When has Lady Indecisive ever lost an argument or failed to get her way?"

I open my mouth to loudly proclaim and then, after a second, I close it. He's right.

Trent suddenly groans and falls back in his chair. "Oh my gawd! That's what this Lame Jane act of yours was all about. You thought that was how Gran and Mom landed their men!"

"I did not!" I tell him hotly.

"You did so! Right up until you heard your biological clock ticking, you were tearing up the town. Then I'm betting some helpful Hollywood hussy told you no guy would ever try to get to first base with you, let alone sweep you off your feet, if you were one step ahead of him all the time. You took one look at Mom and Gran and thought weak is where it's at."

He's so right, I can't stand it. What an idiot I've been. I park the car in front of my place and sit for a moment.

Trent yawns until his jaws creak. "Thank God you finally figured it out. Now help me get my bag into the house and let me get some sleep. When and where are we meeting Nolan?"

"We kept it loose 'til we knew what you might be craving."

"Tell him I'm so overdue for authentic Mexican food, I may faint," Trent grins.

"You got it, brother." I give him a hug and a kiss, grab my purse and hit the road.

With Trent's words echoing in my ears, the first thing I do when I get to Slum Central is cancel the remaining dates on my calendar. I've got way too much on my plate now and lots of ideas simmering for new projects. I text my apologies to Richard the florist, Stewart the sports agent, and Oscar the hotel owner from Beverly Hills. The only two I can't reach are a school teacher named Phil, who expects me to join him for lunch in less than an hour, and an art gallery owner named Michael, who invited me for dinner next Monday night. He's off the grid for the next few days, his secretary tells me, so I decide to leave it alone. What's one more dinner date, I figure.

On my way to meet with my team to make sure we're on top of things, a text from Mitzi stops me in my tracks. *You were right. I was wrong. Please forgive me. Can we talk?*

Wow! I text back *Give me five minutes* and then I corner Nolan in our office, asking him to find a great Mexican place for tonight. As I head out to meet teacher Phil, I dial Mitzi's number. It's a fifteen minute drive to the salad bar I chose because the food is amazing and the prices are reasonable.

Mitzi picks up right away. "I'm so sorry, Lana. Tad was being such an asshole that night. He has apolog--"

When I hear her ramping up, I cut her off. "I'm sorry, Mitz. I can't keep doing this," I tell her calmly. "We need to make some serious changes."

"What?" I've clearly caught her off guard.

"I love you like a sister, hon, but these dramas are a never-ending nightmare. I don't know if you see what you're doing, but it never stops. None of us are therapists. We're friends. And friends give back. But there is so much happening with you sometimes the rest of us feel invisible. Think about why we started getting together in the first place, to share and support one another. It's not supposed to be all about me, or Jonah, or Kat, or you."

"But we *are* there for one another. And it's not my fault that Tad-" she begins.

I stop her again and sign off. "I'm walking into a meeting, Mitzi. I've got to go. If you're ready to own your part in these troubles, we'll see you at the pub tomorrow." And I hang up. Eeeek.

Ten minutes into my lunch date with Phil, I know two things for certain. This is the most fun I've had in maybe a year. We laugh at everything. We talk non-stop. We act like a couple of kids. And everyone around us is green with envy. The other thing I know without a doubt is that he's not my Mr. Right. Adorable freckles, button nose and personality aside, there isn't a thing about him that gives me that special tingle. Nothing that makes me wonder what he'd be like in bed. In fact, the mere idea of him naked makes me blush.

For the first time in a long time, I've met someone I can't wait to see again to do nothing more than hang out and introduce to my gang. When we hug each other and say good-bye, I invite him to drop in at the pub tomorrow night. Then I hit the ground running – I pick up some food, dry cleaning, booze, snacks my brother likes, and fuel up the car. Back home, I just have time to stow groceries, have a shower and get ready for dinner with Nolan and Trent.

With all the madness swirling around me lately, this evening was long overdue. Over drinks and some of the best Mexican food in town, we have the kind of sibling reunion that becomes the stuff of legend. Solemnly tipsy, shortly before two a.m., we unanimously vote NOT to drink all the tequila in town. We ask the waiter to call a taxi and when he presents the bill, we leave him a lavish tip for great service, good humor, and for putting up with us when we broke into song (Go Broncos!). Do we solve all the problems in the world? Not quite. We make a pact to get that done next time.

Week Four

Thursday, Day 22

*F*ortunately, Trent and I use the same hangover remedy. First thing Thursday we hit the all-day breakfast diner and load up on protein and coffee. While I need to head over to Slum Central, he tells me his plan is to check out The Muckers and Van's security company and follow up on a few other leads. Tonight he's joining me for Girls Night. With Kat in New York, he'll be hanging with Jonah, my new friend Phil from my date, and me. We spend a few minutes talking about Mitzi.

"I think Jonah pegged it when he dubbed Mitzi as a drama queen," Trent says. "You've no idea how many of those I see at work. Practically everyone in the prison system thinks it's all about them. That's why they ignore the rules and feel no remorse. Mostly they just get really pissed when someone tells them they're busted."

"Mitzi's not that bad." I say defensively.

"Maybe not, but that isn't the point. The point is that her guy Tad IS that bad. And I'm willing to bet that Mitzi's dad is the same type. So she's got two of them playing with her head and feeding her need to be accepted by keeping her off-balance all the time. If she doesn't listen to you now, she could get into serious trouble. I mean, look at the broken glass and the injured dog. Look at Tad's attack on you and her knee jerk response to blame you when you defended yourself. Believe me, kiddo, as soon as things escalate to physical violence, it's a downhill slide."

Even though he's freaking me out, I find myself agreeing with him. Tad isn't the first guy I've run into who was all about him. Look at Bossman, for instance.

And then Trent blindsides me. "There was a time when we were worried about you, too, you know. Remember that crazy crush you had on that bad boy we put behind bars?"

I feel my cheeks getting warm. First it was Mom talking about Billy the other day and now Trent is dragging him back from the past. Back in high school, Billy was the cool dude with the roving hands, hot car and risky friends. Caught in a drug sweep, he spent two years in jail, loudly protesting that he'd been framed. And there was Love-Struck Lana, who stuck by him the whole time. I wrote letters. I was there on visiting day. Fortunately, sanity prevailed when he asked me to marry him a month before his release and, shortly after he got out, he married someone else. As soon as he got her pregnant, he was back inside again.

"Whatever happened to Billy?" I ask.

"He's one of our frequent flyers," Trent says. "This time he resisted arrest and things got pretty ugly. He's lucky no one got hurt."

Thanking my own lucky stars for moments of sanity and big brothers, I give him another hug and head off to work. When I reach Slum Central, I find a crowd in the parking lot and a police cruiser with its lights flashing parked in front of Bossman's parking spot. *Oh geez, now what?*

When I get closer, I can't believe my eyes. Bossman's car is gone. In its place there's this garden statue of a thief sneaking off with a lantern, all aglow. If the disruptions weren't getting tedious, this prank would be funny. By now, we're just impatient to get back to work.

At noon, Amy orders pizzas so we don't have to go anywhere. Sitting around, chowing down, she asks how the GRAND Plan is unfolding. I figure, what the heck and by the time I finish telling the sordid story, I have everyone in stitches.

After Amy finally stops giggling she says, "Why didn't you walk out on any of these losers at the first sign of trouble?"

Nolan jumps in. "I'll tell you."

I can't wait for this.

"Lana kept waiting for them to wake up. She always expects people to have a better side. But most of the time, the crap they give you is all they've got." He suddenly fishes in his pocket and pulls out a crumpled bill. "You know what? Here's twenty bucks. I'm willing to bet you won't tell a single one of those email pals of yours that they blew it; that their referrals were assholes, losers and jerks."

To my total surprise, everyone agrees with him. In a flash, they're all adding money to the pile.

"So you're saying I have the instincts of a hopeless *New Girl*?"

"Pretty much," Nolan nods.

"Well, shit." I fold my arms across my chest. "That totally sucks." I reach out and grab the money on the table. "Good thing I'm willing to change!" I grab my gear and head home.

You wouldn't think it would take me all afternoon to write one stupid email, but it does, because I have to get inside the head of the woman who kept giving second chances to people who didn't deserve them. While it's clear to me now that I was trying to squeeze myself into a role that was too shallow and too small, I thought I was doing it for a cause. I honestly thought the price tag on 'happily ever after' meant lowering my standards. Why didn't I follow up with that first guy, Tony? Because I didn't think a great single guy was what you got in a husband. Does that mean I was selling my Dad short or dismissing my Mom? A little bit of both.

Why did I forgive Skylar's greasy hair, dirty clothes and disgusting BO? When Ethan and Van thought it was funny to scare me half to death out in the desert, why didn't I call them on it? Why did I even speak to Jason after his attack? And why, as Nolan pointed out, didn't I tell any of those so-called friends of mine what I thought of their lousy loser choices? In every case, the reason is the same. I thought that's how the marriage game was played.

When Poppi asked why I was letting unworthy men decide my fate, I thought his insight was amazing. Now I'm looking at the bigger question: Why was I so eager to give up my identity in the first place? What was prompting me to cast myself as the doting, spectator wife in fantasy lives that revolved around these unworthy men? Within seconds of meeting Van, I was picturing our future in his tiny house. I saw myself watching from the porch as Jason played catch with our kids. In my daydreams, I left America to be with Henri in Paris and Lotar in Germany. The minute I met Skylar, I wondered if our kids would become rock stars or Oscar winners. Not once did I wonder how any of these men might fit into the career I am building or the world I live in.

It's abundantly clear to me now why I chose Jonah, Mitzi and Kat to be friends. We were all so desperately chasing dreams that we couldn't see what was right in front of us. With that thought firmly in my head, I write the follow up email:

To: Group Message
From: Lana Fray
Subject: The GRAND Plan

Hey Matchmakers,

It's me again. The first thing I want to say is that you guys are awesome! When I reached out for help, you were there for me, sending more referrals than I ever dreamed of. In fact, I've had so many dates in just three weeks that I'm writing to say this gig is up.

Did I find Mr. Right? I'm sure you've all got your fingers crossed, hoping I've chosen the man you sent, but the answer is No. None of them delivered romance. On a much more positive note, what they did help me find was something even more valuable: my confidence. It turns out that this GRAND Plan was exactly what I needed to learn to stand up for myself and give Life a chance to just flow.

So thank you. Thanks for helping me see what I was meant to see all along: how fabulous life can be when you don't give up on yourself.

Thanks a million!

Lana

With my email all done, I put my calendar away and get ready for Girls Night.

Sunday	Monday	Tuesday	Wednesday	Thursday	Friday	Saturday
				WEEK ONE [1] The Plan	Nolan's [2] Birthday	Tony? [3] Skylar
Skydive - Van [4]	~~Jason~~ [5]	~~Doug~~ [6]	Henri [7]	WEEK TWO [8] Frank The Girls	~~Jason #2~~ [9]	Hiking Ethan [10] Poppi
Skydive - Van #2 [11]	Jeremy [12]	Lotar [13]	~~Paavo~~ [14] ~~Skylar #2~~	WEEK THREE [15] The Girls	Wine [16] Tasting	~~Jason #3~~ [17] Van #3!
Stewart [18]	Barry [19] Greg	Joey [20] Gale	~~Richard~~ [21] Trent Arrives Phil	WEEK FOUR [22] Girls/Trent	Poppi, [23] Trent	~~Oscar~~ [24] Hiking Trent
~~Poppi~~ [25] Trent Leaves	Michael [26]	Stewart [27]	Muckers [28] Pitch	DEADLINE [29] Girls/Vote	THE WINNER [30]	My [31] Birthday

When I reach our booth, Jonah and Phil are already there. As I squeeze in, taking my favorite corner spot, I see Trent on his way over with Mitzi on his arm. As soon as she notices me, she plants herself in front of me.

"I just have two words for you," she says with her arms folded.

I brace myself.

"The first is 'Thanks' and the second is 'Love'. I've no idea what I did to deserve friends like you guys, but I promise: I will never take you for granted again."

"Does that mean you're done with the drama?" Jonah asks bluntly.

"Yes," Mitzi says, with her chin up.

"And Tad?" Jonah is speaking for all of us.

Mitzi nods. "I'm done with him too. I knew I couldn't do it alone, so I called my father and told him what's been happening." She grins. "It was like lighting a fuse and waiting for the explosion. Tad won't be back if he knows what's good for him."

"Good. It's your turn to buy the next round," he announces. "Let's see what that looks like with no moaning, kvetching or Tad-worshipping, for a change!"

There's a long silence while every eye is on Mitzi's face. Then, without blinking an eye, she claps her hands. In no time flat, our drinks and munchies materialize. Clearly, Mitzi had called ahead and set it up. Now that's the kind of drama I can live with!

Friday, Day 23

When I reach Slum Central Friday morning, I see Johnny waiting by the car. As we exchange friendly waves and I head inside, I find myself wondering how much time he really spends on cement finishing.

As soon as Amy sees me, she points me in the direction of Bossman's office. I tap on the door and walk in. After Bossman's confident mood on Monday, I'm totally unprepared for the tired, anxious face I see peering back at me. Poppi is sitting in one of the guest chairs and a guy who looks vaguely familiar is sitting in the other.

Bossman clears his throat. "Uhh, yes. Good morning, Lana. You know Mr. Vitale, of course."

This is no time for nicknames. "Good morning, sir. It's a pleasure to see you, as always."

"Good morning, Miss Fray."

Poppi has dropped the accent. Okay then.

Bossman continues. "And uh, this is, uh…"

"I'm the son of this asshole's old and faithful partner," the other man says. "The one guy who had this jerk's back. The one guy who never suspected he'd be robbed blind."

When the guy folds his arms, something about the way he moves triggers a memory. "You're the carpet repair guy I tripped over in my office the other day!"

I suddenly feel my knees wobble when I flash back to the ugly nail gun he was using. I hate to think of the damage he could have done with that thing.

"…Clayton Benjamin," Bossman completes his introduction as if we hadn't said anything.

"Hello." I nod.

Bossman clears his throat again. "Mr. Vitale suggested that we invite you to sit in on this meeting because..."

"...because he's afraid I'll sue their collective asses for kidnapping, extortion and anything else I can think of if there aren't any witnesses to this little party," Benjamin says. "Have a seat."

I pull up a chair and sit down.

Poppi calmly opens his briefcase and pulls out a leather-bound folder. "Mr. Benjamin, I am a businessman who does his homework. This folder contains copies of police reports, personnel interviews and insurance estimates acquired by my private investigator relating to a number of 'pranks' that you have claimed credit for in recent weeks."

"Big deal," Benjamin shrugs.

"Not including the multiple medical and emergency response procedures performed in the last twenty-four hours, the estimated value of the damage you have caused is well in excess of half a million dollars."

Benjamin shrugs again.

Poppi opens the folder and takes out a single page filled with a column of figures. "On my instructions, my investigator has also done some digging. According to public records, at the time your father's partnership with Mr. Bozmund was dissolved, the business was valued at slightly less than two hundred thousand dollars. To walk away, your father agreed to a lump sum payment of one hundred thousand dollars from Mr. Bozmund. In addition, the title to the building where the business was conducted was also transferred to him. He chose to sell that building the following year and when that transaction was completed, he received a total of seventy thousand dollars, after fees and taxes."

Poppi hands the page to me. I look at the numbers briefly and then I pass it to Benjamin. Poppi closes the folder and continues.

"What those numbers mean, Mr. Benjamin, is that your father realized more than one hundred and seventy thousand dollars when he walked away from a business valued at less than two hundred thousand dollars. In other words, your father was not robbed blind, as you allege. If anything, he acquired the lion's share at the time the partnership was dissolved."

If I'm stunned by these details, Clayton Benjamin looks pole-axed. Go Poppi!

Poppi takes another sheet of paper out of the folder. "With that inaccuracy out of the way, Mr. Benjamin, what we must address at this time is not the matter of real or imagined unfinished business surrounding the break-up of an old partnership. Our focus today is the fallout resulting directly from your admitted campaign of mischief, assault and vandalism. In other words, what we must determine here and now is the manner in which you propose to address the damages your actions have incurred. Do you have any thoughts?"

If I were Benjamin, I'm thinking, I'd want a lawyer.

"I want a lawyer," Benjamin snarls.

Poppi nods. "That is very wise. Do you currently have one on retainer?"

"No."

Poppi nods again and looks at Bossman. "In that case…"

Bossman punches the buzzer on his desk and a few seconds later Amy opens the door. Two cops walk in, read Benjamin his rights, put him in hand-cuffs and walk him out. When the door closes, Bossman and I breathe audible sighs of relief. Poppi merely smiles as he returns the folder to his briefcase and places it on the table beside his chair.

Bossman says to Poppi, "I owe you big time, Vitale. In spite of what you might hear about me on the street, I'm a guy that pays his debts. But I've gotta ask one question."

Poppi smiles his encouragement.

Bossman continues, "What happened to your accent?"

Poppi turns to me and winks.

To thank me for my help, Bossman gives me the rest of the day off. When I get home, I find Trent waiting to take me to lunch before we hit the shops for early birthday treats. When the waiter has delivered our food, I give Trent the update on this morning's prankster capture. Trent follows with a detailed report on Poppi and The Muckers.

"Giovanni Vitale is an honest man, Lana. He's got a ton of friends in high places and some very big, very lucrative contracts. The story he puts out for public consumption is true. He did come from Sicily. He did choose to steer clear of the old bosses and the bent noses, even though there was a lot of pressure to do things the old school way. By the way, just because *he* chose the straight and narrow, that doesn't mean the whole family is clean. He's got a couple of cousins and at least one uncle who are in it deep."

"And what about his digging methods?"

"Totally cool. Because he didn't want to get tricked into working for the mob, and because he knows first-hand the sneaky methods the mob uses to hook innocent people, he got in the habit of hiring squeaky clean cops to do the digging before he signed on dotted lines. Fast forward to the present and nothing's changed. He hired Van because he carries top security clearances."

"Okay, but where is the connection? How did Van end up on Poppi's radar in the first place?"

"Poppi's grandson."

"Which one?"

"Sandro. Turns out he and Van met in the Navy."

"Wait... who?"

"Sandro, the middle guy. Giovanni Junior, Gina, Sandro, Maria, Antonio."

"I never heard of him."

Trent gives me a wide-eyed look. "Really? Gee, there's a surprise. You'd think the first thing they'd tell a reality TV producer is that one of the family is a shadow ops guy who builds dossiers on everyone they meet."

Though I'd prefer to slug him, I have to laugh. "Fine. I'm an idiot. Now, what about the way they're getting their information on me?"

"There are no bugs or wire taps on you," Trent reassures me. "I double-checked everything. That means they've got to be getting their information the good old-fashioned way."

When I raise my eyebrows, he grins. "They ask."

"What does that mean? Who did they ask? Who gave my secrets away?"

"Seriously? Where's the secret when you email a hundred people and they tell everyone they know? When you're suddenly going out every night wearing a totally different wardrobe? You don't think the people at Café Aroma or the pub where you hold Girls Night aren't wondering how this whole thing is going to work out for you? Are you seriously telling me it hasn't occurred to you that everyone who cares about you wants to see you happy?"

I'm stunned. In the first place, I can't get over how sensitive my big brother is. In the second place, the idea that so many people have been watching out for me is pretty humbling.

Trent stops me with a suddenly serious look. "There's one more thing I need to tell you, kid. It looks like I dropped the ball when I told you that your guy Jason was on the up and up."

"You know, I've been wondering about him. He was tripping all over himself to confirm a third date with me and then, when I told him to give me a call, he just slipped off the radar."

"Yeah, well he didn't give you the slip without a little help," Trent says dryly. "He got busted."

"WHAT?"

"Like I said, I dropped the ball there. It turns out that his name isn't Jason and he's not an electrician. He's a low level drug dealer and his name is Ricky. He and Tad the Cad go all the way back to reform school, by the way. Oh, yeah, and since most dope dealers end up developing a taste for their product, those mood swings you mentioned make a whole lot more sense."

I'm stunned, but the more I think about it, I'm not all that surprised. What does bother me is the background on Tad. "Does Mitzi know about this?"

Trent shakes his head. "I thought she should hear it from you. Maybe it wouldn't hurt to ask Sandro to put a report together. I'm thinking Mitzi's control freak father would like to know."

I'm nodding my head. Given Mitzi's description of the way her father dealt with Tad's removal, that report is exactly what he'll want to make sure Tad keeps his distance. Even though it took a second look at Jason to find the truth, I'm glad Trent came through. It's good to know that Jason is where he belongs.

Trent gives me a brotherly nudge. "Come on, kid, let's hit the road. We've got birthday presents to buy before our date with Poppi. After your rave review of that restaurant of his, I can't wait."

Saturday, Day 24

aturday morning, Trent and I head out early. We're going hiking today with Jonah and Trevor and, aside from the fact that I love spending time in the hills, I can't wait to see if my match-making strategy is working out. On the drive up, Trent continues to rave about last night.

When Poppi first greeted us, there was an interesting twinkle in his eye. We learned what he was up to when reached our table and Poppi introduced us to his son, Sandro, who grinned as he presented Trent with a detailed dossier on my brother's investigations into The Muckers in general and Poppi in particular. It could have been an awkward moment if either one of them had had an axe to grind. Instead, it gave them a bond to build on and in no time they were trading crazy stories that kept us in stitches. Right up until the food arrived, that is.

From that moment on, the only words my brother spoke were, "Ohhh" and "Ahhh" and "Well, if you insist" as Poppi's beaming chef looked on. When the coffee and cognac and pastries arrived, Trent looked as if he'd died and gone to heaven.

With the ice thoroughly broken, Poppi shared the reason he hoped I might consider leaving reality TV. "When Lana said audiences should see why we are different – how American ways are not the old world ways we know and follow – I asked my son to have her checked out," he told Trent. Then he had turned to me. "I reached out to you because there are so many wonderful stories, Bella, and no one is telling them. If this interests you, I would like discuss the possibility that you might take this on."

I was blown away. "Produce documentaries, you mean?"

Poppi nodded. "It would mean many months of research and travel," he cautioned. "Many countries, many people, many towns. And while I think this would suit you well, I am wondering about your GRAND Plan Mr. Right." He smiled a mischievous smile. "Is it his dream to be the one who sits at home, watching the children, waiting for your adventure to end?"

Even though my cheeks were burning, I'd had to laugh and seconds later, Trent and Sandro had joined in. Whether his documentary dream for me ever comes true or I follow my own path, I loved him for making the offer and caring enough to tease me like that.

Even though we managed to empty Poppi's bottomless cognac bottle, Trent and I are in good shape this morning and that means we won't be dragging a couple of hangovers up the side of the mountain. When we reach the base of the trail and hook up with Jonah and Trevor, I find their chemistry and Jonah's smile two more things to love. The four of us have a great time that afternoon and, by the time we call it quits, we're more than ready for food. Trevor insists on hosting dinner, so we all head over to his place and hang around his gourmet kitchen, trading stories, while he prepares a masterpiece meal fit for a king. By the time Trent and I get back to my place, we're ready to hit the sack.

Sunday, Day 25

After a quiet late brunch on Sunday, I take Trent to the airport. It's a happy/sad good-bye. This may be the best visit we've ever had and I wish it was just beginning. At the same time, I'm so ready for some quality 'me' time that I'm almost impatient for him to be gone. At the gate, we take a few minutes to watch the people and enjoy the easy silence between us.

"So, what do you think, kid?" he asks. "Should we do this more often?"

"Is that my loving brother talking or the guy who fell in love with Poppi's restaurant?" I grin.

"If it's a bit of both, is that so wrong?" he grins back.

"I needed this even more than I thought I did," I tell him, all joking aside. "It's great to have friends to confide in, but no one knows you like family. No one really gets who you are."

Trent nods.

"We didn't spend enough time talking about you," I add. "I feel kind of bad about that."

"It's all good. You were there for me when my shit hit the fan. Let's say it was my turn to bail you out this time and leave it at that."

I can feel the tears building and I don't want this visit to end on a weepy note. We give each other big hugs and I watch as they process him through security. When he heads for the boarding ramp, he turns and we both wave.

Walking back through the terminal to my car, I decide that it's time to blow off the cobwebs and hit the road. This time I take the Pacific Coast Highway and follow it north for a couple of hours. On the way back, I remember how good Donnie's Captain Morgan martini tasted last week and I decide to make a pit stop. Donnie's face lights up when I walk in and when I throw my arms wide and say, *Ta Daa,* he bursts out laughing.

"Now this is more like it! I'm assuming we're celebrating with the Captain?"

"You know it! I just put my brother on a plane for home after a kick ass visit. I think he deserves a proper good-bye toast."

As I watch Donnie work his magic, I notice the same guy with the sleeve tattoo that I'd seen last week. Just like last time, he smiles and I smile back.

When Donnie places my martini in front of me, he says softly, "Just so you know, if that guy comes over, he's okay. He's one of our Thursday regulars. Last Sunday was a first. He got here about an hour ago and I have a feeling he was hoping you'd stop in. He asked what your name was. Since he's a nice guy, I told him."

"You're the best, Donnie." I raise my glass to him and take my first sip. Nectar of the Gods.

A few minutes later, the guy slips into the seat next to mine.

"Mind if I join you?" he says.

"Be my guest," I tell him.

"So, instead of 'do you come here often', can I be honest with you?" he asks.

"Go for it," I reply.

He signals to Donnie that he needs a fresh drink. When he asks if I'm ready for another round, I shake my head. "Soda water is my chaser of choice," I tell him.

"It made me crazy that I had to leave early last Sunday, right after you'd smiled. I don't normally do Sundays. It was one of those spur of the moment, grab a cold beer things. So I came back today, hoping I'd see you again. When you smiled this time, I decided to take the plunge."

"Just to set the record straight," I tell him, "I'm not here to meet anyone."

"Fair enough." He offers me his hand and we shake. "Let's start again. I'm Eddie. You're Lana. We're both regulars on different days, so it's not like we're total strangers. Last week you looked like you were carrying the weight of the world on your shoulders. Today you're sitting on top of it, enjoying the view. Wanna talk about it?"

Donnie brings our drinks and this gives me a chance to tease him. "So, you're giving my name to every stray dog in town?"

Donnie grins. "Just the ones who tell me they want to buy you diamonds and furs."

"Really!" I turn back to Eddie. "So what kinds of trinkets are we talking about?"

"It'll never be anything but genuine fakes for you, doll!" he grins.

"So I think I'm jealous," I tell him. "I thought I was Donnie's favorite."

"I'm only his favorite on Thursdays," Eddie confides. "I come here for trivia night."

"You don't look like a trivia kind of guy."

His gleaming white smile is a great contrast to his dark tan. "You can't judge a book by its cover, girl. Not only do I play, I even win." He swivels toward me and plants his black boots on the kick bar of my stool. "So I want to know your story. Why the frown last week? Why the big smile today? What's going on?"

I decide to throw caution to the wind and dive right in. Within minutes, he's wiping his eyes, howling with laughter at the crazy cast of characters I've spent the last three weeks with.

"Okay, you know what? You need to celebrate the fact that you survived this ride. Donnie, get us a couple of shots of Paradisos." Eddie suddenly pauses. "Hang on a second. I'm forgetting my manners. Are you okay with tequila, girl?"

I nod. I'm in a safe place. My favorite bartender is watching my back. I'm having a couple of drinks with a great guy who has a great sense of humor. After three days of Trent therapy, it feels like I've finally got my old self back. When our drinks come, we clink glasses. When we slap the glasses back on the bar, Donnie holds up the bottle. I'm tempted, but I shake my head. Eddie shrugs and orders a beer instead.

With no pressure to find my one and only Mr. Right, our conversation flows naturally. I'm not analyzing him, I'm simply enjoying his company. Eddie and I drink our drinks and eat the munchies Donnie delivers as we talk and laugh and trade insults like old friends.

Sometime later, Eddie glances at his watch.

"Somewhere you have to be?" I ask.

He gives me an upside down grin. "New puppy. I've got to let him out and get him fed and take him for a walk. Unless you want to meet my buddy, Tank, I'm gonna have to call it quits."

Part of me wants to, but I'm torn. I look over at Donnie. To my surprise, he winks. Okay then!

"Why not?" I tell Eddie as I reach for my wallet.

"Put your money away, beauty," he says. "This one's on me."

Outside, I head for my car, but Eddie links my arm through his.

"I'm just a few blocks from here. Let's walk."

A few minutes later we reach a cottage that must have been a guest house once upon a time. When Eddie unlocks the door, we're bombarded by a puppy whose black and tan body and square-nosed head tell me Tank is a shepherd/pit bull mix. He's so wiggly and excited, I can't help but laugh. He rushes outside to take care of business. When he rushes back in, I kneel down and love this adorable puppy up.

Finally, Tank loses interest and runs off to find his toys. When I stand up, Eddie and I are just inches apart. We just stare for a moment without moving. When he slowly starts to grin, I can't stand how sexy he is. So I lean in and kiss him.

In the next second, I'm in his arms. His hot, slow, insistent kiss is like nothing I've ever felt. My body shivers when his hands caress me here, there and everywhere. When I feel him easing my tank top out of my jeans, I grab for his belt. We stumble-glide across the hall into his bedroom and fall onto the bed. He holds my gaze while he works me out of my clothes and gets rid of his.

He starts kissing my neck, taking little nibbles that make me moan. As he works his way down, he spends time at my nipples, doing magical things with his tongue until I'm ready to scream. When he moves on I sink back, totally ready for anything.

"I have a condom?" he frames it as a question, giving me the power to stop this or carry on.

When I smile, he grabs it out of the night stand.

With both of us ready and willing, we're totally in sync. Hands lingering, exploring, teasing. Kisses probing. Heat intensifying. And then…

"Howwwwwwwlllll!!!"

We're suddenly motionless. A second later, hysterical laughter banishes any hope of recapturing the moment.

"Oh my god," I'm wiping the tears and clutching my aching sides.

"If he wasn't so cute, I'd kill him," Eddie finally manages to say. "That's gotta top all your dating disasters put together."

"You win," I tell him as fresh giggles take over.

Eventually, the laughter dies away. The silence is easy. When he gently kisses my shoulder I turn my head and smile. Once again, we're inches apart. Once again, he smiles that sexy smile. Once again, I lean in and kiss him. And right on cue, Tank comes bumbling in and jumps on the bed.

"You need to take this little guy out for a walk," I tell him.

"You want to join us?"

I shake my head with a smile. "Maybe next time."

When we're dressed again, he pulls me into his arms. A long slow kiss later, he gives me a playful slap on my butt as we head for the door.

Back at my apartment, I send Trent a text. *Love who we are and what you do.*

After that, I grab a shower and jump into bed. I don't even try to wipe the smile off my face.

Monday, Day 26

*I*f we weren't under the gun to get *Meet the Muckers* ready to present to the network, I'd be tempted to take the day off and celebrate the newly liberated me. But that will have to wait. Right now, our baby needs my total focus. A successful pitch is all about anticipating questions, hitting hot buttons and giving more than anyone asks for.

Lucky for us, our idea is so fresh and Ethan's footage is so good, the only thing our network insider wants to know is if we can find any vintage footage and add that into the sizzle before it gets screened by their top executives. What they're really hoping is that we use images that make people wonder which mob bosses Poppi is related to.

We're so busy that it's five o'clock before I know it. I race to get home and get changed for my final date with Michael, the art gallery owner. I decide not to mess with success and opt for my favorite little black dress, classic pumps and diamond earrings.

Outside the restaurant, I smile at a tall, handsome guy in an Armani suit as he steps off the curb and crosses a narrow alley that runs between this building and the next. As he raises his hand to wave back at me, BAM, out of nowhere he's tackled by a homeless woman.

Seriously! First he's Mister Fashion Fabulous and then he's Mister Helpless in the clutches of Octopus Annie. The whole time, she's yelling "Help me!" like her dress is on fire and he's doing this crazy two-step to move them beyond the alley and into the action in front of the restaurant.

All of a sudden, everyone sees them. Three valet parking guys get into the game while two casual bystanders grab their cell phones and start taking pictures. In a few seconds, they've got Octopus Annie under control. A second or two after that, a squad car pulls up. One of the valet guys gives us the nod and we slip inside the restaurant before anyone asks us for statements.

I'm standing there thinking the worst is over when things suddenly go horribly wrong. Assuming the last thing Michael will want now is any more unnecessary attention, I'm totally unprepared when he stops in the middle of the restaurant, clears his throat and announces, "I'm with the most amazing woman here!"

I laugh it off and turn away, hoping the hostess will rescue me. No such luck. The desk is empty and Michael doesn't know when to quit.

"No, seriously," he raises his voice. "I *am* with the most amazing woman here. I mean, prove me wrong, Lana. Do you see anyone more amazing than you?"

At this point people are beginning to sense a scene in the making. All eyes are on us.

Gritting my teeth, I smile and say quietly, "You're embarrassing me, Michael. Please stop."

Thankfully, the hostess returns at that moment and whisks us off to our table. She leaves us with menus and tells us our server will be with us shortly.

Once we're seated Michael leans back in his chair and puts his arms over the bannister next to our balcony table. He leans in and says "You are the most amazing woman here." He smiles and looks at me expectantly. I look at him confused and say nothing. He leans further in "... and luckily YOU are with the very most amazing, handsome man here, yes?" He leans back pleased with himself.

Luckily, the waitress interrupts this awkward moment carrying glasses and a pitcher of ice water, Michael tells her to bring a bowl of freshly sliced lemon and lime.

When she heads off on this errand, Michael leans back and steeples his hands under his chin. "I'm going to guess what your drink of choice before dinner is. I'm very good at it, you know."

I sit there patiently while he stares for a long moment. "Margarita," he says smugly.

I shake my head.

"Screw driver?" Another shake.

"Don't tell me you're a Cosmo girl!" I shake my head again.

"Daiquiri?" "Gin and tonic?" "Whisky Sour?

When the waitress returns, I cut to the chase and ask her to bring me a glass of Chardonnay.

His voice dripping with scorn, he says, "Don't you like any hard liquor?"

"I'm in the mood for Chardonnay," I reply politely.

"What about a Cape Cod?" he says. "Have you ever had one?"

When I tell him no, he smiles and tells her to get me a Cape Cod. Then he tells her he wants something that sounds like *blablabla*.

When the waitress looks confused and asks him what ingredients go into his drink, he waves his hand like royalty dismissing a slave and says, "Ask your bartender. He'll know."

Am I embarrassed? Yes. Am I annoyed? You bet. So why am I still here? Maybe I'm too busy trying to make sense of the last ten minutes, starting with the homeless woman, followed by the loud, crowd-gathering compliment and his stupid game of Guess My Drink. In any case, I've about reached my limit.

Michael squeezes a mixture of lemon and lime into his water. When he's done, he asks if I want my water boosted the same way.

"No thanks," I tell him.

He smiles as I say it and picks up a lemon, squeezes it into my water and pushes the whole thing under the surface with his finger. I'm slack-jawed, unable to speak.

At this point the waitress comes back with the drink I didn't order. "Sir," she tells Michael, "the bartender doesn't know what your drink is. Is there something else you'd like instead?"

Michael sighs heavily and tells her to bring him a Grand Marnier, neat.

Cringing at the thought of Grand Marnier before dinner, I remind the waitress that I had asked for a glass of Chardonnay.

"Oh!" She looks confused. "I thought the gentleman wanted you to drink this instead."

I take a breath and let it out. "What the gentleman wants isn't the point."

To my everlasting astonishment, the waitress turns to Michael. "Is that okay, sir?"

Michael waves his hand again, and the waitress rushes off to do his bidding. I decide that if I get my wine, I'll stay long enough to drink it. If the waitress comes up with another reason not to take me seriously, I'm out of here. A minute, she's back with my glass of Chardonnay and Michael's Grand Marnier. I take a sip. Cold and crisp. Though he doesn't know it, Michael has fifteen minutes and I'm done.

He's looking at the appetizers and asks if I want pot stickers. I tell him no. He orders six and when they arrive, he immediately puts two on my plate and piles on the sauce.

"I said I didn't want an appetizer."

"It has been my experience that women who are obsessive about their looks don't take care of themselves. You need to eat, Lana, or you'll make yourself sick," he replies.

And with that insufferably rude remark hanging in the air, I'm done. I take a last sip of my wine and put my glass down, tuck my purse under my arm and stand up.

"If you need the restroom, it's around the corner," Michael says.

"This evening was a mistake, Michael, and rather than prolong it any further, I'll say good-bye. Thank you for the glass of wine." With my shoulders back and head high, I walk away.

"Wait!" he calls, but I keep walking.

As I reach the door and give the valet my parking stub, the final piece of the puzzle falls into place and my transformation is complete. Just because someone agrees to meet me doesn't mean I owe them anything. And just because my email contacts forwarded names of men they knew doesn't mean I have to like them. The fact that looms large now is that these men weren't chosen because they were wildly popular. It was exactly the opposite. And if I hadn't been trying so hard to create fantasy endings that were never meant to be, I'd have seen it sooner.

Tuesday, Day 27

*T*oday we're putting the finishing touches on the sizzle reel. We add the footage the network asked for and now it's time to double and triple check every detail. When we break for lunch, I'm surprised how relieved I am – that Bossman hasn't ruined everything, that Poppi has turned out to be one of the good guys, that the [malicious] prankster is behind bars, and maybe most of all, that I don't have to go on any more of those disastrous GRAND Plan dates.

I'm enjoying a quiet evening, heating up some Minestrone soup I'd made from scratch and froze a few weeks ago. I may watch a movie. And then again, I may just have a bubble bath and go to bed. I'm so surprised when the doorbell rings that I sit for a moment, assuming it isn't mine. Well, not assuming as much as hoping. It rings again so I look through the peephole and almost pass out when I see Tad standing there with a huge bouquet of flowers. I grab my cell phone and send Mitzi a text: *Tad's here. Please come now!* To be safe, I also send the same text to Nolan, Jonah and Ethan. My cell phone has a recording function and this seems like the perfect time to use it. I press the button, put the cell in my pocket and hide behind the door. With any luck, he'll give up in a minute or two and go away.

Nope. This time he holds his finger on the doorbell for several seconds. When I still don't answer, he starts pounding on the door with his fists.

"I know you're in there, Lana," he calls. "I was watching you through the window before I came to the door, so you might as well let me in. Save us both a whole lot of trouble."

I feel the panic rising in my throat as I text Nolan: *Where ARE you???*

His '*6 blocks*' reply isn't much comfort. It takes less time than that to cause bodily harm.

"What's it gonna be, Lana?" Tad's voice comes through the door. "Do we do this the easy way or what?"

Nolan's '*2 blocks*' update gives me the courage I need and I open the door.

"Good evening, Lana," Tad says, as if he hasn't just threatened me. "I thought you might like a nice bouquet of roses. May I come in?"

"No."

"I admire your loyalty, but it's okay. I broke up with Mitzi. I didn't want to hurt her, but I can't hide it anymore. I need to be with you. You're the perfect woman for me."

"It's a nice speech, Tad, but no dice."

"I'll be a better man. I'll get a job. Just give me a chance."

"I'm closing the door, Tad. You need to go."

Instead of doing the right thing, he pushes past me into the living room, dropping the roses on the coffee table and sitting on the couch. When he reaches for the remote and turns on the TV to a football game, I text Mitzi "Tad's here." Seconds later, my phone rings.

"Excuse me, Tad. I need to use the bathroom."

He nods without turning away from the football game and I answer the phone as I walk into the bathroom and lock the door.

"What's he doing there?" Mitzi says.

"I don't know and I can't get him to leave. Get over here as fast as you can. I'll leave the line open so you can hear everything."

"I'm on my way." She says and I can hear her car keys jingling in the background.

I put the phone, still connected to her, back in my pocket and rejoin Tad in the living room.

"I'm back," I tell him.

"Just a second," he says distractedly. "The Steelers are doing really well!"

A minute later, the team gets a touchdown and he jumps up with a big cheer. I can't believe how quickly he's made himself at home.

"Okay Tad, that's it. Your team won and now you need to go," I say firmly.

"Lana, you need to stop fighting it. We can be great together. I can prove it if you give me a chance. Just because Mitzi and I were together doesn't mean we can't find our own happiness."

I can hear Mitzi's voice in my pocket, so I laugh to cover the sound.

"What's so funny?"

"I just can't believe you would do this for a pittly five grand. And the gig is up, no more GRAND plan."

"It doesn't have to be. Plus, five grand is a lot of money," he blurts it out before he realizes what he's doing. Then he shrugs. "Listen, I'm not going to say the five grand isn't important, because I don't want to lie to you. But you are the real prize. We're meant to be together. Why can't you see it?"

"Maybe Lana's distracted by all your lies," Mitzi says as she walks through the door.

He's really surprised to see her. He looks back and forth between us, not sure what to do.

"Mitzi," he finally mumbles, "you shouldn't be here."

"It's the other way 'round, Tad. There's nothing here for you. Lana has asked you to go and you've ignored her. Just like you did after the wine tasting on Friday night."

"I told you what happened on Friday. She came onto me. She hit on me first."

"Mitzi, I do believe he's lying, yet again," Jonah says as he and Trevor push through the door.

Nolan and Ethan are right behind them. "Lana thinks you're an ass, Tad. She always has." Nolan says shaking his head. Ethan nods in agreement.

"That's not true. She's always wanted me. You know it's the truth, Mitzi. She's tried to break us up for years. I'm the only one who tells you the truth. THEY are the liars."

Mitzi stands firm and I'm relieved to see no tears. "It's over, Tad. Just go. I'm done with you."

"Yeah, well we'll see about that. You made promises to me. I'm holding you to them."

He slams my front door hard. The next thing we hear is the sound of his truck starting.

As I put my arm around Mitzi, Jonah hugs us both. Trevor locks the door while Nolan goes to my cupboard, grabs glasses and pours us all some wine.

Wednesday, Day 28

*I*f there were roosters in the valley I would be hearing them now. The sun hasn't even risen when I pack up my computer and head out the front door. I'm exhausted from the previous evening. Tad was always a jerk, but knowing his reputation made last night the ultimate scary showdown.

As I drive, I forget about Tad and start focussing on the network pitch. The hard work we've put in is behind us and our moment of reckoning is finally here. I'm dressed for success today, in black tailored slacks and a crisp blue button up. Even though this is just a conference call, I need the boost that comes with looking like a professional.

As I park the car and grab my computer, someone clears their throat behind me. I turn and find Nolan and Ethan standing there. Ethan has coffee. Nolan has a bag from the local donut shop.

"Donut for your thoughts?" he grins.

"I'm so nervous," I mumble as I bite into my favorite gooey treat.

"This one's in the bag, Lana," Ethan says. "It's solid gold."

The Bossman walks past just at that moment and signals the three of us to follow him into the conference room. As we pass Amy she flashes two thumbs up. Everyone is rooting for us, but the thought that I might let them down makes me feel sick. I finish my donut, toss the wrapping and settle gingerly into the plush leather seat closest to the speakerphone.

"Let's make money," Bossman says as Amy buzzes to let us know the network is on the phone.

We get past the introductions fairly painlessly. The network is represented by two executives, a man and a woman. I'm grateful that a woman's involved so I can highlight the hot, sweaty Italians causing traffic jams and the military back stories affecting their family lives.

"You've seen our updated sizzle with the historical footage. What do you think?" Bossman says.

The woman jumps in. "It looks great, but sell me on the real hook. Why would anyone tune in week after week after they get used to the spectacle?"

Bossman points to me. Sweat beading on my forehead, I dive in.

"The hook is that this show is the next big thing in reality TV," I tell her as I wind up for the pitch. "It's much more than *The Godfather* meets *Greensburg*," I begin. "And it's more than a Sicilian family that went straight. When Giovanni Vitale came to America, he gambled on something much bigger than a legitimate business that he hoped would be in every mall, plaza and square in LA someday. What he saw when he got here was an opportunity to start over in a new land, making a new home, and a new life.

"When we *meet the Muckers*," I continue, "we get a chance to revisit our own history as people who came to America with a dream in their hearts and hope in their eyes. We get to be reminded why and how this country became great – because it was built by people like Giovanni and his family – people who loved this new world so deeply that they were prepared to fight and die for its freedoms – because that's what America means to them – because that's what America means to every family whose lives have been touched by the sacrifice of war.

I'm almost done. "The bottom line is that you get an American success story that touches all of us. On top of that, you get road rage. You get graft. You get greed and corruption. You get hard work and tough choices. You get restless wives and jealous husbands. I mean, forget pool boys – these guys have the hottest bodies in town!"

I take a breath and the room is silent. I lean back in the chair signaling to Bossman that I'm done.

"But will our male viewers be jealous? Will the men holding the remotes change the channel to avoid these guys?" The male executive sounds like he's gritting his teeth.

Nolan grins. "Not when they see how turned on their women get."

Bossman cuts him off. "We think it's got enough gutsy moves, big machines, military contacts and mafia links to satisfy the men," he says. "And let's not forget the American Dream."

The woman takes the lead again. "You know what? I like the whole package and I think the flag waving nails it. I also think the young man is right. Men do want their wives to be all turned on."

When I hear that, I grin. "In that case," I toss in, "you're gonna LOVE the next show we've got planned!"

"Really!" the woman says. "Now that's very interesting. Mr. Bozmund, with your permission, I'll have my secretary set up a preliminary discussion call with Lana early next week. I like to strike while the iron is hot."

Bossman blinks. "Of course!" he says, having no idea what's going on.

The woman continues: "Okay, we need to discuss this on our end and see how The Muckers fits into our fall line-up. Thanks for your time, everyone. You'll be hearing from us shortly."

And just like that, we're done. Well, not quite.

"And just what the hell was THAT little dance all about?" Bossman growls. "I don't recall green-lighting a next show with you."

Nolan looks equally puzzled and not a little hurt and, since he's the one I care about, I jump in to explain. "I'm really sorry I did that without warning, but the timing was too perfect to pass up. Here's what happened: I had lunch the other day with this bright, funny, gorgeous man who told me he was in marketing. Ten minutes into our meal, when I ask him to describe what he does, he says: "Let's just say that what I coach people to achieve gives them a whole new lease on life.""

Bossman's scowl hasn't faded. "He's one of those evangelist life coaches. So what?"

Nolan, on the other hand, is grinning from ear to ear. "I'm thinking he motivates his clients to say Hallelujah for a whole different set of reasons, am I right?"

I grin back at him.

Bossman still doesn't get it, so I tell him: "He's a gigolo, Carlton. Think Richard Gere in Armani suits, circa 1980, updated to the here and now, coming to you, live and in color, every week."

Bossman's eyes actually roll back in his head and for a second I wonder if the idea has killed him or it was the shock of hearing me call him by his given name for the first time in ten years.

"Brilliant," he finally says. "Now listen to me, Red. Whether we get the nod on the Muckers or not, I want that sizzle reel ASAP. Now get out of here. Take the day and have some fun."

On our way out, Nolan stops me to ask, "Does your gigolo know anything about this?"

"Well of course he does," I laugh. "All we have to do now is get him under contract to us!"

As I head home after our celebration lunch, I suddenly realize that I'm totally exhausted. For the first time in a month, the only person I need to think about is me. After a long, relaxing bath, I curl up with a good book and turn in early.

Thursday, Day 29

*T*oday I get to sleep in. I treat myself to breakfast and then a manicure and pedicure. The crazy thing is, in spite of all the ups and downs, I'm looking forward to my thirtieth birthday more than I could ever have imagined.

Sunday	Monday	Tuesday	Wednesday	Thursday	Friday	Saturday
				WEEK ONE[1] The Plan	Nolan's[2] Birthday The Muckers	Tony?[3] ~~Skylar~~
Skydive - Van[4]	~~Jason~~[5]	~~Doug~~[6]	Henri[7]	WEEK TWO[8] Frank The Girls	~~Jason #2~~[9]	Hiking Ethan[10] Poppi
Skydive - Van #2[11]	~~Jeremy~~[12]	~~totar~~ Erik[13]	~~Paavo~~ ~~Skylar #2~~[14]	WEEK THREE[15] The Girls Poppi	Wine Tasting[16]	~~Jason #3~~[17] Jonah! Van!
~~Stewart~~[18]	~~Barry~~ Greg[19]	~~Joey~~ Gale[20]	~~Richard~~[21] Trent Arrives Phil	WEEK FOUR[22] Girls/Trent	Poppi,[23] Trent	~~Oscar~~[24] Hiking Trent
~~Poppi~~[25] Trent Leaves Eddie!	~~Michael~~[26]	Tad![27] ~~Stewart~~	Muckers[28] Pitch	DEADLINE[29] Girls/Vote	THE WINNER[30]	My[31] Birthday

At five o'clock I walk over to Café Aroma. I grab my favorite table and tell Penny that this week we're celebrating Girls Night with her.

Jonah is the first one to arrive. Mitzi's next. Phil wanders in smiling And Kat follows last. As I watch them hug Penny and grab their drinks, I smile. Who could ask for better friends?

Jonah is the first one to ask and that seems right. "Well, girlfriend? Who gets the five grand?"

"I'm keeping it," I raise my glass. "I sent 100 emails and met enough losers, whackos and weirdos to push me to my limits and beyond. On the upside, I came face to face with reality and found out who I am. I also have enough horror stories to dine out on for months to come. So, although it might sound crazy, I hereby proclaim the GRAND Plan a great success."

"Let's drink to that!" Jonah laughs.

And we do.

Friday, Day 30

I'm up early. Tomorrow is my birthday and, since Nolan and I have today off, we're going to meet for breakfast and tie down the details for the party. I've got one foot out the door when the phone rings and I almost decide to ignore it. A second later, I'm very glad I change my mind.

"Hello?"

"Hey, Lana. It's Van."

Wow. My heart suddenly does a flip flop. "Hey, stranger! What's up?"

"Listen, I know it's really last minute, but Sarah and I got to talking about you."

"Well, how cool is that!"

"Sarah wants to know if you'd like to go on a birthday picnic with us after I get back, a couple of weeks from Sunday. Just a casual meet and greet."

"You bet!"

"Great. See you then." He says with a smile in his voice.

I hang up and float out the door on my way to Slum Central with the biggest grin. This no strings single life is totally working for me!

I arrive at Slum Central to find the Bossman standing in the parking lot with, of all the lame things, one of those Swisher Sweet cigars.

"You're late, Miss Fray," he says. "But that's okay because I have a cigar."

I nod, wondering if the last few weeks have finally pushed him over the edge.

"And why do I have a cigar, you're wondering? It's because cigars are for celebrating."

I'm still nodding, because nods are for calming crazy people.

Then he drops the nut job act. "We got it Lana! You sold the network on the whole deal – no conditions, no demands. They're on board. We got the go ahead to start mucking it up ASAP!"

As his words hit home, my eyes grow bigger than saucers. I'm so excited I almost hug the Bossman. At the last second, I come to my senses and opt for a high five.

"Have you told the team yet?" I ask

He shakes his head. "It's your moment." He makes a little shooing motion. "Go get 'em."

Still a little off balance from the sincere smile on his face instead of the usual sneer, I run off to find the team. The first thing I see in the bull pen is a cake that says "Congratulations." News travels fast in the jungle. I scream when I see Nolan.

"Dude, we did it!"

"We sure did!" He picks me up and spins me around. Sam is next. Then it's Amy's turn. I'm caught up in Ethan's bear hug when my phone rings and he laughingly sets me down. I try to grab it in time but it goes to voice mail, so I leave it until after we've finished celebrating with cake and more hugs. When I check my phone later and see that it was my mom who called, I duck into my office for some privacy while I listen to her message.

"Lana? Are you there, dear? It's your mother. (pause) Shirley. Trent says everything's fine, but I'm never sure whether everything is fine when he says that or everything's going to hell in a handcart and he just doesn't like to worry me. I was at the store picking up cucumbers to make those pickles you like and that's when I ran into that girl... you know, the one with all the tattoos: Felicity? Fanny? Freddie? What is her name? Anyway, she told me she was really disappointed that you had called off your GRAND Plan. Well, I have to admit that I was at a loss for words. What with Ginger, our new horse, and the washing machine and the insurance adjuster and the contractor and our trip to Vegas, I haven't been checking my emails the way I should. Anyway, she rambled on and on ... Sonya? Sandy?

Sammy? What IS her name? ... It was something about a huge surprise she'd wanted to spring on you, but couldn't reach the man before you'd called the Plan off because you'd found yourself. And good for you, honey! We all lose our focus now and then. Lord knows, there were times when I was your age and I-- but that's not why I called. Well, you know how I hate to encourage people who prattle on and on, but that girl had the oddest smile on her face ... Tina? Tammy? Tony? I'm sure it's one of those boy/girl names. Anyway, I finally said that since she couldn't surprise you anymore, wasn't it a shame that she couldn't share her clever plan with someone else, and the next thing you know she was telling me every sordid detail. Sometimes it's so easy, I'm ashamed of myself. The thing is, dear, the man she was planning to surprise you with was Billy! Well, you could have knocked me down with a feather. Apparently he's out again... something about an early release under some kind of pardon, but how could that be remotely possible? She also said something about him landing a job in the diamond industry and I thought to myself, who in their right mind would trust that boy with diamonds? Well, I feel much better now that you know. It's wonderful the way these mother-daughter chats work, isn't it dear? Such a comfort. Oh, there's your father. I'd better go. He wants to know which chapel to book to renew our vows while we're in Vegas. I love the man to death, even if he can't make a decision about the simplest things. Love you, honey."

It's a good thing I'm sitting down. In what may go down in history as the bombshell call to end all bombshell calls, my mother has simultaneously thrilled and horrified me beyond belief. Focusing on the great news first, how perfect is it that she and daddy are planning to renew their wedding vows in Vegas? This is a trip I am NOT going to miss! Then, taking a deep breath and staring the bad news in the face, it looks like Billy is up to his old tricks. How he managed to scam someone into granting him a pardon is one of those stories I don't want to hear from the horse's mouth so I'm going to call Trent. After that, I'm calling Mom. Aside from confirming Vegas details and making sure she knows that I love her crazy messages, I need to tell her how much I want to hear those 'lost my focus' stories of hers.

I stick my head out the door and get Nolan's attention. "Hey, I've got a couple of family calls to make." When he gives me two thumbs up and his best grin, I grin back. No need to tell him I'm taking care of other business before I share the news about our new show.

Trent answers right away. "So I'm guessing Mom called," he says.

"Exactly."

"Okay, the bottom line is that Billy did get out and it isn't a scam."

"And you were going to tell me this when?"

"I was going to tell you right after I got off the phone with Sandro and told him to put a couple of extra guys on you."

"Which was when exactly?" I ask a bit annoyed.

"Five minutes ago."

"I know that should comfort me, but somehow it doesn't."

"Okay, look: I feel the same way, but what's the alternative? Send you off to live in a yurt somewhere, surrounded by body guards? You've got a life to live."

"Good point."

"And in any case, the likelihood that Billy would try to hook up with you is slim to none. This whole diamond deal means he's up to no good and he knows you're not going to put up with that shit again. Why would he take the risk that you'd call the cops the minute you laid eyes on him after his lawyer just got him out? Even for Billy, that would be incredibly stupid."

Even though the small voice inside my head is still making an unhappy humming sound, I can't argue with his logic. "You're right."

"So are you okay?"

"Yeah. And listen, thanks for making the call to Sandro."

"Hey, what's the point of having connections if you don't use them?"

I have to laugh. "And speaking of connections, do you think it's too late for me to pull some strings in Vegas and surprise Mom and Dad a little?"

Now it's Trent's turn to laugh. "What've you got in mind?"

"I'm thinking Poppi probably has a few favors he can call in."

"Love it! And I think he'll be thrilled when you ask him."

I start to grin. "Especially since the network just gave us the green light on the reality show."

"NO!"

"YES! We just got the word this morning!"

"And you were going to tell me when?" He asks with a laugh.

"Okay, no fair! Mom's news about Billy was a total game changer."

"True enough. Okay, sis, get back to me when you hear from Poppi. Whatever he dreams up, I'm in. And don't lose any sleep about Billy. I'm keeping tabs on him from my end and I've got Sandro's word that he won't let anything happen to you."

As soon as we hang up, I call Poppi. Luckily, I catch him by the phone.

"Bella, what a nice surprise!"

I quickly tell him the good news about the show and, as I predicted, he's delighted. Before the dust settles, I also tell him about my folks.

"Tell your mother everything is taken care of. Whatever she wants, all she must do is ask."

I thank him and place the next call. When Mom answers, I play her game.

"Mom? It's your daughter. Lana."

Her laughter on the line is music to my ears. Why have I waited so long? Maybe I needed the time to grow up a little. When I tell her how grateful I am that she let me know about Billy, I hear a slight change in her voice. It takes me a second to realize that she's smiling and I'm suddenly wondering how long it's been since I heard that sound in her voice over the phone. When I tell her about Poppi's offer, I hear something else I've never heard in one of our calls: Silence.

"Mom? Are you okay?"

"Darling, I'm quite speechless."

"So I can tell Poppi it's okay? You don't mind?"

"Mind? Sweetheart, I'm over the moon! Tell that lovely man that we accept with great pleasure, but only on one condition: He must promise to kiss the bride."

"I'm sure he'll be happy to oblige. Okay, I've got to run. I'll call you later. Love to Dad."

After that, I follow up with Poppi, who laughs with delight when he hears about my Mom's reaction. Then I tell Nolan I'm heading out to clear my head and get some rest. Tomorrow's my birthday and I have a feeling it's going to be a busy day.

Saturday, Day 31

After my quiet, early night, I head down to Café Aroma for my birthday breakfast. When I'm done, Penny brings me a Latte. I sink back in my chair and close my eyes with a contented smile.

"Excuse me," I hear a voice say, "Is this seat taken?"

I open my eyes just enough to see a finger pointing to the stuffed chair next to mine.

"Help yourself," I smile and close my eyes again.

After a minute, my curiosity gets the better of me and I open my eyes again. The guy looks vaguely familiar, which doesn't surprise me. I'm in here all the time. The other thing I can't help noticing is the book he's reading: The Alchemist, by Paul Coelho, one of my all-time favorites.

"That's a great book," I tell him.

"I'm enjoying it. I'm launching a new business and I'm a bit scared. You won't tell anyone?"

"Your secret is safe with me. What kind of business?"

"It's an offshoot of my grandfather's company. Right now I advise businesses thinking of expanding their infrastructures and upgrading their locations. What I plan to do is something more creative and I'm a little worried that I'll lose my passion when it becomes a daily grind."

"Wow. A new career and a passion? That's pretty cool. May I ask what your passion is?"

"Documentaries."

"A man after my own heart." I say it without thinking and then, when I realize how it must have sounded, I blush. "I mean, I just love documentaries."

"No worries. Plus you look even prettier when you blush."

He reaches out his hand to me and I shake it.

"I'm Tony," he says.

I can't believe it. Today of all days. "And I'm Lana."

"You may not remember," he says, "but I met you here about a month ago? You were meeting some guy."

"Yes. That would have been Skylar." I laugh.

"And where is Skylar these days?" he asks carefully.

"We parted ways," I reply politely, hoping that's enough information.

"So, does that mean you're single?" he raises his eye brows slightly.

"Why yes I am, happily." I suddenly realize how that sounds. "Oh... wait. Happily doesn't mean I want to stay that way forever, it's just that... Okay, you know what? I'll just shut up now."

Tony's face lights up with the best looking smile I've ever seen. "Strangely enough, I get it. And if you're up for a date next Saturday, and you're willing to give me your phone number, I'd love to take you to dinner. I know this great little restaurant."

"I'd love to," I tell him as I write my number on a napkin and hand it to him.

When he takes the napkin from me, he takes my hand and gently kisses it. When I look surprised, he grins.

"It's a family custom."

"I like it."

"I'm glad. Until Saturday, then, Bella."

"Until Saturday, Tony."

As I head home, it hits me: He just called me Bella. And Tony is short for Antony. Is it possible?

We'll have to see. And even then, who knows? Right now, I'm enjoying each day as it comes, meeting people without the stress of trying to fit into some little box. I still want to be married someday, but not until I find a partner, a best friend, and an all-around good guy. Until then, I'm leaving things in the hands of Destiny.

Mind you, with the way Destiny's been working overtime lately, I wouldn't be surprised if she has me engaged by the time I'm thirty-two.

Not that I'm rushing things.

CPSIA information can be obtained
at www.ICGtesting.com
Printed in the USA
FSOW01n0751111214
3806FS